The Battle of Poitiers

Charles Martel and 'Abd al-Rahman

Novels of Islamic History in Translation Series

Written by Jurji Zaidan and published by the Zaidan Foundation.
(in historical chronological order)

The Conquest of Andalusia
translated with an Afterword and Study Guide by Roger Allen

The Battle of Poitiers
Charles Martel and ʿAbd al-Rahman
translated with a Study Guide by William Granara

The Caliph's Sister
Harun al-Rashid and the Fall of the Persians
translated by Issa J. Boullata with a Study Guide

The Caliph's Heirs
Brothers at War: The Fall of Baghdad
translated with an Afterword and Study Guide by Michael Cooperson

Saladin and the Assassins
translated by Paul Starkey with a Study Guide

The Battle of Poitiers

Charles Martel
and 'Abd al-Rahman

A historical novel describing the Arab invasion of France at the beginning of the eighth century up to the banks of the Loire River near Tours. And the reasons for the failure of the Arab invasion and how the Franks, under the leadership of Charles Martel, united and saved Europe.

Jurji Zaidan

**translated from the Arabic
with a Study Guide by**

William Granara

With an Introduction by the Zaidan Foundation

The Zaidan Foundation
For Intercultural Understanding, Inc.

7007 Longwood Drive
Bethesda, MD 20817
Email: george@zaidanfoundation.org
www.zaidanfoundation.org
Tel: (301) 469-8131
Fax: (301) 469-8132

Table of Contents

Introduction...vii

Translator's Acknowledgements... xv

Author's Historical Introduction...1

1. The Conquest of Bordeaux 5

2. Hani and Maryam 19

3. Maymuna 43

4. Two Secrets 49

5. The Lovers' Encounter 59

6. A New Plot 75

7. The Two Hanis 87

8. Salma in Bordeaux 99

9. A Strange Apparition 113

10. With Duke Odo 119

11. Who is Roderic? 131

12. The First Secret 159

13. On the Battlefield...175

14. Hani and Maryam 189

15. Charles' Messenger...207

16. War 217

Study Guide...233

The Battle of Poitiers
Charles Martel and 'Abd al-Rahman

Introduction

About the Novel[1]

Less than a hundred years elapsed between the birth of Islam in 622 AD—the year in which the Prophet Muhammad had emigrated from Mecca to Medina, that emigration (*hijra*) marking the beginning of the Islamic calendar—and the date of the Muslim invasion of Spain in 710 AD. By that time the Islamic faith had spread rapidly to both east and west: Syria, Iraq and Egypt first, but then east towards India and west along the Northern shores of Africa. From then on, as is well described by Jurji Zaidan in the author's historical introduction to the current novel, the Muslim caliphs were set on conquering the European continent. They first tried unsuccessfully to do so from the east with the siege of Constantinople in 717 AD and then from the west. They crossed the Pyrenees from Spain and set out to conquer France and a fragmented European continent that was backward and in disarray compared to the far stronger Byzantine Empire. They would thus try to reach Constantinople from the west on their way to Damascus, which was the seat of the Umayyad Caliphate in those times.

Jurji Zaidan wrote three historical novels set in Spain, or al-Andalus (Andalusia) as the Arabs called it. The first was *The Conquest of Andalusia*[2] which took place just before and during the conquest of Spain in 710 AD

---

1 First published in 1904 in Arabic as *Sharl wa 'Abd al-Rahman,* Cairo, Dar-al-Hilal.
2 First published in 1903 in Arabic as *Fath al-Andalus aw Tariq Ibn Ziyad* and translated into English as *The Conquest of Andalusia* by Roger Allen. It was published in 2011.

and which led to an Arab presence of almost eight centuries in the Iberian Peninsula ending in 1492 AD with the fall of Granada, the last piece of Spanish territory under Islamic rule. The second was the current novel, *The Battle of Poitiers*, whose events follow closely those described in the earlier novel culminating in the epic Battle of Poitiers in 732 AD. The third and final novel[3] is set during the reign of 'Abd al- Rahman al Nasir, the Umayyad ruler in Spain from 929 to 961 AD at the zenith of Islamic civilization in Spain. He was the first Arab ruler of Spain to be called Caliph and that novel includes a detailed description of the great luxury, wealth and level of development of Andalusia, its relative tolerance of religious diversity and its particular interest in literature, poetry, the arts, and the sciences.

The Battle of Poitiers pitted 'Abd al-Rahman al-Ghafiqi, Arab soldier and emir of Spain, against Charles Martel, "the Hammer", leader of the Franks. 'Abd al- Rahman had conquered parts of Southern France and had become its governor in 721. In 732 AD, when the growth of Frankish power threatened the Muslim position in Spain, he led an army across the Pyrenees into the dominions of the Franks. His army met the Franks, led by Charles Martel, near Tours, France, later that year. Charles Martel (688?-741) was the mayor of the Palace of the Merovingian Frankish kingdom of Austrasia (in present northeastern France and southwestern Germany). He was the son of Pepin of Herstal and the grandfather of Charlemagne, whose rule solidified the Carolingian dynasty. Although he was engaged in many wars against various kingdoms before he established his authority as the ruler of the Franks, his greatest victories were against the Muslims from Spain. When they invaded France, Charles defeated them at the Battle of Poitiers near Tours following an indecisive outcome on the battlefield after the Muslims withdrew. The progress of Islam, which had filled all Christendom with alarm, was thus checked for a time. Subsequently, Charles drove the Muslims out of the Rhône valley in 739 AD, when they had again advanced into France as far as Lyon, leaving them without any of their possessions north of the Pyrenees beyond the Aude River.

Zaidan provides vivid descriptions of the siege of Constantinople and the ensuing military confrontation as well as the Battle of Poitiers. Not only does he describe the details of warfare such as military strategy, the

---

3 *'Abd al-Rahman al-Nasir,* first published in Arabic in 1910 and not translated into English.

disposition of battle formations, and the arms and attires of Christian and Muslim armies. But also and importantly he describes the human and social aspects of war—with commentaries on how each side viewed the other and how the social and tribal composition of the Arab and European armies affected the course of those battles.

The novel depicts the political climate and social mores of Spain and other areas that came under Arab rule. One of the more distinctive attributes of Zaidan's approach is the continuous and perceptive commentary and reflection on political and social organization and particularly on human behavior, sentiments, and motivations under varying conditions. Zaidan also analyses the power of a common religion or language in unifying people from different cultures—a theme found in many of his other works. Last but not least is the contrast between the tolerance of Islamic rule in which religious minorities were able to preserve the freedom to worship in exchange for a tax compared to the Christian areas where there was no such tolerance. This situation prevailed for many centuries. It culminated in the thirteenth and fourteenth centuries, a period that proved to be a golden age of tolerance and achievement for the various communities living in Spain. This came to an abrupt end with the Christian re-conquest of Spain which led to the Inquisition and the expulsion of both Jews and Muslims.

Zaidan's adventures usually unfold against a textured backdrop of history, culture and politics, and *The Battle of Poitiers* is no exception. Romance and intrigue provide the central plot of this historical novel that are woven into the events culminating in the Battle of Poitiers. Maryam, the novel's heroine, was not only young and beautiful but she was a woman of extraordinary honor, by birth and accomplishment. Like any man, she fought with great courage in several battles. But she also had the grace of women and had many suitors: Hani, captain of the Arab cavalry and Bustam his rival and chieftain of a Berber tribe. Last but not least 'Abd al-Rahman, the Arab ruler of Spain and southern France, is also enamored with her. Who will win her heart and how will all these relationships unfold in the context of the historical events?

The novel is replete with mystery—the identity and genealogy of many of the principal characters are shrouded in secrecy and suspense reigns for long before their true identity is revealed. Who is Maryam's father? And is

Salma really her mother? What is Salma's true identity? Who is that grandson of Maryam's servant, Hassan, whom he has never seen? Is Maymuna, slave and concubine of 'Abd al-Rahman, really the servant of Lumbaja the daughter of Duke Odo or is she impersonating someone else? Not only are we kept guessing on the true identity of many of the novel's main characters but we are surprised to learn that so many of them lived at various stages of their lives in both the Muslim and Christian worlds. As we learn their origins and their true loyalties we begin to piece together the game of spies and counter-spies that is played out, with each promoting his or her secret agenda in a web of fast-paced actions that influence the outcome of the Battle of Poitiers.

Jurji Zaidan—The Historical Novelist

Jurji Zaidan (1861–1914) was a prolific writer who at the dawn of the twentieth century sought to inform and educate his Arab contemporaries about the modern world and the heritage of the Arabs. He is considered one of the most prominent intellectual leaders who laid the foundation for a pan-Arab secular national identity. Pioneering new forms of literature and style in Arabic, he founded in 1892 one of the first and most successful monthly journals, *al-Hilal*, a magazine that is still popular today in its 120th year. The *Dar al-Hilal* publishing house in Cairo remains one of the largest in the Arab world. It is a fitting tribute to Zaidan's legacy that new studies reassessing his contributions, and translations of many of his novels—this one among them—are being published one hundred years after his death.

Zaidan was one of the pioneers in the composition of historical novels within the modern Arabic literary tradition and in their serialization in magazines. New editions of the entire series of novels are still being published almost every decade and widely distributed throughout the Arab world – a testament to their lasting popularity. Zaidan's novels were not just for entertainment; national education was his primary goal. The twenty two historical novels he wrote cover extensive periods of Arab history, from the rise of Islam in the seventh century until the decline of the Ottoman Empire in the nineteenth. The stories depicted in these novels are grounded in the major historical events of various epochs. The particular manners, lifestyles, beliefs and social mores of those periods, as well as political events, provided the context into which Zaidan weaved adventure and romance, deception and excitement. They were therefore as much "historical" as "novels," reminiscent of the historical novels of Alexandre Dumas in France and Sir Walter Scott in Britain, though Jurji Zaidan's novels more closely reflect actual historical events and developments.

Over the last hundred years Zaidan's historical novels have been translated into many languages; every novel has been translated at least once; many into four or more languages. To our knowledge there are almost one hundred translations of individual novels in more than ten languages—most in Persian, Turkish/Ottoman, Javanese, Uighur (in China), Azeri, and Urdu – but several also in French, Spanish, German and Russian. Three translations of the present novel were made in Persian. What is noticeable, however, is that not a single one has been translated into English until the present time.

The Zaidan Foundation has so far commissioned the translation into English of five of Jurji Zaidan's historical novels and more are being planned. The *Battle of Poitiers (Sharl wa 'Abd al-Rahman,1904)* is the second novel set in Spain, following the appearance of the first novel in this series, *The Conquest of Andalusia*. Two other novels cover the 'Abbasid period, during and after the reign of Harun al-Rashid, at the zenith of Arab and Islamic power and civilization: *The Caliph's Sister – Harun al-Rashid and the Fall of the Persians (al-'Abbasa Ukht al-Rashid,1906)* and *The Caliph's Heirs – Brothers at War: the Fall of Baghdad (al-Amin wa'l-Ma'mun,1907)*. The fifth novel, *Saladin and the Assassins (Salah al-din al-Ayyubi,1913)*, takes place at the time of the Crusades.

The Zaidan Foundation[4]

The Zaidan Foundation, Inc was established in 2009. Its mission is to enhance understanding between cultures. To this end the Foundation's principal objective is the international dissemination of the secular and progressive view of the Arab and Islamic heritage. Its first program is the

---

4 More information about the Zaidan Foundation and its activities can be found on the Foundation's website at www.zaidanfoundation.org

study and translation of the works of Jurji Zaidan. Our audience is the broader English speaking world: the United States, England and Canada to be sure, but also English-speaking Muslim populations with little or no knowledge of Arabic such as Bangladesh, India and Pakistan. To achieve its objectives, the Foundation supports directly or through educational or other institutions, the translation and publication of historical, literary and other works, research, scholarships, conferences, seminars, student exchanges, documentaries, films and other activities.

Acknowledgements and Thanks

The Zaidan Foundation was fortunate to have Professor William Granara from the Center for Middle Eastern Studies at Harvard University translate this novel. He is professor of the Practice of Arabic on the Gordon Gray Endowment and director of Modern Language Programs at Harvard. He teaches Arabic language and literature and directs the Arabic language program at Harvard University. He studied Arabic at Georgetown University and received his PhD in Arabic and Islamic Studies at the University of Pennsylvania. He is also the former executive director of the Center for Arabic Study at the American University in Cairo and the former director of the Arabic Field School of the U.S. Department of State in Tunis, Tunisia. He writes on cross-cultural encounters between Islam and Christendom throughout the Middle Ages. In addition, he lectures and writes on contemporary Arabic literature and has published translations of Egyptian and North African fiction. His work on literary criticism focuses on post-colonialism and cross cultural poetics.

Many people have generously contributed their time and energy to the Zaidan Foundation, helping to craft our mission and goals, designing and advising on the implementation of our programs and reviewing studies and translations. Foremost among these are Ambassador Hussein A. Hassouna, ambassador of the Arab League to the United States, Ambassador Clovis F. Maksoud, professor of International Relations and director of the Center of the Global South at American University, as well as Edmond Asfour and Bassem Abdallah – all members of the Foundation's Advisory Council. Professor Thomas Philipp was instrumental in helping launch the Jurji Zaidan project following our fortuitous meeting after several decades. Last but not least my greatest debt is to my wife Hada Zaidan and our son

George S. Zaidan for their support of all aspects of this project. The original idea of the Jurji Zaidan program came from Hada who had more than a marital interest in this project as her grandfather, Jabr Dumit, was one of Jurji Zaidan's closest friends. In addition to their general and unstinting support, both she and George Jr helped design the program and made detailed reviews and many suggestions on the products sponsored by the Foundation.

George C Zaidan
President
The Zaidan Foundation

Washington DC
March 2012

Translator's Acknowledgments

Embarking on a venture of translating a novel and meeting the challenges that lie therein are never the work of any one individual.

In bringing Jurji Zaidan's *Battle of Poitiers* to English, I benefited from the assistance and advice of several friends and colleagues whom I wish to acknowledge. Khaled Al-Masri, Sayed Elsisi, and Eric Calderwood have all displayed wisdom, patience, and generosity in advising, explicating, arguing, challenging, and editing. Without their input, this undertaking would have been lonely and unsuccessful.

My thanks also go to George Zaidan for his vision and devotion to this magnificent enterprise of bringing the literary treasures of Jurji Zaidan to contemporary Anglophone readers, and for including me in this project that will most assuredly make a substantial contribution to both Arabic and world literatures.

William Granara

Dramatis Personae

'ABD AL-RAHMAN AL-GHAFIQI

(*'Abd al-Rahman*),   ruler of the Arabs in Spain

CHARLES MARTEL,   leader of the Franks

HANI,   captain of the Arab Cavalry

DUKE ODO,   prince of Aquitaine

BUSTAM,   chieftain of a Berber Tribe

MARYAM,   daughter of 'Abd al-Aziz Ibn Musa

SALMA,   mother of Maryam, a slave and wife of Roderic, Visigoth King of Spain

MAYMOUNA,   servant of Lumbaja, the daughter of Duke Odo, a slave and concubine of 'Abd al-Rahman

HASSAN,   servant to Maryam

Glossary of Arabic Terms

'abaya: a cape-like garment worn over a robe or other outerwear.
dinar: a coin minted usually from gold.
dirham: a coin minted usually from silver, and of lower value than a dinar
Emir (var: amir): prince, or commander
howdah (Arabic: hawdaj *p.* hawadij): a litter or tent-like structure placed on top of a camel for women and children.
jubba: a knee-length garment worn by men on formal occasions
People of the Book (Arabic: ahl al-dhimma): a legal status for protected people, usually Christians and Jews, who have concluded treaties with Muslims.

Author's Historical Introduction

The Muslims invaded Spain in the year 711 AD (92 AH[1]) under the command of the Berber[2] Tariq Ibn Ziyad, an officer of Musa Ibn Nusayr, the Umayyad governor in North Africa. Musa had by this time approached eighty years of age, and when Andalusia[3] was conquered it became a province subordinate to his rule. The governor at that time resided in the city of al-Kairouan whence he commanded his viceroys in Andalusia. After the 'Abbasids rose to power in the east, Andalusia became an independent Umayyad state.

When Musa's preparations for invading Spain were fully underway, he consulted the caliph who gave his consent but also cautioned him. Musa was reluctant to overextend the Muslim forces, since they were highly outnumbered at this time by the population of the country they intended to conquer. He launched a campaign drawing mostly from the Berbers, the indigenous population of North Africa, and he appointed one of their own, Tariq, to lead them. When the armies of Tariq and Roderic clashed in a fierce battle, Roderic was killed in 711 AD, and the conquest of Andalusia entered the annals of history. Within the span of a single year, the cities of Cordoba, Malaga, Toledo and others became part of greater Andalusia, where the feet of the Muslims were firmly planted.

---

1 AH short for *hijra* denotes years in the Islamic calendar which begins in AH1 (622AD) when the Prophet Muhammad emigrated from Mecca to Medina.

2 In this novel Jurji Zaidan uses the Arabic term 'barbari' to describe the indigenous peoples of North Africa. We have thus translated it as 'Berber.' More recently however, that term has come to be regarded with disfavor by the people whom it describes, the preferred term being the one by which they describe themselves: 'Amazigh' (plural 'Imazighen').

3 Spain was then known to the Arabs as al-Andalus or Andalusia in the west.

When the news of this speedy victory reached Musa, he wanted to get directly involved, and so he sent word to Tariq to desist from advancing further into enemy territory. He mobilized an army, comprised of Arabs and Berbers, and crossed over to Spain from another direction. He captured Almeria (Almerida), Saragossa (Zaragoza) and other towns, and when he saw how easy it was for him to conquer these places, he penetrated further into the peninsula until he reached the Pyrenees Mountains and entered France. When he arrived at the city of Narbonne, he resolved to continue his conquest of Europe and reach Damascus by way of Constantinople. It was his hope to conquer the whole of the civilized world at the time, especially since Europe lay divided and in disarray.

As these conquests progressed, disagreement began to fester between Musa and Tariq. When it got out of control, the caliph in Damascus, Walid Ibn 'Abd al-Malik, summoned them to his palace to investigate the matter. They arrived in Syria in 713 AD, with Musa bearing vast amounts of booty and slaves as gifts. In the meantime he left his son, 'Abd al-Aziz, in control of Spain, who, in turn, made Seville his headquarters.

During these hearings in Damascus in 715 AD, the caliph died and his brother Sulayman Ibn 'Abd al-Malik assumed the caliphate. There had been some residual animosity between him and Musa, and so he rebuked the North African governor severely and had him imprisoned. Then he instructed one of his agents in Andalusia to kill Musa's son, 'Abd al-Aziz. When they brought his embalmed head back to Damascus, the caliph summoned Musa and showed him the head. This gravely affected the father, and soon thereafter he died.

We do not know what happened to Tariq thereafter. Whatever the case may be, the Arabs in Andalusia did not abandon the idea of conquering Europe after Tariq and Musa's departure from the scene. They waited for the right moment to resume their conquest, but tribal rivalries stood in their way. Then, in 717 AD, they resumed Musa's plan but from a different route. The caliph Sulayman dispatched a massive army under the command of his brother, Maslama. These forces set up a blockade around Constantinople and remained there until Sulayman died and Umar Ibn 'Abd al-Aziz was proclaimed caliph. He recalled the army, having ruled out the conquest of Europe from this route, and took the decision that this would be better done from Andalusia.

A series of commanders followed, one after the other, capturing many cities in the south of France. But they failed to establish a permanent foothold in any of them. Until the year 730 AD when the governorship of 'Abd al-Rahman began.[4] He was a resolute man, pious and dignified, jealously protective of Islam and Muslims. He took it upon himself to resume the conquest of Europe from Gaul, Germania, and the Holy Roman Kingdom until he reached Damascus. The capital city in the meantime had been transferred to Cordoba, and 'Abd al-Rahman chose a number of battalions to launch an invasion on Frankish territories—which they called at that time "the continent." However, he took the utmost precautions to avoid the pitfalls that had plagued his predecessors. He examined closely the causes of their failure and made great efforts to avoid them. He assessed the situation in the provinces of Andalusia personally, and he inspected the local governors, removing those he found weak or overly ambitious. He replaced them with men who displayed intelligence and good judgment. He restored churches and property that had been usurped or pillaged to their rightful owners. He restored to the citizens the rights they used to enjoy in the time of Musa Ibn Nusayr. During his tour of the towns and villages, he preached to the Muslims in their mosques, urging them to struggle in the service of God (*jihad*) to conquer Gaul and what lay beyond it, so that Islam would prevail throughout the world. His words had a powerful impact on all Muslims, Arabs and non-Arabs, and they came in throngs from many directions—North Africa and Egypt, Syria, Hejaz, and Yemen. Among them were Arabs and Berbers, as well as new converts to Islam from Egypt and Syria, from the various tribes and ethnic groups. They stood shoulder to shoulder to perform the jihad for the sake of their faith, all in response to 'Abd al-Rahman's call. They put their trust in him because of the resolve, virtue, justice and sincerity for which he was well known. They rallied around him and organized themselves in groups according to their tribes and ethnicities, vying to outdo each other in their obedience to the man they considered their great leader.

---

4 'Abd al-Rahman Al- Ghafiqi led the Andalusian Muslims into battle against the forces of Charles Martel in the Battle of Tours (October 10, 732) for which he is primarily remembered in the west. From the Yemeni tribe of Ghafiq, he relocated to Ifriqiya (now Tunisia), then to the Maghrib (now Morocco), where he became acquainted with Musa Ibn Nusayr and his son 'Abd al-Aziz, the governors of Andalusia. *Translator's Note*

Chapter 1

The Conquest of Bordeaux

In the days of old, France was called Gaul, or to some Gallia, at a time when the shadow of the Roman Empire had been gradually fading away from its lands. A Germanic tribe, which the historians refer to as Merovingians, came to rule it, and the first of their kings was Clovis who ascended to power in 481 AD. Succession to the throne passed to his sons and grandsons until the beginning of the eighth century when their dominance weakened and their kingdom dissolved into many parts. Power eventually fell into the hands of numerous figures throughout the realm, as happens within many a nation in decline.

In those days the king's chief minister was a man named Charles who hailed from the tribe of the Franks. Gaul had now been divided into provinces: the southern province, which they called Septimania, and whose major center was Narbonne, had fallen into the possession of the Muslims. To the north was Aquitaine, whose major center was Toulouse. This was a huge province ruled by the Frankish prince, Odo. Bordering Aquitaine to the north was the Loire River, to the east the Rhone River, to the south the Pyrenees mountains, and to the west Guyenne. The province of Neustria, later Austrasia, was located to the north, and the aforementioned Charles ruled this province in addition to all the other provinces of the upper realm.

Each of the provincial rulers, called dukes, sought to gain power over all the others, thereby strengthening Emir 'Abd al-Rahman's resolve to conquer their lands by exploiting their weaknesses and rivalries. He mobilized his forces and ordered them to march on a jihad to conquer every inch of their territories.

During the campaign he discovered that one of the Muslim commanders on the eastern border of the Pyrenees did not see things the way he did. The general, whose name was Munaydhir, was the leader of the Berber forces. He was renowned for his bravery, but he felt no sense of solidarity with the Arab commanders against whom he harbored bitter resentment. Unfortunately this was the case with many Berber commanders. Munaydhir had concluded a pact with Odo, Duke of Aquitaine, upon which the duke offered the hand of one of his daughters in marriage, a beautiful maiden named Lumbaja. When 'Abd al-Rahman became aware of this pact, he set out to combat Munaydhir, but with the utmost caution and restraint. When he finally succeeded in finding him, he killed him on the spot, seized his property and women, and sent Lumbaja to the caliph in Damascus. Immediately thereafter 'Abd al-Rahman resumed his conquest of the Frankish lands. He penetrated the areas to the north while several of his battalions captured many towns, amassing along the way stunning amounts of booty. The Franks, by now gripped with fear, were unable to defend themselves. When the Arabs reached the city of Bordeaux, famous today for its wine, they conquered it by force, arrested its governor whom they thought was Odo, beheaded him and sent the head back to the caliph in Damascus, as was the custom in those days.

Bordeaux was known at that time as "Bordighallia." It was a fortified city surrounded by high walls with lofty look-out towers. The Romans counted it among the greatest cities of Gaul in terms of knowledge and culture. It even boasted a Roman theatre which they called the 'Ghallius Amphitheater.' Bordeaux was also home to a cathedral, the Church of the Holy Cross, whose ruins are still in existence today. When the Muslims arrived they camped on the outskirts of the city. From there they launched attacks and pillaged its vast riches. When the fighting died down, they gathered all the booty, prisoners of war, and slaves, and lined them up in a public square in front of the campsite. Emir 'Abd al-Rahman then selected one of his officers, Hani by name, to oversee the division of the spoils among the troops. This Hani was a commander of the cavalry, the most vital segment of the Muslim army at that time since Arab skill in horsemanship was the crucial element in the Muslim victories, especially in the lands of the Franks.

Hani was a young man not quite twenty-five years of age. He stood out among 'Abd al-Rahman's soldiers for his valor and his exceptional skills in combat and horsemanship. 'Abd al-Rahman had great affection for him and promoted him above the other commanders in spite of his tender age, and despite the animosity between their two tribes. 'Abd al-Rahman was a scion of the Bani Ghafir of Yemen, while Hani hailed from the Qays, one of the major tribes of the Hijaz, and the rancor between these two tribes continued to fester at that time. Hani, for his part, reciprocated both love and respect for 'Abd al-Rahman. The two men made a solemn pact to stand united in this battle and to avoid the follies of jealousy and divisiveness to which others before them had succumbed in their attempts to conquer 'Europe.' And so 'Abd al-Rahman was unwavering in his decision to delegate to Hani the responsibility of dividing the booty after the capture of Bordeaux and distributing the slaves among the officers and soldiers, as he delegated to him all responsibilities that required trust and confidence.

It was now the beginning of autumn in the year 733 AD, and the vineyards that flourished along the outskirts of Bordeaux were blooming with grapes. Hani had, by now, proven himself to his soldiers. He would routinely mount his steed and accompany them on their daily rounds throughout the lands, encouraging them to remain patient and steadfast. His intimate relationship with 'Abd al-Rahman and the preferential treatment he received from the revered emir, however, provoked resentment, even among some of the senior officers.

Hani was tall and broad chested, and people recognized him immediately. Wherever he appeared, his outstanding qualities were easy to detect. He was in the prime of youth, with clearly defined features, prominent eyebrows, high cheek bones, piercing eyes, a small nose and mouth, a prominent chin, a sparse beard, and jet black hair, with a face ever smiling but nonetheless dignified.

One day, as was his custom, he was riding his black stallion, the one he preferred above all others for its easy stride, graceful gait, and stamina on the battlefield. There was never a battle from which Hani, mounted on this stallion, didn't return victorious, and there wasn't a single soldier among the army of 'Abd al-Rahman who wasn't familiar with Hani's attachment to this horse. Some even held the view that Hani was too preoccupied with his beloved horse to entertain thoughts of other earthly pleasures—such was the degree to which he tended to its every need. He adorned its saddle with gold and equipped it with a silver bridle and stirrups. Across its forehead he hung a large pearl medallion he picked up during one of his expeditions in Gaul and which he had remolded into the shape of a star. The horse, in turn, was equally attached to Hani. When it heard him calling or spurring it into battle, it was always quick to respond. It would take off in battle like an eagle spreading its wings and soaring in flight. And when Hani commanded it to stop, it stopped in a split second.

During the late afternoon of that day Hani mounted his stallion as if he were about to climb a mountain, donned in a crimson 'abaya and turban. He girded himself with his sword. His name was engraved on its blade and the hilt was encrusted with precious gemstones that shone in the sunlight. He then ordered his men to divide the spoils of war into separate piles, putting the prisoners of war to one side, women and children to another, and weapons, utensils, jewelry, and other possessions to a third. Next he summoned his senior officers who formed a large group. Many of these were North Africans on whom the Arab armies depended for the campaigns into the Iberian peninsula and France. Although they were a valiant and ferocious people, they were not sincere in their support of the Islamic cause, especially given the Arabs' arrogance at that time towards non-Arabs, even toward those who accepted the Muslim faith. The Berbers accompanied them on their expeditions, more in their desire for their share in the booty than for their support of Islam. Some of their tribes participated in holy wars pretending to be Muslims, even though they were Jews or pagans. Such was the case as well with other non-Arab segments of the army—Slavs, Franks, and Greeks, for example—many of whom were former captives or slaves purchased by the Arabs and raised under the protective cover of Islam. That day when the officers gathered around Hani, he ordered that the precious utensils and other looted objects be brought to him, and he commanded that they be divided into fifths, in accordance with Islamic law. He set aside his fifth and distributed the remainder to his officers, according to the number of soldiers they commanded.[5] Whenever he discovered a dispute erupting among them over an item or the manner in which the booty was divided, he would intervene and quickly settle the score among the squabblers.

When they had finished dividing the booty, they turned to the matter of dividing the slaves. There was quite a large number of them, and most of them had been bound together with ropes and chains. When they were brought to Hani, he addressed his officers:

"These slaves are part of the spoils of war, but dividing them is not feasible at this time. So, put them up them for sale. Where are the merchants?"

No sooner had he finished this last question than a crowd of Jewish merchants from Kairouan, Cordoba and other Muslim cities appeared. They had accompanied the campaign hoping to profit from such trade. One of them stepped forward, wearing a wide black turban, and sporting both a long beard that reached his chest and a large eagle-shaped nose. He was cloaked in a bulky robe with broad sleeves, and he was carrying a large purse filled with gold dinars and silver dirhams.

"For how much will you buy these prisoners, Harun?"

"Whatever my lord commands," he responded.

"Were we not anxious to continue the battle we wouldn't be putting them up for sale at all. Instead we would be putting them to good use or perhaps extracting a ransom from their kinfolk. No doubt many of them come from wealthy families who would be willing and able to pay a handsome sum for their release. But we're pressed to move on, and we haven't much time, so, make the purchases." Hani spoke in a dignified but straightforward tone.

Harun for his part was scheming a way to pay the lowest price possible. "My lord speaks the truth, but buying such a large number of them will cost us an arm and a leg for we must transport them for sale to Spain, North Africa and Syria, not to mention the costs of feeding and clothing them."

---

5 In Islamic law, and in the tradition of ancient Arabian warfare, the leader of the victorious army was entitled to the first pick of the booty, and the remainder was divided among the soldiers.

Hani had no patience for haggling, and since he wanted to finalize the sale and get on with the matter of selling the captives, he made an offer: "Buy each prisoner for one dinar, but leave us their personal possessions, and let them take a bit of clothing to cover themselves."

Harun laughed as he began to stroke his beard and lay it over his chest. He feigned surprise at such a high price. "Isn't it enough that I pay so much for so many of them, and then you demand to keep all their possessions except the shirts on their backs?"

"Our price is final and the sale is concluded," insisted Hani as he pointed to his scribe. "So pay him when he finishes counting the numbers and adds up the bill."

He then walked his horse over to the other side of the square where they kept the women and children captives. Harun followed him and suggested to Hani that he sell them only to him. Another merchant, who was a witness to the sale, spoke up in protest. "You bought all the prisoners for yourself, so leave the captives for us." When Harun responded to this merchant crudely, some of the other merchants sided with him while others came to the defense of his competitor. When the fracas grew to a violent pitch, Hani shouted above the din: "Calm down! We'll sell them to you all."

When they reached the area where the captives were kept, Hani trotted his horse to the far end. They had been placed in rows, the women separated from the children. Hani slowed down the horse's pace, scrutinizing the faces carefully. The women pleaded with him, weeping and wailing, some shouting that they didn't know any Arabic, others fretting because he wasn't looking directly at them. When he reached the last row he saw what he was looking for—a young, beautiful woman the likes of whom no human being had ever laid eyes upon. She was next to an older woman who couldn't be more than forty years of age. There was a noble, dignified air about them. They remained absolutely silent amidst the hysterical clamor of the other women and children, and they sat motionless, not moving an inch. There wasn't the slightest trace of fear or worry on their faces. The older woman had a fair complexion, blond hair and blue eyes. She twisted her hair into a bun and set it on top of her head, which she covered with a black headscarf. She wore a black robe that covered her entire body, making her seem as though she were coming from a convent. She sat on a rock with her head bowed as if mulling over a ponderous matter. She held a leather purse in her hand, clutching onto it for dear life.

The young girl was tall, well built, and well proportioned. She stood close to her mother. She too was dressed in black, and one hand rested on her mother's shoulder. Her arms were exposed from the elbow to the wrist. Her natural beauty was fully evident. There was a healthy and radiant look in her face. One would guess she was about fifteen years old, twenty at the most. She had an olive complexion, jet black eyes, and long, black lashes. Her eyes had a piercing but delicate look. One could tell by the way she stood that she was healthy and strong, but at the same time she was endowed with a feminine softness that melted men's hearts. She wore a simple black frock that was open from the neck to the uppermost part of her chest. She braided her beautiful chestnut hair into two long braids that hung down her chest and reached the top of her waist. Her hair was covered with a headscarf that draped over her shoulders and back.

Hani approached at the moment the young girl was turned toward her mother, speaking to her in a whisper. When he reached them the girl glanced toward him and studied his face. He too stared at her closely. He then ordered one of his slave boys to bring them to a secluded place where he usually went to rest. No one paid any attention to this since it was the custom for commanders to choose for themselves whatever they desire from the spoils of war. Hani returned to the middle of the crowd and called out to the merchants: "How shall you divide these captives among yourselves?"

Harun stepped forward. "The price of a young girl or a woman differs according to the degree of her beauty, intelligence, health, or some skill she may possess—such as singing or dancing, sewing or cooking, for example. If it pleases my lord, command that each one of us be allowed to choose whomever we desire, on the condition that whoever has the first choice pay the highest price, the second choice the next highest price, and so on and so forth."

Hani found this suggestion most reasonable and agreed to proceed: "Who steps forth to make the first bid, let him pay five dinars for the first woman, and one dinar for the first slave boy. Who comes second, let him pay half that price." As Hani made these announcements he beckoned to his scribe and entrusted him to complete the transactions, setting the prices, and allocating to the soldiers their legal share of the booty. With that done, he mounted his horse and set out to visit his two captives.

✼ ✼ ✼

The sun was beginning to set and the Muslim soldiers were returning to their camps, leaving the division of the booty to the commanders in charge of completing the sale of the captives and dividing the totals among themselves. They were seated in a tent next to the pavilion of Emir 'Abd al-Rahman, and among them was a Berber chieftain named Bustam. Along with his tribe, he had converted to Islam only in his greed to gain the material rewards that come from pillage and plunder. Bustam was strong-bodied and ill-natured. Anyone who laid eyes on him shivered in fear at the mere sight of him, with his huge skull, wide, flat face, and large nose with massive nostrils. There was hostility in his eyes and a sharp, penetrating look that cut through anyone or anything that had the misfortune of crossing his path. Compounding his terrifying mien were two intensely thick, bushy eyebrows that were bridged by a thick tuft of hair, making it seem as though he had one long eyebrow. Added to that, he had a dark, oily complexion that gave him a hard, crude look. And his thick, bulbous lips made him look lewd and lecherous. He was the chieftain of one of the largest Berber tribes. When he heard about 'Abd al-Rahman's campaign against the lands of the Franks, he made a public display of embracing Islam and professed to join the jihad all in the name of his new faith. But what he really wanted was the plunder. However, the likes of him did not fool Emir 'Abd al-Rahman. But he was compelled to turn a blind eye in order to win their support, especially because the Berbers had proven themselves to be fearless and skillful in battle. Bustam, alone, could charge the enemy gates, dodge a barrage of arrows, and fight hand to hand with a band of knights. His heart knew no fear. And when a battle was won and the time came to divide the plunder, Bustam stood first in line to select what he desired from the loot. 'Abd al-Rahman dealt with him patiently, always cautious against rattling his cage, lest his anger and fury lead him to stage a revolt against the Muslim army. Such a revolt could draw in the various Berber tribes as well as the battalions of non-Muslim partisans who were recruited for this campaign. Many of these harbored resentment towards the Arabs for their superior achievements and success in securing higher positions of power and amassing greater wealth.

The Arabs found themselves no less embroiled in their own rivalries. The tribes from Yemen competed with the tribes from the Hejaz. And the Ummayad Arabs vied with the Hashemite Arabs for the right to occupy the caliphate. However, the non-Arab Muslims often paid little attention to these petty jealousies, especially in times of the jihad, since they were the *crème* of Islam. As for those who feigned conversion to Islam in their desire to reap its worldly rewards, they were sooner or later subjected to derision, as their true intentions became all too well known.

It was a matter of general agreement that Bustam had conducted himself with exceptional courage during the battle for Bordeaux. It was he who personally stormed the estate where the two women were residing, and he who took them into custody and assigned one of his soldiers to bring them back to the camp where they were added to the plunder. It was his intention from the beginning to select the girl for himself as soon as she was put up for sale. He hadn't anticipated anyone standing in his way or competing for her. So, Bustam ordered one of his soldiers to keep an eye on the young girl and not let her slip from his fingers. But when the soldier saw Hani pick out the girl and her companion for himself, he dared not speak up to object, but rushed back to inform his master. Bustam shouted at him angrily: "Go back and tell that Qaysi tribesman that the girl belongs to commander Bustam. She's mine, and I won her with the edge of my sword!" As the soldier stood dumbfounded, Bustam realized he wouldn't deign to address Hani in that manner. Bustam taunted him: "What's wrong with you? Why aren't you going?"

The messenger turned around and made his way out of the tent, dragging his feet while he sunk his nails and rubbed them into the thick, tangled hair that stood on top of his head like a huge turban. He was holding under his arm a leather pouch that contained all the items of booty he earned from the last battle. There was no other way to keep them than to carry them on his person, no matter how heavy they were. As the Berber moved away at a snail's pace, turning around frequently to guard against anyone who might follow him and rob him of his loot, Bustam continued to keep his eye on him. The more he watched, the more his anger flared at the thought of the soldier's insolent hesitation to carry out his order. He called out to the soldier to come back, and when he stood in front of him, Bustam shouted: "Apparently, you're afraid of him? So, don't talk to him, just go yourself, and take whomever wishes to accompany you, and bring me back the girl."

The soldier set out once again in the same manner he did before. This time Bustam flew into a blind rage and picked up a Roman dagger which he had acquired by killing its owner simply because he wanted to possess it. He rushed toward the soldier and stabbed him with one hard thrust that killed him instantly. He then yelled out to a group of soldiers sitting in a nearby tent. "Go ahead and help yourselves to this coward's loot. All that he's carrying and all that remains in his tent are now legally yours!" The soldiers pounced on the corpse and ripped open the pouch, grabbing its contents and nearly coming to blows in their greed. Bustam put the dagger back in its sheath, jumped on his horse, and returned to the square. Since he had already learned of the whereabouts of the two women, he headed in their direction, without passing by Hani or confronting him on the matter.

Meanwhile, Hani was still preoccupied with the sale of the captives. When he finally finished his business with the Jewish merchants, he mounted his horse and galloped toward the women who were roughly a mile away. The sun set behind the buildings of Bordeaux, casting its last rays over the remnants of its fallen castles until the darkness settled over victor and vanquished, killer and killed, as well as over all the Muslims who remained resolved to continue their conquests and enjoy the rewards of their successes. It set over the defeated city of Bordeaux and its people, the slain menfolk whose women were taken into captivity while their homes and churches were plundered.

Had Hani's excitement and desire not taken over his heart, and his feelings for the captive not clouded his vision, he would have thought that what loomed over the horizon of Bordeaux was nothing more than twilight. His beet-red blushing had so intensified that anyone who saw him at that moment would have guessed it was the result of all the bloodshed from that day. His mind was lost in the fog of something only a person afflicted with the same thoughts could identify and understand. It was love—a love that strikes people like a sickness from out of nowhere. It may start with but a mere glimpse, eyes hardly meeting—then emotions are aroused and two hearts become inescapably attracted to and intertwined with each other. But not every man experiences this kind of love. It only afflicts some eyes and some hearts. When eyes exchange looks that lead to a mutual understanding, feelings are aroused and hearts awaken. The lovers, having found each other, blissfully unite as they recognize each other with only a glance. This is exactly what happened to Hani that day. He had never seen this young maiden before. His eyes fell upon her for the very first time in front of the gate of the city, as he supervised his soldiers unloading the booty and captives. She was among those being brought out by a band of Berber soldiers carrying out Bustam's orders. He spotted her as she walked by, garbed in a black frock and headscarf. She kept her head bowed down, looking at no one, and clinging close to her companion. When she reached the entrance of the gate, she heard him calling out to his scribe, inquiring about the number of captives taken from the estate. Then Hani gave his scribe an order. "Do not count this one among them!" His voice pierced her ear like an arrow that went straight to her heart. She couldn't help but look up at him, and at that moment he saw in that glance what no preacher could preach or writer set to paper. What her look conveyed was a plea, a cry for help and a need for affection—it was an act of submission with dignity and honor. He responded in kind with a glance in which she read a clear response that set her heart at ease. All this interaction happened in a split second, while the throngs of people, crying and weeping, hoping and fearing, remained oblivious to what was going on between them.

Hani resolved to marry her and be with her forever the moment he laid eyes on her. He had remained unmarried all this time because of the solemn decision he took as a young boy to devote himself to the jihad, and to fight the Franks until the Islamic conquest of Europe was complete. For this reason he answered the call of 'Abd al-Rahman to join the battle. But when his heart began to flutter he couldn't help but think about marriage. Most people who wish to marry seek it in this manner—that is, by falling in love. Some even spend long years thinking about it but do nothing until their heart is suddenly awakened by a glance or a word, and only then do they make a concerted effort to act.

Hani decided not to breathe a word to anyone about the girl after completing the sale of the captives, so intent was he to have her for himself. He strapped the bridle onto his steed and made his way toward her. As he drew near, he saw a horseman close by. Although it was twilight he could detect from the kind of horse and the battle gear that it was a Berber soldier. He spurred his horse to a gallop, not worried in the least about this girl he loved because he was secure in the fact that there wasn't a single soul among the Muslim troops who would dare to speak to her after he publicly staked his exclusive claim to her. But jealousy is love's strongest and clearest warning sign. It is blind and deaf, neither responsive to reason nor receptive to advice. And so Hani galloped at full speed straight to her as his heart pounded in his chest. When he saw the horseman standing next to her and was close enough to hear him speak to her with threats and promises, he knew immediately who it was. "Bustam," he shouted. Bustam turned toward him with eyes flashing sparks of rage. "What do you want, Commander?"

"Get away from these women. I have selected them for myself," he replied.

"How can that be, when it is I who captured them," retorted Bustam.

Hani was determined to persuade Bustam to concede the girl, either by offering someone more beautiful, or by compensating him with whatever money or property he wished to have. "Suppose you did in fact capture them," he said smiling. "But you also saw that I rightfully selected them for myself. Why don't you relinquish them for my sake, and you can have whatever you desire from my portion of the booty?" As he spoke, he pretended to be busy stroking the mane of his stallion and acting as if the matter were of little concern to him, concealing the deep-seated feelings of jealousy that suddenly threatened to overwhelm him.

Bustam answered, unable to conceal what he himself was really thinking. "That won't happen. If you want to share my portion of the plunder, then take the older one, and leave this one for me."

Hani responded calmly but with an explicit threat in his tone: "I'm not interested in sharing. This girl belongs to me. So go back to your camp and take your portion of the booty, as well as the prisoners and captives we sold to you."

Bustam, seething in anger and shock, stood his ground. "No one can take away what I lawfully plundered, not even Emir 'Abd al-Rahman himself. Isn't it enough that you Arab tribesmen degrade us and lord over us for everything we do? You treat us as if we weren't Muslims. But you know full well that I can stand in your way and send you packing, and you won't be able to conquer a single town."

The threat weighed heavily on Hani, and he gave thought to what evils may occur if he were to anger Bustam, especially since he had no real interest in Islam or commitment to the Muslims. His anger and the anger of his tribesmen would provoke a serious rift that neither Hani nor 'Abd al-Rahman could control. But his youthful impetuosity got the better of him, especially since he now stood between him and the woman he loved. He put his hand on his sword and slowly removed it from its sheathe. He started to attack Bustam, swinging at him without aiming at any particular part of his body. Then suddenly the woman came forward and took hold of the reins of his horse and addressed him in Arabic: "Stop fighting over us. We're nobody's property. Enough quarreling, please." She spoke in the Yemeni dialect with a slight foreign accent. The two men froze in silence, stunned by her Arabic.

This, however, did nothing to deter Bustam from pressing ahead with his demand to keep the girl. Hani's threat in the presence of the women, especially now that it was revealed that they understood Arabic, had rendered him all the more adamant. Bustam turned toward the woman and spoke: "You are, in fact, my booty. You are free to go with this man should you choose to do so. But this girl is mine. He slid off his saddle as he spoke and stood straight up on the ground. He held his hand out to the girl expecting to take hold of it. But she moved further away from him, staring at him distrustfully but without losing her composure. He jumped back on his horse and followed her. When Hani saw his brazen act, he couldn't control himself any longer. The girl's apparent disgust with Bustam delighted him but he realized that his reasoning and restraint would have no effect on this Berber. He whispered to his stallion still brandishing his sword in his hand. The stallion leaped forward and neighed loudly as though it were sharing its rider's thoughts and emotions. The woman stood back as her heart pounded, when all of a sudden they all heard the sound of a horse's footsteps coming toward them from the direction of the camp.

"Hani, Hani," cried out the voice, "put your sword back in its sheathe!" They turned around and saw the horseman approaching. Before they could even see his face they could tell from the horse and his clothing that it was Emir 'Abd al-Rahman.

Chapter 2

Hani and Maryam

Although 'Abd al-Rahman was a man of medium height, he was endowed with an imposing appearance. He had a most radiant face, with a wide beard and a prominent forehead. His black hair was sprinkled with white. His eyes were huge but not bulging, and his nose was eagle-shaped. He had a sharp but intelligent look about him. He wore a thick, black 'abaya and his head was covered in a large white turban. The moment he arrived everyone grew silent. He turned toward Hani.

"I see you're quarreling with each other and divided into factions. I expected as much ever since I heard Bustam talking to his messenger. I feared a fight would erupt among my officers just at this time when we're in the direst need to stand united. I waited for Bustam to get back, but when he didn't, I came to you right away, and thank God I arrived just in time."

Everyone marveled at the emir's watchful eye over his troops and his resolve to keep them together. The pang of a guilty conscience struck Hani at that moment since he had vowed to 'Abd al-Rahman that he would stand by him .

"It's never been my intention to compete with another Muslim over anything, no matter how valuable. But Bustam is contesting my choice of a young captive girl whom I chose among hundreds of women we sold in public auction. And what would happen if we had sold her to one of the Jewish merchants? What would he have done then?"

Bustam interrupted in protest: "It was I who obtained her from her seller with a price he accepted."

The older of the two women stepped forward and facing 'Abd al-Rahman she spoke with firmness and composure. "I am standing before 'Abd al-Rahman al-Ghafiqi, the emir of this army, I presume?"

'Abd al-Rahman, taken aback by her Arabic, replied: "Indeed, it is I. And how did you know that?"

"I recognized you immediately by the way you attend to your troops. I had heard that about you. These two men are quarreling over us, but we belong to neither one of them. We belong to another man whose identity I will reveal only to you!"

As she addressed him with a fearlessness unheard of among prisoners and captives, he stood in awe. This awe was compounded by the combination of her poise and her simple black clothing which pleased him. He darted a quick glance at the young girl and was immediately overwhelmed by her beauty. His curiosity about these women got the better of him, and he continued to probe. "Tell me, please, what you wish to say."

"I shall not tell you anything here and now," she responded. "But I will tell you in private."

'Abd al-Rahman turned to two of his special forces and ordered them to bring a pair of horses to carry the women back to his pavilion. When he asked the woman about the young girl, she simply replied: "She's my daughter."

Hani stood nearby but remained silent. He was confused by all the talk about the mother and daughter, and he feared that something the mother might say could stand between him and the daughter. In this brief instant he became drawn to her, especially since he felt that the young woman seemed attracted to him. He even felt that she may be falling in love with him. So while the emir was speaking to the mother he seized the opportunity and moved quietly closer and spoke in a tone that couldn't disguise his amorous feelings. "What's your name, young lady?"

"My name is Maryam," she answered, in proper Arabic. The soft ring of her voice delighted him, and he was especially charmed by her slight lisp that turned her "r" into a hard, guttural "g," making her say, "My name is "Maghiyam."

"My name is Hani," he continued. "Will you memorize my name the way I memorized yours?"

She immediately understood what he really meant to convey by this question, and she responded in kind. "I memorized it even before I knew it! And how could I not, having seen of its bearer what I have now seen?"

Hani was delighted by her intelligence and quick wit. He felt strangely at ease with her and he answered by imitating her lisp in a playful and affectionate manner. "I pray this will be a blessed acquaintance!"

Maryam smiled and his heart was instantly captivated. Her cheeks flushed crimson and she bowed her head bashfully. Bustam was watching them closely with evil in his heart, but did not dare utter a word, especially in the presence of 'Abd al-Rahman. A few moments later the two horses arrived and they all rode back to the camp. Hani didn't take his eyes off of Maryam for a moment as she mounted the horse with such speed and agility that he thought she must have been born on the back of a horse. His passion for her was growing by the minute but he couldn't shake an unsettling premonition that he would be separated from her. When they arrived in front of 'Abd al-Rahman's pavilion, the largest and most prominent of all the military tents, 'Abd al-Rahman turned to Hani. "Go back and take charge of the army, and perform your duties in the manner I have come to expect of you, and remember, we are now in enemy territory. As for you, Bustam, my brave officer, go about your business and put aside this matter that has erupted between you and Hani. We're about to embark upon a series of conquests, and you will fall upon booty and captives many times more numerous than what you have lost."

As soon as his two senior officers departed 'Abd al-Rahman beckoned Maryam and her mother to follow him into his tent. The woman was still clutching on to her purse which she had strapped to her forearm. She kept one of her hands over it in fear that someone would come and snatch it from her. 'Abd al-Rahman dismissed all the members of his elite guard and inner circle of advisers, and remained alone with the two women. He was eager to hear their story, and so he sat down by a corner of the tent on a thick carpet on which they had laid out his portion of the booty. He sat the two women in front of him. Both of them removed their headscarves and outer cloaks. In the soft glow of a lantern 'Abd al-Rahman saw the face of the woman and beheld its exquisiteness despite the waning of her youth. He then looked at Maryam and caught a glimpse of the bewitching beauty of her eyes and her sublime features. He offered a silent prayer of praise to the Creator for such a magnificent creature. He then turned his attention to the mother, most anxious to hear her story. "Where do you come from, my sister, and what information do you have to tell me?"

"I will tell you my story in good time, but my goal for now is to help this army achieve what it has set out to do."

'Abd al-Rahman was taken aback by these words. He also detected a slight accent even though she spoke in fluent Arabic. He wanted to get to discover who she really was. He continued to probe. "But what brought you to these parts? The way you speak suggests you're not originally an Arab. And your clothing appears to be that of a non-Muslim woman. This goal of yours seems difficult for me to believe, so why don't you just come out with the truth."

The woman stared at him in astonishment. "I do not sit before Emir 'Abd al-Rahman al-Ghafiqi with the intention of concocting a fake story, but I see that his impressions about me are incorrect. Whether I am or am not an Arab or Muslim need not prevent me from wanting to help the Arab or Muslim army. It should not come as a surprise to my lord, the emir, that there are in this and in other Christian and Frankish cities many who would prefer an Arab Muslim victory over that of the Franks."

'Abd al-Rahman bowed his head as both his amazement and confusion increased. But he decided to sit patiently in the hope of eventually finding a clue that might reveal her true story.

"I don't completely understand what you're telling me," he added. "Are the people of these lands hoping for a Muslim victory over their own rulers?"

"They've been hoping for this ever since they heard about the conditions of the Spaniards who came under Arab protection because they saw them going from slavery to freedom, and from oppression to justice."

"But have they now changed their minds?"

"Yes," she replied.

"Why? Please tell me."

"It's no secret to my lord that when the Muslims conquered Spain twenty-two years ago they treated the population gently and justly. They didn't force people's allegiance nor did they shed innocent blood. Those who opted to remain in their faith were allowed to do so, while those who had been enslaved and then embraced Islam were given their freedom. They were given rights as well as obligations. The Visigoth rulers treated these people as their property, forcing them to work as serfs in their homes and fields. When the Muslims came and conquered their lands, they gave the people the choice between conversion or the right to purchase legal protection. They made it clear to the Spaniards that whoever was a slave and converted would become a free man. A significant number of those enslaved quickly converted in their desire for freedom, while only a tiny fraction of them, those who displayed unusual courage or some exceptional skill, had previously been granted freedom under the Visigoths. But even those few emancipated during the rule of the Visigoths and the Romans before them did not enjoy all the rights granted to free men. Their status was something between a slave and a freeman. With the Muslims, however, those who embraced Islam were granted full rights, and even the Spaniards who remained as Christians maintained their right to practice their religion openly, to follow their customs and rituals, and even keep their institutions, such as their system of government and courts. The Spaniards felt as though they moved away from oppression to liberation with the Islamic conquest. And that feeling spread throughout all these parts. That's why Musa ibn Nusayr found the conquest of these lands so easy. He was determined to conquer all of Europe before returning to Damascus by way of Constantinople, but the Muslims assassinated him, just as they killed his son 'Abd al-Aziz, after him.[6] If it weren't for these pernicious deeds, the Muslim conquest would have been completed at that time, and these lands which you came to conquer would have fallen into your possession twenty years sooner. But the rulers of these lands that succeeded Musa and his son

---

6 Musa ibn Nusayr (640-716AD), an Umayyad general of Syrian origin, was instrumental in the Muslim wars of conquest in North Africa and Spain. According to many historical accounts, he died a natural death, but his son 'Abd al-Aziz was assassinated by Arab forces. *Translator's Note*

were men with personal ambitions, and they treated the Christians and the non-Arab Muslims with contempt. Ill-will spread and the conquest became more difficult, as more and more people came to believe that it was preferable to remain in their own state and in their own religion."

The woman stopped speaking at that point and lifted her hand to wipe her mouth. 'Abd al-Rahman sat speechless, astonished at her wisdom and her command of facts. He studied her features, wondering who she could possibly be. But he remained patient, hoping that at the end of her story there would be answers to the mystery of her identity. He took advantage of her silence and decided to bait her.

"It seems to me that you're more familiar with the facts than most of our own men, and more determined than they to protect Muslim interests!" Taking a deep breath he continued. "The matter is exactly as you say, my sister, and I assume word reached you that I've been exerting all my efforts to rectify the situation before embarking on this new war of conquest. I decided not to march forward before visiting all the cities and towns of Andalusia the Muslims conquered from the Franks. I inspected their governors and removed those whom I found to be weak or ambitious. I replaced them with wise and intelligent men who govern all the citizens fairly, regardless of religion or ethnicity. I returned to the Christians what some Muslim commanders plundered from their churches. I restored to them all the rights promised to them by Musa ibn Nusayr and his son 'Abd al-Aziz. In fact, I made these adjustments acknowledging that Islam commands us to do so, and with the realization that the Companions of the Prophet Muhammad were only able to achieve success in their conquests by striving to rule with compassion and to treat their new subjects with kindness and justice."

The woman replied as she adjusted her headscarf, exposing her features which revealed how deep she was in thought. "I've learned about all you've done and are doing, and everything you intend to do, and for that I was anticipating your victory. But I see a contradiction in what I heard, and frankly, I fear the outcome."

"How so?" he reacted, taken aback by her audacity.

"I suppose you know what I know in this respect, but shouldn't what you yourself have just witnessed between Hani and Bustam be sufficient to illustrate what I'm saying? Was not blood nearly shed between them on account of this young girl?" She pointed to Maryam who sat next to her listening with interest and curiosity, as if she were hearing all of this for the first time.

As 'Abd al-Rahman took in the woman's words he sat twirling the sides of his mustache and pulling at his beard with the tips of his fingers. There was a look of intense interest in his eyes as he continued to probe the woman.

"What you actually saw was no more than a rivalry between two commanders over the prize of a beautiful captive. There's nothing unusual about that."

She contrived a polite laugh and continued. "Emir 'Abd al-Rahman is clearly aware that the reasons for this rivalry are the bad feelings among the commanders and their differences concerning the goals of the campaign. Many of them joined the campaign only because of the plunder and looting, especially the Berbers and other tribes like them. They do not understand the true meaning of jihad and 'conquest.' Nor do they know what Islam really is about because they came to embrace it only for its worldly rewards. Those of them with such misguided motivations have no concern for what the people want or why they are angry. You can see proof of that in what I myself saw during the fighting today. Some of your own men made no distinction at all between residences and places of worship, or between monks and common folk. They pillaged the cathedral of Bordeaux, one of the most revered churches of the Gallic people. Now, in addition to their contempt toward the Muslims, the Gauls believe that the archbishop is going to help them take their revenge against the Muslims.

"How is it that they pillaged the cathedral?" 'Abd al-Rahman interrupted. "I personally ordered them to protect it and show respect to the priests and monks." He then stood up, clapped his hands, and called out to his servants standing guard at the entrance of the tent. A young man, slight of build and garbed in a simple tunic, rushed in. "Bring Hani to me at once!" The servant made a gesture of obedience, and just as he was about to leave the tent the woman spoke up: "I neglected to ask you to free my servant. He was taken prisoner despite his old age, and despite his Arab ethnicity." 'Abd al-Rahman yelled out to the servant to order Hani to bring the old man from among the prisoners. He then asked the woman. "What's his name?"

"Hassan," she replied.

"Tell Hani," he ordered the servant, "that an old man named Hassan has been taken prisoner and that he should bring him to me."

When Maryam heard Hani's name her heart began to pound. She had been sitting with her head lowered, but now she perked up. Her cheeks flushed red, and a sparkle twinkled in her eye. The three of them sat quietly, waiting for Hani's arrival. 'Abd al-Rahman kept his eyes averted as he fiddled with his beard, fearing that some precipitous action might muddle his thoughts, or perhaps confuse or obstruct them. The woman for her part remained silent, awestruck by the way in which he was sitting. Only a few minutes passed before they heard the sounds of a horse's trot. When it neighed 'Abd al-Rahman recognized the sound of Hani's black stallion and knew that he had arrived. The servant reappeared at the opening of the tent and announced what the emir already knew.

"Show him in," 'Abd al-Rahman ordered.

Even before the servant had the chance to turn around, Hani entered the tent as if he were entering his own home, such was the close relationship between him and the emir. He was still wearing his red 'abaya, armed with sword and light weapons. When 'Abd al-Rahman saw him, he flashed a smile, welcomed him, and asked him to take a seat next to him. Hani sat down with his gaze fixed on Maryam and her mother as he adjusted his robe and settled into his seat. Maryam sat demurely, with eyes bowed but stealing a glimpse of Hani every few seconds to watch his every move. An elderly man, garbed in traditional Gallic dress and wearing a small turban had entered right behind Hani. His hair had turned ashen and he sported a long, thick beard. He was frail of physique and his forehead and neck had become severely wrinkled. His cheeks were sunken, and anyone who laid eyes on him would guess he was in his nineties. But to see him walk or hear him speak one would say he wasn't a day over sixty. He entered the tent wearing a knee-length tunic fastened at the waist with a leather belt. His lower legs were exposed, covered by thick hair under which the skin could not be seen. He covered his feet in sandals made from the local Bordeaux leather. 'Abd al-Rahman beckoned him from the entrance of the tent to sit, and he came in and complied politely.

'Abd al-Rahman turned to Hani. "I imagine you've had a trying day. You must be exhausted."

"There's no exhaustion in war if your goal is victory, as was the case today in our victory over this city, which came with the help of God's and Emir 'Abd al-Rahman's sword."

"The emir had no hand in this matter," 'Abd al-Rahman replied. "Our victory is owed to you, to your troops, and to all the Muslim forces. But I didn't summon you here to talk about that. I called you here on a matter of grave concern. So lend me your ear!"

Hani stepped forward and pricked up his ears. "I wish to hear what the emir has to say."

"Do you know the reason why the Muslims succeeded in conquering so much territory, from the days of our first holy wars until now?" he asked.

"I know that God granted them victory by allowing them to come together and join forces, and this is what we aspire to do in every struggle in which we engage," he responded.

"I agree. You have been my right hand in keeping this huge army of warriors together, especially given their different backgrounds and conflicting goals, even if some hardships had to be endured along the way. But there's another factor that aided our pious ancestors in their conquests and in establishing a new system of governance. Do you know what it is?"

Hani bowed his head and pondered the question carefully. 'Abd al-Rahman kept his eyes sharply focused, seemingly anxious for a speedy response. "What I know is that the Islamic state rests on justice and compassion," he finally replied.

"This is what I was getting at," affirmed the emir. "Justice is the basis of the power to rule, and compassion toward the citizens assures their obedience and affection. This has been the case among the protected peoples, the Christians and Jews alike, and especially the monks and priests who oversee the churches and synagogues. Both the Koran and the Prophetic sayings and traditions have instructed us not to harm them. And so whenever our patriarchal caliphs dispatched an army into battle they commanded it to treat the conquered peoples gently, and that they not inflict any harm on them. And they instructed that their houses of worship and those who watch over them were not to be violated. Didn't you know that?"

"I do, indeed, know this," Hani insisted, "and how often did we speak about the violations committed by some of the rulers of Andalusia in this regard, and we vowed to prevent such violations."

"Then what is the meaning, pray tell, of your assault on the Bordeaux Cathedral today, plundering its vessels and harming its clergy?"

An expression of anger mixed with bewilderment flashed over Hani's face. He lowered his eyes for a moment and then looked up, shook his head and spoke: "May God damn Bustam for his greed and disobedience! I personally warned him against such atrocities during the battle. I could see how ravenous he and his men were to loot treasures. Having heard about the gold and silver vessels in the cathedral, and anticipating that greed would lead him and his tribesmen to plunder, I interrupted the fighting to tell him pointedly, 'I'm warning you not to allow your men to enter a single church or synagogue.' Total silence was his reply and I knew then and there that he had no intention of heeding my warning, given his greedy and vicious nature."

Before he could go on, 'Abd al-Rahman spoke: "So you think Bustam has a hand in this?"

"It could only be him. No one else would be so brazen as to disobey my orders. Later, when the booty was being divided I noticed one of his men carrying a solid gold cross and another with a sterling silver censer. These could only be found in a church."

Once again 'Abd al-Rahman clapped his hands and called out to his servant. "Go and bring me Bustam." Then he turned back to Hani. "I'm going to speak to him calmly, knowing how ill-tempered and vindictive he is. If I anger him I run the risk of tearing the army apart."

"What is it about this dangerous ally and his tribe you can't do without?" asked the woman.

'Abd al-Rahman sighed a deep sigh. "If we cleansed our army of these unsavory elements, we would be removing the fiercest and most numerous of them. The many legions that make up our army come from Berber tribes, Slavs and Serbians, Copts, Nabateans, and others. And there are many among them who still adhere to their Jewish, Christian, Manichaean, or atheist beliefs even though they profess allegiance to Islam in public. The Berbers are the bravest of people—they fear neither death nor the enemy. It could rightfully be said that it was they who actually conquered the Iberian peninsula and then turned it over to us. So if we were to rid ourselves of them, this next phase of conquest would be nearly impossible. The Arabs even today remain too few in number to undertake this campaign alone, and so deploying the Berber battalions in this war will be of the utmost importance. But this requires us for the moment to exercise skillful politics in dealing with them and to avoid provoking them. What incites them is the spoils of war, and this leads, frankly, to our giving in to their demands. We do this to keep them happy which, in the end, is in the best interests of Islam."

Maryam's mother marveled at 'Abd al-Rahman's shrewd intelligence and open mind. "An army created with you as it's leader can only emerge triumphant and victorious," she said.

Beaming with delight at the woman's compliment, 'Abd al-Rahman turned toward Hani and placed his hand on his shoulder: "This is my right hand, the leader of our cavalry." Hani was visibly embarrassed and just as he was about to say something the servant entered and announced that Bustam had arrived. "Let him in," ordered 'Abd al-Rahman.

Bustam entered with his robe open in the front and his turban half falling off the side of his head, with one hand dragging his sword and the other holding a half-eaten bunch of grapes. When he realized he was in the presence of the emir, he took a few steps back and tossed the grapes outside the tent. Then he came back inside, swaggering confidently. However arrogant he appeared, he remained diffident toward 'Abd al-Rahman, given that the emir never once failed to treat him with the utmost respect. 'Abd al-Rahman was a shrewd politician who knew full well that real power rests on affection and leniency, not on boorishness, arrogance, and coercion. Thus, he greeted the Berber chieftain with a warm and welcoming smile and invited him to take a seat. Bustam sat down while casting his gaze around the corners of the tent. When he spotted Maryam and Hani he knew instantly that this summons was in some way connected to them.

"We've asked you to come, commander," 'Abd al-Rahman addressed him, "to ask you about a matter that concerns us greatly, since our goal is the same, that is, to raise the banner of Islam."

Bustam was delighted by the flattering remarks, especially since the Arabs were accustomed to treating the Berbers as though they were merely clients. He responded, "O Emir, whatever wish you command will be my honor to obey, for I am eternally at your service!"

"God bless you, and may He bestow His benefits on the Muslims through your sword," he intoned. "But the matter for which we brought you here concerns the Christians of this city who have raised a complaint against some of our soldiers for pillaging one of their churches. As you well know, the Christians are 'People of the Book' and are thus entitled to our protection, as God has commanded us, and that their churches and places of worship shall not be desecrated. More than ever, it is imperative that we treat the people of these towns kindly especially since we're about to embark upon the conquest of areas more resistant than those we've already taken—areas ruled by men who oppress their subjects with more cruelty than those we defeated. So, if they see us as being tolerant and fair rulers, they will help us. For this reason I have been instructing you, under the command of our brother, Hani, to respect all their places of worship. Therefore, I ask that if you have any information about this church or who plundered it, I implore you to help us retrieve all the stolen items."

"I cannot deny, Emir, the seriousness of this matter. Until today, we have been obeying these orders and respecting the sanctity of the churches. But this morning I saw something that shook me to the core. I couldn't hold myself back from taking revenge and ransacking this church. I saw in some of the houses throughout the city a number of Muslims—men, young boys and even women—being used as slaves! True, I can't deny them the right to practice slavery since we, ourselves, do the same with those of them we capture. But I saw Muslims with feet bound in iron shackles, and Muslims, burdened with heavy loads over their shoulders, being lead into the vineyards to work like animals. After seeing these horrific scenes I couldn't control myself from exacting justice, and so I plundered everything I could get my hands on, and I made sure not to leave out a single church or a single monastery." When Bustam had finished what he had to say, 'Abd al-Rahman turned toward the woman to gauge her reaction.

"I readily admit," she said, "that the Franks treat their Arab prisoners much more harshly than the Muslims treat their Frankish prisoners, even if both groups alike buy and sell these captives like commodities. And when the prisoner comes under the roof of his master, he or she is used however the master wishes, to till the land or work in the home. These prisoners remain as slaves, as do their children and several generations to follow, unless their families or acquaintances ransom them with handsome sums or some other form of payment. But with Muslims, emancipation from slavery is an easier matter than it is with the Franks. Concerning the matter of shackling feet, as far as I know this is done to prevent escape. Maybe in these cases they tried to run away and failed, and so their feet were bound to prevent them from trying again."

'Abd al-Rahman cut her short and turned to address Bustam. "Let's suppose that what you say happened. But what is important in the end are the consequences. If we were to behave the way they do, how would we be superior to them? What kind of victory could we expect in this life and what kind of reward could we anticipate in the afterlife? What matters to us is that we conduct ourselves the way the Koran and Islamic custom instruct us to, and that we live our lives according to the ways of our pious forefathers. Furthermore, our desire to go to war for even a little of the booty leads to our failure and stands in the way of our mission, and thus we lose twofold the spoils of war. Not to mention the ignominy that would follow us!"

Then he turned to Hani as his eyebrows arched in an expression of concern. "I don't need to remind you that we are following the righteous path in achieving something more precious than gold and silver. We are striving to conquer this entire continent. If we succeed in doing so, we gain not only riches but souls as well. We also spread Islam to the many tribes of Christians, atheists, and God knows how many more. We will take possession of the cities and their people. Our flag will wave high over Rome and Constantinople, not to mention the countless number of other Christian capitals. Our vagabond will become a prince, and our poor man will become a rich man. And you, Hani, will gain much of gold, silver, and precious gems. You will possess more than you desire of slave girls and young servants. If you think I'm mistaken, say so!"

Hani was quick to realize that 'Abd al-Rahman was aiming his remarks to Bustam even though he was staring at Hani as a ploy to extract a reaction from the Berber chieftain. Bustam replied with his familiar contrived charm. "You're absolutely correct! They say the Berbers and other client groups never received their fair share of the booty from the Arabs until you assumed the leadership. Your predecessors, and even many Arab commanders until today, regard non-Arab Muslims as slaves. If they fight in a battle, they don't receive their rightful share of the rewards. And we're not blind to this favored treatment!"

"I have treated you with absolute fairness because all Muslims are brothers," 'Abd al-Rahman insisted in his defense. "Now, you must hasten, you and Hani, and retrieve the church's vessels so that we may return them to their rightful owners."

Bustam arose basking in the praise and respect 'Abd al-Rahman showered on him. He even momentarily forgot the rage he felt toward Hani because of their feud over Maryam. Boorish and uncivilized people like himself are the quickest to forget a grudge because their hearts do not retain emotions. If someone crosses them, they react, loudly and publicly, never holding anything back. This was exactly the case with Bustam's claim to Maryam because he wasn't emotionally attached to her the way his rival was. For his part, Hani stood up and followed Bustam out of the pavilion, but he left his heart behind, perhaps as collateral for Maryam's heart. She herself felt as though her heart had stopped beating the moment Hani left, and she was terrified that her feelings would be clearly visible on her face. And so she pretended to adjust her headscarf. When the two commanders were out of sight, the woman turned to 'Abd al-Rahman: "Would my lord the Emir grant permission that my daughter be escorted along with my servant to a safe place where she could remain under your protection? I will then finish what I must tell you, and we will see what can be done."

"Servant," shouted 'Abd al-Rahman as he clapped his hand. One of the young attendants quickly entered. "Accompany this elderly man and young girl to the women's tent. Prepare it with all that is necessary to welcome them, and treat them as guests in our custody."

The woman, satisfied, turned to Hassan: "Go, my good man, with Maryam. You are in the emir's protection. Stay by her side until I arrive."

With the servant leading, the elderly Hassan walked out limping with the aid of his cane. Maryam walked behind him.'Abd al-Rahman speculated that the woman wanted to be alone with him to reveal her secret. When the two of them were alone, he took the initiative and spoke up: "Please, first and foremost, sister, tell me your name with which I may address you."

"If that's the reason you need to know my name, you may call me Salma."

"I must confess, Salma, that I find your situation very strange. The more I hear you speak the more I find myself eager to know who you really are. Am I correct in thinking you wish to be alone in order to let me in on your secret?"

Salma began to relax and unfastened her outer cloak. She set down the purse she was cautiously holding onto and looked 'Abd al-Rahman straight in the eye with a very intense expression on her face: "My sire, you are speaking with a woman who is neither an Arab nor a Muslim, but someone who holds them in the highest regard. I beg you, my lord, to be satisfied with what little you know about me for reasons which will soon become apparent, God willing. For now, I pledge my devotion to serving the cause for which you have come, and I will do whatever I can to contribute to your success."

'Abd al-Rahman was taken aback at the way she insisted on concealing herself. It even occurred to him that this may have been part of a plot or scheme. "And what assurances do we have that you're telling the truth?" he asked.

"Your suspicion of me is reassuring," she replied. "Had you not reacted that way, I would have thought you were weak. One who commands such a massive army as yours should always stand guard against plotters and tricksters. If you don't harbor some degree of suspicion toward every person who crosses your path, you will always face the danger of betrayal. If I were to reveal to you my reasons for being here, it would be too easy for you to believe me. For now, it's enough that I'm placing my daughter and myself as pawns in your hand as proof of my truthfulness. And if you detect the slightest sign of betrayal or deceit on my part, then you may act as you see fit."

Salma's words awakened him to the deception and cunning that surrounded him, and he responded in a tone that implied a greater degree of suspicion: "And how are we to be certain she's really your daughter? There's no resemblance between you. She looks like an Arab and you do not!"

Salma lowered her eyes for a moment and then looked up. "The only way you can know for sure is to ask the girl herself, or ask the old man. He's an Arab and a Muslim, and he's the only person who knows my secret. But he won't reveal it until the right time. So, go and ask them." As she spoke, her sincerity came through clearly in the tone of her voice and in the glimmer of her eye, and her diffidence and seriousness were clearly manifest in her facial expressions. 'Abd al-Rahman's intuition told him she was telling the truth, and that alone was enough for him.

"I believe you, Salma, but tell me, how long must we wait before you divulge your secret?"

"The secret is not tied to any particular time but it's contingent upon a certain event, and it cannot be revealed before this event takes place."

"What might this event be?" he asked.

"I cannot tell you at this time. But the purity of your intentions in conquering these lands and the speed with which you complete this project will bring us close to it. It is for this purpose that I devote myself to you. And if my lord permits me to assist him, I will gladly do so."

'Abd al-Rahman lowered his head in pensive silence for several moments. He was convinced that the key to the secret was knowing the identity of Maryam's father. He then lifted his head and started to speak to Salma as the tips of his fingers played gently with the tip of his sword. "There's no problem with holding onto your secret. But I ask of you one thing and I hope you can answer me honestly."

"If I can, then I will," she replied.

"I want to know who the girl's father is and where he is now."

The question caught Salma off guard and the blood rushed to her face. Her whole expression suddenly changed and a look of depression flashed from her forehead to her mouth. She lowered her eyes but didn't utter a word. After a long silence she lifted her gaze, her eyes awash in tears.

"Behold: you see me dressed all in black and you ask where he is?" She spoke with difficulty as she pulled onto the edge of her headscarf with her thumb and index finger.

'Abd al-Rahman regretted having asked the question about his whereabouts.

"It wasn't my intention to remind you of the passing of your husband. I just wanted to know his name. I don't see any problem in my knowing that, especially since you and I are here alone. I also give you my solemn word that I will not reveal any information you give me to a living soul. I'm not asking you to divulge your secret, just the name of your husband." He spoke these words expecting a simple answer from her. But his insistence on knowing the name of her husband angered her.

"Perhaps I've made a mistake in offering my services to you. Why all this insistence and pressure? If revealing the name of that poor man were possible, I would have done so, sparing you the trouble of asking the question. I don't see the benefit of telling you his name at this point. You will come to know everything in good time."

'Abd al-Rahman was baffled, and his desire to know her secret only grew stronger. But he decided not to persist any further, careful to protect her feelings and desirous of her support. Instead, he took another approach. "Very well," he responded. "But one question remains, and I hope that my asking it won't end in failure like my previous question."

"Speak your mind," she replied.

"I see that your daughter is of the utmost beauty. She's now of marriageable age, and you yourself are alone. Why don't you marry her off to a young man who can take care of her? I have no doubt whatsoever that you can find a person who will be acceptable to you and deserving of her beauty and sophistication."

Salma looked up at 'Abd al-Rahman as the sullen look disappeared from her face. She seemed more relaxed now as she spoke. "This is a question I have no problem answering."

"What is your answer," 'Abd al-Rahman asked delighted.

"The girl was betrothed when she was a child."

"To whom?" he inquired.

"To a man who became a Muslim, who was inclined toward Islam and Muslims, and who detests tyranny and tyrants. He's brave, courageous, broad-minded and kind."

"And his name?"

"In point of fact, I'm not certain what his name is," she answered.

"Does your daughter know him?"

"Neither I nor my daughter know him. No one knows about any of this except the two of us."

'Abd al-Rahman was confused and irritated by such riddles. "How can this be, Salma? Are you toying with me?"

"I swear by God Almighty I'm telling the truth," she answered.

"How could your daughter possibly be engaged to a man whose family name or title you do not know?"

"His title I do know."

"What is it?"

"He is referred to as '*The one who has conquered the land of the Franks with the sword,*' and '*The one who aids Islam through truth and justice.*' "

'Abd al-Rahman understood immediately that she was referring to him since no one else could be described in such terms. But he played along, feigning ignorance. "And when and where will this marriage take place?"

"At any time of the betrothed's choosing," she replied. "But it can only take place on the other side of the Loire River." She darted a look at him in a way that suggested she was awaiting his reaction.

'Abd al-Rahman understood that linking the marriage to a place beyond the Loire River was intended to hasten the Muslim conquest and crossing the northern borders into Aquitaine, the very area in which his army was headed. His head swam with thoughts of his success and his heart opened to the thought of Maryam. He had indeed taken note of her exceptional beauty since he first laid eyes on her earlier that evening, but since then he became preoccupied with matters of war, victory, and disputes among his officers. Now that he heard Salma speak, however, his thoughts immediately turned to Maryam and, giving more thought to how beautiful she was, he began to entertain feelings for her. This is of course in the nature of men. They may see a young girl and become attracted, but for some reason they don't pursue her. But when the slightest glimmer of hope arises, their feelings grow deeper, often to the point of obsession. This is not limited to love, but exists with other human aspirations. A man may aspire to power, but his ambition is thwarted by weakness or poverty. But if perchance an opportunity arises, he suddenly develops an insatiable desire for it and will go to the greatest lengths to attain it. Now, 'Abd al-Rahman could harness his energies toward two goals simultaneously since Salma's words stimulated his desire for victory and aroused in him a desire for Maryam. But pursuing the matters of finding out the name of her husband and the reasons for dedicating herself to his victory had run their course for now, and he was content to take this up on another occasion. "Let's put aside this matter for the moment," he said, "and tell me what you intend to do to help us in this new conquest?"

"I bear not a sword with which I can defend you or fight alongside of you, but the knowledge I have of these lands and their conditions could facilitate your campaign."

"And what is that?" he asked.

"Is the Commander 'Abd al-Rahman aware of the fact that the Gauls who are the original inhabitants of these lands are not the Franks who are fighting you and standing in your way? Are you aware that Duke Odo, the governor of Aquitaine, and his army are no dearer to the hearts of the Gauls than the legions of Muslims and their leader? "

"How do you explain this?" he asked.

"The inhabitants of these lands are a mixture of Romans and Gauls. The Gallic people were once a large nation. They were nomadic and free until the Romans arrived in the century before Christ and conquered them under the leadership of the famous Caesar. They remained under Roman sovereignty for five centuries until the Roman Empire began to crumble and the land was invaded by Germanic tribes from the north, just as Arabian tribes invaded it from the south. The Franks, one of the Germanic tribes, completed the conquest and occupied it. Merovius was the first of their rulers. The right to rule passed down through generations of his family until a succession of weak kings prompted ministers and commanders to compete for power and divide the empire into petty fiefdoms. Aquitaine became one such fiefdom, and the Loire River extends along its northern border. Duke Odo governs it now. Beyond the Loire lies the province of Austrasia whose governor is Charles, the prime minister of the last of the Merovingian kings. Both these men are Franks, but each one looks upon the other with deep suspicion. And the populations look at each of them with loathing because they know full well that each man covets the other province for his own selfish interests. And now, you have come to conquer, and the Gauls find themselves caught in the middle. In the end, it doesn't matter to them who is victorious, as long as they see that their interests and well-being will be safeguarded."

'Abd al-Rahman cut her off at this point: "The Gauls naturally favor the Franks because they're Christian like them!"

"It's not like that, my lord," she replied with a smile. "Religion has no part in this war. The Frankish tribes were driven to conquer this land by hunger for power and greed for wealth. That's why they were divided. For example, Odo, the governor of Aquitaine where we are now, is on his guard against Charles of Austrasia whose power he fears. Each one of them has exerted great efforts in turning the other's population against their ruler, but all the people detest both men because they fail to see how either will promote their own best interests. As you well know, it's because they oppress their subjects and usurp their property and wealth. Not like the Arabs who, when they first conquered the Iberian peninsula, left the people the freedom to tend to their own affairs. Nor did they try and coerce them to change their religion. The best of these new rulers were Musa Ibn Nusayr and his son 'Abd al-Aziz. Had 'Abd al-Aziz not been killed as soon as he was, he would have completed the conquest of these lands. The Spaniards felt that they had gone from repression to liberation during his reign, but it wasn't long before they were made to taste the bitterness of tyranny from the Muslim commanders who followed him. And then power was passed down to your family. I learned that you were on the march, guided by the hand of God, on a mission to bring kindness and justice to the 'Peoples of the Book' by honoring the treaties that guaranteed to protect their safety, their places of worship, and the right to practice their own faith. As I realize all this now, I am convinced that if the Gauls are guaranteed their personal safety and the safety of their families and livelihoods, they will be a tremendous help to you in the conquest. Don't forget that the Jews, Christians, and other groups in this country will come to your aid as long as they're reassured of your resolve to safeguard their peace and freedom of worship after the conquest is completed. What appears as zealotry on the part of the Christians comes only from a sect of the clergy, those of the old Roman guard whose interests lie in defending the Church, and from those Gauls who joined them. Also, bear in mind that there are many among the Frankish tribes who converted to Christianity only to gain power and wealth, just as some Berbers and other tribes in your ranks have embraced Islam!"

When 'Abd al-Rahman heard her say all of this, he took comfort and pride in his fair and gentle treatment of Christians and Jews. "You know that I have done this of my own accord. And what do you plan to do in this regard?"

"I will gladly undertake any mission on which you send me. In my opinion it would be best to send me in advance to the place you plan to conquer. There I could persuade the people to open their hearts to the Muslims and their leader. This of course would be on the condition that you help me in this endeavor by treating the Christians of Bordeaux with kindness and justice, and by respecting their churches and practices and not offending their dignity and sensitivities. If you succeed, it will be easy for me to convince them that the Muslim conquerors are men of their word, who fear the Lord and live by justice. I will remind them that Muslims are not what they suspect—cruel and greedy. Neither are they a people without a religion that deters them from committing atrocities. Or without sympathy in their hearts that would prevent them from ruthless and reckless behavior. I would tell them that many of their people were made to believe all these horrors because some of the Muslim soldiers who carry the banner of Islam were interested only in pillage and murder, soldiers who were not guided by a wise and just leader like Emir 'Abd al-Rahman who will make amends for the crimes they committed, as we have all seen this evening."

'Abd al-Rahman continued to be amazed by both Salma's wisdom and solidarity with the Muslims. "Do as you see appropriate," he responded, "and I will treat the Christians of Bordeaux as you suggest. What do you think will appease them?"

"What would appease them," she answered, "first and foremost, is that you guarantee their right to practice their faith and safeguard their churches and temples. Then, free the captives by ransom. Finally there's a matter of grave concern that you should be mindful of. You must prevent the sale of Muslim slaves to the Jews."

"The Jews are the merchants to whom we sell captives for money, and whoever of the local population wishes to ransom a captive, he may do so for a price," he explained.

"But some Jews purchase the captives to punish them in revenge for what they previously suffered from them. Often Jews purchase Christian captives and then kill them in secret. And so avoiding this would be deemed best in any case." Salma hardly finished speaking when they heard a great commotion outside the tent. Within seconds Hani stormed in, followed by servants carrying sacks of vessels. "Only with the greatest difficulty were we able to collect these stolen vessels since they had already been distrib-uted as booty!" he announced. He then ordered the men to empty the sacks in front of the emir. They laid out on the carpet before him candelabras, crosses, and chalices, some of which were solid gold and silver. There were also various pieces of cutlery, spoons, plates and figurines, as well as pieces of gold chipped off from the larger statues they couldn't carry off. When the servants left, only 'Abd al-Rahman, Hani, and Salma remained in the tent. 'Abd al-Rahman turned to Salma: "Here are the vessels, so what shall we do?"

She replied: "I think you should have them returned to the archbishop in Bordeaux with a messenger informing him that these objects were pil-laged from the church without your knowledge, and that you're returning them with your apologies. The messenger should inform him that the cap-tives will remain in the camp until tomorrow evening, and that anyone who wishes to ransom a captive may do so without any obstacle. I myself will go to the archbishop after the messenger returns. I'll take advantage of his satisfaction with this Muslim sense of fair play by asking him to dispatch envoys to convince the populations of the areas located on your path toward the Loire River that the Muslims will treat them more kindly than the Franks. The messenger should also tell the archbishop that if the Muslims enter their cities as conquerors, they will leave the people free, in the practice of their faith, in their local government and courts of law, as well as in all other personal matters, just as was done with the Andalusians at the time they were conquered."

'Abd al-Rahman could not find any words to add to or change in Salma's advice, and he continued to be overwhelmed by her levelheadedness and wisdom. "So let it be as you say, and let everything that has happened between us remain secret." Then he turned to Hani. "I entrust to you, a man of honor, the task of returning these precious objects and relaying this message to the archbishop."

Hani, by now, had grown more in awe of Salma than 'Abd al-Rahman, especially given that she was the mother of the young girl who captured his heart at first sight. He seized the moment and commanded the servants to carry the sacks ahead of him, and then followed them to carry out this mission. Salma arose from her seat and asked 'Abd al-Rahman to take her to her daughter to spend the night there and prepare for her mission the following day. To favor her with special treatment, he summoned Hani to come back. "Send me an elite guard to escort this woman to the women's quarters." Hani saw in this errand an opportunity he couldn't miss. "Such a lady deserves only the utmost respect. Since I'm going in that direction, it would give me the highest honor to escort her there myself." 'Abd al-Rahman approved of the idea and smiled. "May God bless you, but she deserves even more than that!"

Salma left with Hani and 'Abd al-Rahman remained alone, overwhelmed by the events of that evening. He took satisfaction with the success of his mission thus far, and he felt the powerful urge to review his troops before settling in for the night.

Chapter 3

Maymuna

When we last saw Maryam she was departing from 'Abd al-Rahman's pavilion with her servant Hassan. They were taken to a tent by one of the emir's guards. Nighttime had pitched its own tent on her thoughts that remained focused on Hani. She felt something drawing her to him, but she couldn't put her finger on it. All her mother's words on the importance of her future seemed to vanish from her mind. She was hearing nothing of the sort at that moment.

When she was a little girl her mother succeeded in persuading her to learn Arabic. She also taught her how to ride a horse and master equestrian skills and other forms of exercise. As a result, Maryam's physique developed and her muscles grew strong, blossoming into a young woman of strong character, self-confidence, and courage. But her feminine soft side prevailed, and while her physical activities gave her great bodily strength her face maintained the radiant glow of the full moon.

She walked behind the guard as Hassan strode by her side keeping the brisk pace with the help of his cane. He was wrapped in his 'abaya and wearing a skull cap fastened to his shaved head that looked like a second layer of skin. They walked along a road teeming with foot soldiers of every tribe. Some of them were in tents pitched by the side of the road, while others walked in front and behind them. There was boisterous commotion among them, and disputes over the division of the spoils of war erupted. Items of high value, such as clothing, jewelry, gold and silver utensils, and carpets were the clear bones of contention. What stood out the loudest among the arguments was the claim that some were not getting their fair share of the loot, or receiving items of little value or of no use. Maryam heard some of the officers reprimanding or threatening their soldiers. You can only imagine what she felt when she heard Hani's voice booming from a tent only a few steps away as he tried his best to convince some of them to turn over the stolen vessels from the church. Her heart began to beat quickly and she longed to stop and listen to what he was saying and take comfort in the sound of his voice. She harbored the hope that her tent would be nearby so that she could catch a glimpse of him as he passed by. She called out to the guard who was escorting them. "Where is the tent we're going to?" He responded: "Outside the camp, my lady." "Is it far from here?" she asked. The guard turned around and pointed his finger toward the horizon and explained to her that the tent was out in the direction where the light of a fire was burning beyond the outskirts of the camp. Maryam fixed her gaze on the light and realized how far away it was. "Why did they pitch a tent so far way?" she asked. "Those are the women's quarters," he replied. "It's customary that they be set up away from the camp. When we arrive, you'll see a number of tents for the wives and daughters of the officers, commanders, and other high-ranking soldiers. Were it not for the servants and eunuch slaves, you'd think you'd be entering a city inhabited only by women."

She grew silent as they walked along, with Hassan right behind, listening contently to the sound of his sandals and cane softly tapping the ground. When they finally arrived at the edge of the camp, she heard sounds coming toward them from the direction of the tents, and she froze in her tracks. Hassan, noticing her fear, spoke to comfort her. "Don't be afraid, my girl, the camp guards will ask us for a password for safe passage, and if we don't respond, they'll think we're the enemy."

"Why is that necessary, and what do we say?" she asked.

"The servant will know it." Then he turned to the young man to ask him, and he immediately responded out loud to the guards, "Toledo and Cordoba!" Then Hassan turned to Maryam: "That's our password for the night." The guards didn't ask any further questions, and Maryam and Hassan were allowed to pass, continuing to walk behind the servant until they reached the tents. Maryam heard for a second time the same questions and the same password. The servant led them toward a secluded tent in front of which a large bonfire was burning. Maryam realized it was the one he had pointed to earlier. As she got closer she recognized some white-skinned Slavs who were often sold into slavery in these parts. In addition, there were the dark-skinned who had joined the expedition back in North Africa, and most of these were eunuchs. She scrutinized the tent and saw that it was rectangular in shape, made of a heavy red material, and rested on wooden columns wrapped in cloth. She estimated it to be about fifty square feet, enclosed by a wall made with the same material and fastened to the ground with pegs and rope. The roof of the tent, again of the same material, was propped up by thick sturdy posts. The tent inside the wall was divided into small 'rooms' and open spaces separated by walls covered in a heavy green material, also supported by columns.

While she was inspecting the tent one of the eunuchs approached them. She could tell by his face he was a Slav. Maryam's guide greeted him, and, after introductions were made, they came to an agreement on the arrangements. The guide explained to the eunuch the nature of the assignment which brought him there. Just before the Slav disappeared, he spoke in broken Arabic. "I'm going in to see the matron, the caretaker of this tent. I'll bring her out so you can meet her." He left while the guide, Hassan, and Maryam waited outside. When he returned, he spoke only to Maryam: "Please go in, my lady. Your servant can wait with us out here."

Maryam fastened her cloak and adjusted her headscarf, arranging her hair in preparation to meet the matron. She entered behind the eunuch and found herself standing in a passageway that lead toward a large sitting room that was aglow with the light of an oil lantern hanging from the top of the tent. There was no doubt in Maryam's mind that it was a lantern that had been pillaged from one of the churches in a conquered area. The ground of the tent was covered with a thick, luxurious carpet on top of which rested every utensil one could possibly need, making the tent look as if it had been inhabited for many years.

She followed the eunuch into the sitting room. When he informed the matron of the emir's orders, she came forward to greet her guest. She was a large woman who moved with great effort. She had a wide face with gigantic eyes. Her voice was hoarse, and her cheeks had sunk with age. She had thick lips, and slight lines of hair sat above her upper lip and on her lower chin. Her neck and chest were buried in necklaces and chains. Some were solid gold and others gold encrusted with gems. She wore bracelets and bangles on her arms, and earrings dangled from her ears and anklets jangled on her feet. Anyone who laid eyes on her waddling on her haunches would wonder how she managed not to fall down from the weight of all that jewelry. If there was any doubt about her strength, it was dispelled by one look at her powerful facial expressions and features. She and 'Abd al-Rahman were related by birth. He provided her with the keys to his pavilion's locks and entrusted to her the management of his wives and concubines—among whom were Visigoths, Sicilians, Byzantines, Berbers and others. As soon as the matron's eyes fell upon Maryam and noticed her exceptional beauty and refinement, she took an immediate liking to her. She greeted her with the utmost warmth, especially after receiving 'Abd al-Rahman's orders to make her feel welcome. For her part, Maryam was at first repulsed by the matron's appearance, but after she heard her speak, she was comforted and even made a gesture to kiss her hand. But the matron prevented her from doing so. "Welcome, my little darling," she greeted her. "What's your name?"

When Maryam spoke her name, she pronounced the "r" like a guttural hard "g," as was her habit, much to the delight of the matron. The woman invited her to take a seat on the carpet and in no time several servants appeared bearing trays of food. Maryam ate with relish since she hadn't had a bite to eat since the morning. The matron spoke, asking questions while Maryam answered and ate at the same time. Her thoughts were still dwelling on Hani, and the more she remembered him, the faster her heart pounded. The matron noticed that Maryam seemed distracted and depressed, and she took it as homesickness. When she remembered 'Abd al-Rahman's instructions to give her a special welcome, she thought about what might comfort her and make her feel at home. As the girl sat without saying a word, the matron thought and then spoke. "It seems that an old woman's chatter doesn't suit you, but the emir has asked that I receive you with special hospitality. Perhaps you feel homesick because you were just taken captive and pulled away from your loved ones? Please rest assured you'll be treated like one of the family as long as you're with us. I'll summon one of the women from this tent who's originally from these parts and who learned to speak Arabic. She's extremely beautiful and she enjoys a high status with 'Abd al-Rahman. I'm certain that when you meet her you'll enjoy her company very much."

The matron clapped her hands summoning one of the Slav eunuchs. When he appeared she gave him an order: "Go and tell Maymuna that the matron wishes to see her." When the eunuch left she turned toward Maryam. "I have no doubt you'll enjoy Maymuna. She's 'Abd al-Rahman's favorite woman in this tent. She was once a maidservant to Lumbaja, the daughter of Duke Odo, the ruler of this country. I believe you already know his story with Munaydhir the African, a Muslim commander who was once a governor in the mountain regions that border Spain, and who concluded a treaty with Odo whose contents are still unknown. What we do know is that Odo married his daughter to Munaydhir. But our Emir 'Abd al-Rahman, fearing secrets there may have been in this treaty, killed Munaydhir. He did so during this expedition as he passed through the mountains. The army seized his property, as well as his women and booty, and they sent his wife Lumbaja to the caliph in Damascus. Maymuna was given to 'Abd al-Rahman as his portion of the booty. They say she was the most cherished of Lumbaja's slave-girls, the closest to her in beauty and intelligence."

Just as the matron was finishing her sentence, the eunuch returned with Maymuna. She was wearing a violet robe with long, wide sleeves with the back draped behind her all the way to the ground, accentuating her height and graceful figure. She had long golden hair which she twisted into a single braid she let hang from the back. If you looked at it closely you would see it was a shimmering gold, and if you inspected it even further you would see a glimmering blondness. However she had big black eyes with long black lashes. You could detect in her eyes a sparkle that revealed coquettishness and cunning more than honesty and loyalty. She had a small nose and mouth, thin lips, a wide, prominent chin, and a clear, white complexion. Maryam was instantly dazzled by her beauty and elegance, making her feel all the more grim and depressed, wrapped as she was in her black cloak. Maymuna was quick to sense this and she rushed forward to greet her warmly. Her smile put Maryam totally at ease, allowing her to feel instant warmth that allayed her anxiety. Maryam responded with a smile that did not convey the same feelings, but which only a discerning eye could detect.

Maymuna drew close and greeted her with an embrace as if they had a prearranged appointment, or as if they had known each other for a very long time. With that, Maryam felt even more at ease, forgetting the discomfort and fear she felt when she first saw the matron.

"This is Maymuna whom I spoke to you about a little while ago," said the matron. "I hope you'll find comfort in her company and enjoy your time with her." Then the matron turned to Maymuna. "This is the guest of Emir 'Abd al-Rahman. He sent her to us instructing that we take special care of her."

Maymuna sat down next to Maryam. "Welcome, our honored guest! Where are you coming from, my dear?" she asked in an Arabic tinged with a Frankish accent. Maryam, relieved by her smiling face and her obvious Frankish origins, responded. "I came with the citizens of Bordeaux who were taken captive by this army."

"Did they capture you alone, or were you with someone in your family?" she asked.

"They took me along with my mother and an elderly servant of ours. I left him with the other servants outside this tent."

"I see that you speak Arabic very well, and you say you come from Bordeaux. How is that?" Maymuna asked.

"I don't really know the reason," replied Maryam. "It just happened that way." Maryam kept her answer brief knowing that her mother would not want her to reveal too much information.

"Was you father killed in this battle?"

"No," answered Maryam.

"Was he taken prisoner, or did he escape?"

Maryam remained silent and shook her head in a non-committal way. Maymuna guessed that her father had died some time ago. But she didn't let on to what was going through her mind. "What's your mother's name? Perhaps I may know her?"

"Her name is Salma."

"Well, then she's an Arab?"

"I don't know," replied Maryam.

Chapter 4

Two Secrets

While engaged in conversation, Maymuna studied Maryam's every word and expression, trying to recall whether or not she had ever met or seen her before. She continued to ask questions in the hope that something the girl might say would jog her memory. But when she realized the girl would only answer with terse responses, she decided not to continue her questioning. She turned to the matron and saw that the old woman, with head bowed, had fallen asleep and her snoring was growing louder. She turned back to Maryam. "Why don't we go to my room? You're most welcome to stay there during your visit." Maryam complied. They arose and passed through several rooms before arriving at Maymuna's quarters. When they sat down Maymuna once again tried to remember if she had ever seen this face. Maryam was oblivious to her hostess's thoughts. She herself took to thinking about Hani and all the feelings that were building up inside of her. She wondered about the kind of burning love that arouses the heart. A pang of anxiety suddenly gripped her and a worried look flashed on her face.

They remained silent for a while, each one steeped in her own thoughts. Suddenly the voice of the matron broke the silence, calling out loudly, "Maymuna, Maryam," startling the two women. Maymuna worried that the matron might consider their move to her quarters as improper, and that she might complain to the emir that Maymuna insulted her because it was the matron who had the authority to give the orders inside the tent. These matrons have long exercised tremendous power and influence inside the households of princes, caliphs, and sultans throughout the ages. And in cases where men proved to be weak, it fell upon the matrons to give orders and set prohibitions, sometimes even in matters of state governance. They could remove men from high positions, make appointments and arrests, and decree divorces, as they pleased. So when Maymuna heard her calling, she sprung to her feet. Maryam did the same and they both rushed to the sitting room. When they arrived they saw a woman standing there, covered from head to toe in black. Maryam recognized her mother right away. She went over to greet her with a kiss. When Maymuna got a glimpse of her face the image of what she had struggled to recollect came to mind, and an anxious look suddenly flashed on her face. But she controlled her emotions and welcomed Salma courteously and cheerfully. For her part, Salma recognized Maymuna as soon as she caught sight of her. Her heart beat nervously as she never expected to see that face, especially there, or anywhere in Europe. She returned the greeting, but with coldness and a scrutinizing gaze to see how she would react. Maymuna responded with devious expressions of welcome, flattery, and playfulness.

"I'm doubly delighted that you're here with us. Firstly, I'm glad to have your company, and I'm delighted that my darling Maryam is happy as well; secondly, I'm relieved that my auntie, the matron, isn't angry with me." She forced a polite laugh while pretending to be preoccupied with adjusting her hair. She continued to speak, nervously fidgeting with the sleeve of her dress. "You're most welcome! You're among family here, and your stay with us will be a pleasure to us all."

Maymuna rested her hand on Maryam's shoulder in an attempt to hold her next to her. "Please don't be cross with me if I've become attached to your daughter, like love at first sight! She's so adorable with all the grace and beauty God bestowed upon her. No wonder she captivated the emir's heart and is being honored with such royal treatment."

While Maymuna prattled on, laughing while straining herself to be cordial, Salma watched her closely, and by her accent and the pitch of her voice, she was now absolutely certain she had met her before. She plunged deep in thought and at a loss as to what to do—now that she knew the real identity of this woman who called herself Maymuna and who pretended to have been among the women captured by the Muslim army. Who knows, perhaps she could be of great assistance to them, she told herself. She remained silent several moments longer, wavering between letting on that she knew her and revealing her identity, and between keeping the secret and acting as if she knew nothing about her. But then she realized that Maymuna seemed to recognize her, and she feared she would reveal her own secret—a secret she wanted to continue to protect. So she opted not to speak but to wait and see what would happen.

"I'm delighted to see my daughter attended to by such an affectionate woman like yourself, and in the care of our wonderful matron here, may God give her strength!" As Salma spoke these words, the matron grinned with a big smile that revealed only two teeth in her mouth, one on the top and the other on the bottom. "Your daughter is my guest, Salma, and we honor our guests here," replied the matron. "Unlike the servants and concubines, she is free to do whatever she pleases."

"I put her at your service," Salma, said, "and should you desire to treat her like your own daughter, that would be much to your credit." The matron made an effort to stand up, but because she was so heavy she was only able to rise with the help of her two strong hands, a series of moans, and the support of the tent wall. She rose as though she were carrying a heavy burden on her shoulders, replying just as she was at the point of standing erect. "She's more precious to me than a daughter, and so I'll entrust her to the care of the woman closest to the emir," pointing at Maymuna.

"Rest assured, dear lady, Maryam will be as secure here as she would be in your own lap. Who could possibly look at her and not fall in love with her? But don't think she'll stay merely as a guest. It'll only take one glimpse before the emir falls in love with her and keeps her here with us. Of course, that will only add to our happiness, as we rejoice in her presence among us. "

Maymuna smiled at Maryam as she spoke these words while an expression of shock came over Maryam's face, fearing that her prediction would come true. She dreaded losing her beloved Hani and having all her hopes fade away. Blood rushed to her face and she flushed crimson red as she put her head down. Maymuna read this as a sign of the bashfulness of young maidens upon hearing such complements. The matron abruptly ended the conversation by announcing that it was late and that everyone should go to sleep. She clapped her hands, the sound of her clapping mixing with the jingling of her bracelets. When one of the eunuch servants came into the room, she ordered him to prepare a private room for the two guests.

"Make it close to my room," Maymuna added. "If we can't be in the same room, my darling Maryam, we can at least keep each other company." The matron beckoned to the servant to do as she asked. A few moments later the servant returned announcing that the rooms were ready. Maymuna left, and Salma and Maryam followed the servant to their room. Just before going in they heard the neighing of a horse and Maryam's heart began to pound rapidly, because she imagined it sounded like the neighing of Hani's stallion. Unable to contain herself, she asked her mother if she thought Hani was there.

"He brought me here," her mother replied," but I assumed he went away since he was assigned to an urgent mission involving the archbishop of Bordeaux. Maybe something kept him here."

Maryam saw his remaining at their tent as a promising sign, and her heart told her that he stayed behind to see her. Yet suddenly she fretted and a bewildered look came over her. Had her mother observed her more closely she would have noticed her daughter's bewildered expression, but she was too absorbed in her own situation and too deep in thought about preparing for the following morning's journey to Bordeaux.

Alone in the reception room, the matron moved toward the lantern and took out a folded handkerchief from her pocket. She opened it and removed a solid gold chain strung with pearls. In the center of the necklace was a gold cross ornately encrusted with diamonds and rubies. She laid it out on the palm of her hand, turning it over and over as she smiled. She reassured herself that Hani must surely have intended it as a present to her. She wasn't foolish enough to believe it was her beauty and her graceful figure that aroused his desire and love, but his need of her intercession with 'Abd al-Rahman, who always had the last word on everything as far as Hani was concerned. She took hold of the necklace between the tips of her fingers and held it up to the the lantern, its precious gems sparkling in the light. The matron assumed the necklace was part of Hani's pick of the booty from that day's battle. But she wondered why he wanted to give it to her as a present. And then the reason suddenly dawned on her, and she was relieved. She clapped for the servant. "Go and tell Commander Hani to come to my quarters. Bring him here yourself but come from the back entrance, and do not let anyone see you." She put the necklace back into her pocket and went to her quarters. She sat on a cushion next to the wall. Hani arrived moments later but instead of wearing his turban he was wearing a steel helmet. He unfastened his tunic, revealing his coat of mail underneath. He was girded in a wide belt from which his famous sword was dangling. He rushed into the room and went straight toward the matron who was sitting motionless.

"Welcome, Commander Hani! Please have a seat."

"I have no time to sit, auntie,"[7] he answered. "I have a most urgent assignment to attend to. But I did want to see you before I left."

"God bless you, my son. Is there anything I can do for you?"

He smiled. "I do have a very simple request, which I believe you will not fail to fulfill."

"And what is that, pray tell?"

"You have seen Maryam? I would like to see her and speak to her in your presence so that you may bear witness to my honorable intentions."

"Now?" she asked.

"Of course not now. Tomorrow morning, after her mother departs. I'm confident you will comply with my request, and I count on your discretion."

The matron cleared her throat and bellowed with laughter. She communicated with her eyes that she would do as he asked. He then made a gesture to take her hand and kiss it, but she prevented him from doing so. He turned around and went on his way.

Meanwhile, we left Maryam and her mother retiring for the night, with heads bowed in silence. When they entered the room that had been prepared for them, they found the walls padded with fabric and the floor covered with carpets and furnishings. There was a pitcher for drinking water suspended on one of the walls. They sat on the cushions and when they were settled in, Salma spoke to Maryam. "We should thank God for our

---

7 In Arab culture, 'aunt' and 'uncle' are terms of respect for older people that are close but not necessarily related by blood.

safety and for our success in convincing the emir to do what we want. Our salvation and the salvation of this country rest with him alone. Tomorrow morning I will be setting out to see the archbishop. I may stay with him a day or two in order to accomplish one of my missions. I hope my absence won't distress you?"

"Must you go? And what are these missions that will keep you away so long? I've never been separated from you, and I can't stay here alone with people I don't know. I hope you'll at least leave Hassan here to keep me company."

"I need him to accompany me. Besides, I don't think I'll be away all that long," her mother replied.

"You have me worried. Couldn't you at least tell me why you're going?"

"To tell you the truth, I've agreed with Emir 'Abd al-Rahman to act as a mediator between him and the Gauls, the original inhabitants of this country, provided that he treat them with kindness and tolerance the way Musa Ibn Nusayr and his son 'Abd al-Aziz treated the Christians of Andalusia when they conquered them. I'm going to the archbishop of Bordeaux tomorrow morning to meet with him after the pillaged church property is returned to him on 'Abd al-Rahman's orders. I'm seeking his help to convince the other leaders, archbishops and elders throughout the provinces that the Muslims will better serve their interests than Odo and all the other Frankish rulers, and that I firmly believe their welfare rests with them. And please bear in mind, Maryam, that what I'm revealing to you must remain a secret from every living soul."

Maryam wasn't the least bit interested in what her mother was telling her since her every thought was focused on Hani. She wished at the moment her mother would mention his name so that she might get some information about what he was doing. But her mother ended the conversation and stood up to change her clothes and get ready for bed. Maryam did the same, but when she lay down she couldn't sleep. She was hoping Hani would call out to her, or that someone would call out to tell her something about him. She remained in this state for many long hours until sleep finally overcame her.

✵ ✵ ✵

Maymuna had gone to her bedroom next to the room where Salma and her daughter were lodging. She was thinking hard about what passed between her and Salma. She tried to reassure herself that Salma had come into the camp only to spend the night. She decided to spy on her, to eavesdrop on any conversation between mother and daughter. When she heard Salma revealing to Maryam her intended mission to the archbishop of Bordeaux, she grew gravely concerned since it stood in the way of her accomplishing the goal for which she joined this campaign. She spent a sleepless night, anxiously mulling over this problem and plotting strategies to foil Salma's mission.

Before dawn broke the following day Maymuna got out of bed and put on her cloak. She claimed to be going out to visit a tent close to the emir's pavilion. She would be having her usual morning rendezvous with a soldier whom she claimed used to be one of her personal servants when she attended to Lumbaja during the days of Munaydhir the African. As she was leaving her tent she saw a horseman coming from the direction of the camp. By the uniform and the color of the stallion she knew instantly that it was Hani. She was surprised by his arrival so early in the morning. When he was out of sight, she slipped away to the place of her appointment and waited there until her soldier arrived. He was a Berber who was in uniform. Short, with clipped hair and a slight build, he was about thirty years of age. There was an intense squint in his eyes. When he approached, he gave her a smile that communicated how much he missed her. She returned the smile in a coquettish manner. "Apparently, Adlan, you have forgotten your mistress and ignored your promise. Perhaps the spoils of war have turned your attention away from Maymuna, while her thoughts haven't drifted a split-second from you."

A look of rapture flashed in his eyes. He was totally smitten with this reprimand since it meant he was still in good standing with this beautiful and flirtatious nymph. He also knew full well that the cruel distance that separated them made him desire her all the more. He convinced himself to accept her chastisements as nothing more than a lovers' reprimand. For, there are three kinds of lovers: first, the lover who is satisfied by a mutual love that fills both hearts; second, a lover who is satisfied by giving his beloved a bouquet of flowers or a string of pearls and content with the mere acceptance of the gift, asking for nothing more; and third, an adherent of love who is merely satisfied to render his beloved a service that pleases her, like buying her food she needs, or something to that effect. Adlan was that sort of lover. He was obsessed with Maymuna, and he devoted himself to serving her whenever she turned her charms on him, or pretended to let him in on one of her little secrets. After all, it was to him that she had pledged to be completely satisfied with the services he rendered her, following the murder of Munaydhir, when her world had fallen apart.

To her playful reprimand he could only retort with the gaze of a smitten lover on her lovely face. "How could you say such a thing, my lady, when you know all too well how long I've been devoted to your service. As far as the spoils of war, it should be of no surprise to you what those Arabs left of it, especially today! After they completed our portion of the division, they came back to take it back. And you must have heard that the emir offended Bustam with an insult to end all insults!"

"Commander Bustam? Why did you let him accept that? Why didn't you prod him into demanding his rights? How long must you endure this humiliation?"

"I did try, but his rival is hard to defeat," he said.

"And who is this rival?" she asked.

"It's Hani himself. I think you saw him coming to this tent this morning."

"Yes, I did see him," she answered. "But I wondered why he came here?"

"He came to see that beautiful young girl whom Emir 'Abd al-Rahman sent to you yesterday. She belongs to Bustam as his booty, but Hani snatched her away from him, and 'Abd al-Rahman helped him to do so."

"Is she taken with this Arab, and does she prefer him over Bustam?" she asked.

"Apparently, she's fallen in love with Hani," he replied.

Maymuna then realized that Hani and Maryam had fallen in love and that he came that morning to see her. She saw in this the perfect opportunity to devise a plot that would pit the emir and Hani against each other. "How can Bustam bear such humiliation? How can he accept to let his share of the booty slip from his hands and stand by and do nothing about it? He may be able to accept this, but I will not. Tell him I will do everything in my power to return this girl to him. Tell him this without letting on what's going on between us. Do you understand me, Adlan? It offends me that these Arabs claim the best for themselves while they force you to bear all the burdens and face all the dangers. It is you who conquer all the fortresses and pillage all the booty, and what do you get for it besides fatigue and distress? But don't worry, you'll be happy when you see what I can do."

As she spoke these words she caught sight of a horseman leaving the emir's tent. When she looked closer she could see that it wasn't a man at all, but Salma, heading out on her mission. She could tell by her black clothing and also because Hassan was by her side. She also guessed that Hani would see Maryam once Salma departed. She decided to end her rendez-vous with Adlan. "You should leave now, and go with God's protection." She hurried back to her tent while Adlan remained standing, watching her depart, feasting his eyes on her statuesque figure and silky golden hair. At the very instant she was about to disappear from his sight, she turned around suddenly and flashed him a smile. He felt the earth swallow him up along with everything else on it.

Now convinced of the mutual enmity between Hani and Bustam, Maymuna returned to plotting ways to drive a wedge between Hani and 'Abd al-Rahman to sabotage the army's march to conquest—well aware that its success hinged upon the unity between these two leaders. She already figured that 'Abd al-Rahman had sent Maryam to the tent under the protection of someone else, and that Hani's love for Maryam bothered 'Abd al-Rahman. With that, she decided to ignite the fires of jealousy between them. She headed straight toward Maryam's room but not finding her there, she inquired after the matron. When she was told she was in her room, she was certain that her suspicions were correct. She was suddenly struck by the idea of a scheme she was certain would succeed, and she rushed back to her own room. She called out to a servant who had been one of the servants of Munaydhir the African before he had been taken captive. "Go quickly to Emir 'Abd al-Rahman and tell him that Maymuna sends her greetings, and that she requests an audience with him concerning an urgent matter she wishes to discuss immediately."

"With affection and respect," he replied and departed.

Chapter 5

The Lovers' Encounter

Hani arrived at an early hour that morning in his ardent desire to see Maryam. When he reached the matron's quarters she greeted him warmly but cautioned him to be patient until Salma departed. Moments later, the matron escorted Salma out of the tent and bade her farewell. When she and Hassan vanished from sight, the matron came back inside the tent, relieved to see that Maymuna wasn't there to witness the secret meeting between Hani and Maryam. She went to fetch Maryam and found her distracted and brooding. When they returned to the matron's room, Maryam caught sight of Hani's presence, and was taken by surprise. Her cheeks flushed crimson red and she was overcome with shyness. She pulled her headscarf over her eyes and lowered her head, as the emotion showed in the redness of her cheeks. This made her look all the more beautiful in Hani's eyes. For his part, he was nervously seated, and the time he spent waiting seemed to him like a whole year. When he heard the jingling of the bracelets from behind the door he knew the matron was coming. His heart jumped for joy and he leaped up to greet them the second they entered the room. The matron acted as if his presence was unexpected. "What brings you here so early in the morning, commander?" she asked.

"I came to see your lovely face, auntie!" he replied.

The matron was amused. "I can't imagine my wrinkled face attracting you. It's almost as if I were expecting your visit, so I brought you this beautiful face instead. Do you recognize it?" The matron pointed to Maryam as she spoke. Hani, overwhelmed with passion, smiled. "I recognize it and have become enchanted by it. I wonder, does it recognize me?"

When Maryam heard this she lifted her head and gazed into his face. At first her eyes wilted in love and then glowed with the sparkle of passion, expressing what she felt without the need for words. Hardly able to contain himself, Hani blurted out: "I hear the response."

The matron laughed as she took hold of Maryam's hand, struggling to lower herself down onto a cushion. "How readily you hear without words," she teased.

Hani wrapped his tunic around him and, sitting back down on his cushion adjusted his turban. "My heart speaks to me, auntie, just as one heart communicates with another." Then he turned to Maryam. "Have no fear, Maryam. I didn't come here to disturb you, but only in response to what my heart has been telling me. My instincts have proven correct and good fortune serves me well. I pledge my service to you as I consider you to be among the most auspicious of people."

Maryam took a deep breath as she tried to appease the intense throbbing of her heart which she had never experienced before. She wanted to respond but her bashfulness prevented her. How could she—*she* who never blinked facing men in the thick of battle—now find herself unable to speak before a man who only wanted to please her, who stood before her waiting for a single word uttered from her lips with which to sing her praises and hold on to, like a good luck charm around his neck? But love humbles the mightiest of creatures and renders speechless the most eloquent of people.

Hani could see from her pursed lips and stiff silence that she was holding back something she wanted to say but couldn't, out of diffidence. Consumed by his passion and losing all restraint, he decided to come right to the point. "Tell me, Maryam, and don't be afraid. Don't suppress your feelings. You needn't be embarrassed in front of the matron, for she is the bearer of all our secrets. So, pray tell, do you love me?"

She looked at him directly as she tried to gain her composure. "What value is there in love when it is not reciprocated? You're a tribe of commanders accustomed to having dozens of women. Love can only be real when it happens between two people, not three."

Hani was taken aback and barely knew how to respond. "I'm not such a person," he managed to say. "This woman here in our presence knows me well and she can attest to the fact that I've reached this age without ever having married or taken a concubine or slave girl. You may ask her yourself. She's privy to every single detail that concerns the leaders of this army. Every officer has his own tent where he keeps his wives and concubines. I have no tent, nor have I ever fallen in love with any woman or young maiden. Even the thought of love never occurred to me until the moment I laid eyes on you yesterday morning, and that's when I decided you would be my lifetime partner. And to confirm that, I pledge to you here and now that I will cast my eyes on none other than you. Can you make the same pledge to me?"

Maryam's face lit up and her face radiated with happiness. Her eyes sparkled as she flashed a wide smile that filled Hani with delight. His heart pounded with joy and he couldn't wait for her to reply. "But there is one condition I must set for you and myself. Nothing can happen until the end of this war. But when we return victorious, and I pray God will grant us victory, will you pledge yourself to me?"

"That is precisely my condition as well," she replied bashfully with eyes looking downward. "Because, if I achieve this with you, I will have gained both worldly and eternal prosperity."

"Then, let us vow to hold to this condition," he said. He stretched out his hand to her as if he wanted to say 'take my hand.' She extended her hand slowly, visibly shaken with emotion. He took hold of it and squeezed it firmly, and they were both seized with excitement feeling as though struck by a bolt of lightning.

He stood up. "I will take my leave and prepare to face the enemy. I promise you that I will strive to perform a heroic jihad because I know that it will please you. So, say a prayer for my victory." He then put his hand into one of his sleeves and took out a vial that emitted a powerful scent of a perfume. He held it out to Maryam. "This is a bottle of a special perfume unlike anything you can find in this tent. Spray it only on yourself so that when I come to visit you I will recognize the scent before I arrive, and I will bask in your presence even before I see you. And when you, yourself, whiff its fragrance, you will remember the one slain by your love." His eyes glowed from the heat of his passion as he spoke these words. She extended her hand and took the vial smiling. But then she suddenly thought about their imminent separation and became dispirited. She lifted her gaze toward heaven, and her eyes glistened with the moisture of tears.

During this time the matron managed to fall asleep in her seat. Such conversations were of little interest to her. What mattered most were the expensive presents she received or hoped to receive from future campaigns. In mid-dream, she awoke to the sound of a loud commotion from outside the tent. The sounds of cracking reins and galloping horses startled her as they did Hani and Maryam. Before she was able to hoist herself up from the cushion, she heard one of the servants shout: "Where is the lady, matron?"

The matron arose and shouted. "Who's calling out for me?" She hurried to the entrance of the tent and was met by a servant. "Emir 'Abd al-Rahman wishes to see you." "Where is he?" she asked, as she rushed toward the courtyard. "He's waiting for you in the courtyard," replied the servant. She turned around and went back into the tent. "Please, get on your horse and leave here at once before the emir catches sight of you here," she implored Hani. "He may grow suspicious of your intentions."

Hani started to leave like someone fleeing the scene of a crime but suddenly stopped. "Why don't you go and see to him and not worry about me. I'll leave soon enough." The matron sent Maryam to her quarters before heading out to meet 'Abd al-Rahman. Hani regained his composure and slipped out from the back of the tent and made his way to his stallion. As he arrived, he encountered one of 'Abd al-Rahman's lieutenants holding the stallion's bridle.

"The commander wishes to see you in his tent," the lieutenant announced to Hani. "He's gone out for the moment but will soon be back."

"Who told him I was here?" Hani inquired.

"He found out because your horse is here," he replied.

The matron went back to her quarters to fetch Maryam. Barely out of the tent with Maryam by her side, 'Abd al-Rahman encountered them. Maryam's face was still flushed with the signs of love and her eyes still awash in tears. But when she saw 'Abd al-Rahman she regained her composure and greeted him. For his part, as soon as he saw Maryam he remembered her mother, and began to address her without looking at the matron. "Where is your mother, Maryam? Has she departed?"

"Yes, my lord. She left early this morning," she said in her familiar way of speaking. He was pleasantly surprised by her lisp since this was the first time he actually heard her speak. With his keen observation and sharp perception he could tell she was surprised to see him. He also remembered at that moment seeing Hani's stallion outside the matron's tent, and he deduced that Hani had spent time with her. Pretending not to be bothered by any of this, and making a show of his indifference, he turned to the matron and spoke with a feigned naivety. "Has commander Hani returned?"

The matron didn't know how to respond. Not failing to notice this, he quickly added. "No problem. I'll see him as soon as I return." He then moved closer to Maryam but addressed the matron: "I've instructed you, auntie, to give our guest here the royal treatment. I repeat my instructions that you shower her with the best care, and not deprive her of anything. Don't let her feel homesick in this tent, for she is the most cherished of women to me."

The matron was relieved by his words and her mind eased from fear that 'Abd al-Rahman might have learned of Hani and Maryam's meeting. "I am here at the service of my lord, and—truth be told—Maryam will not be exposed to anyone who does not love and respect her."

The emir cut her off. "Where's Maymuna? Is she in her quarters?"

"I believe she is," replied the matron as she attempted to rush off to look for her.

"Stay here with Maryam, or take her wherever you like," he ordered the matron. "I'll go and get Maymuna myself. I know where her room is."

Maymuna had seen the emir arriving at the tent, and she knew he had seen Hani's stallion because she saw him pointing to it while talking to one of the servants. When she went back inside, she resolved to find out how 'Abd al-Rahman would react after finding the matron with Maryam and Hani. She wondered if he had seen them coming out of the room. But when she heard what went on between him and the two women, she assumed he didn't see the encounter between Hani and Maryam. So she looked forward to breaking the news to him.

'Abd al-Rahman meanwhile went off to Maymuna's room as the servants hovered around him, offering their services or merely standing in fearful attention. As he approached, Maymuna, feigning annoyance over how long it was taking him, rushed to the door with a worried look on her face. When he arrived at the entrance she greeted him with eyes full of love and longing. Although not his lover, she was highly skilled in the art of deception. The gleam in her eyes, her coquettish smile, and her demure manner made her look as though she was madly in love with him. 'Abd al-Rahman, for his part, found her amusing and enjoyed her company, but he viewed her just like any other concubine. Besides, for the sake of the conquest he vowed to renounce the company of women until he finished this campaign and crossed the Loire River. For this reason he came to this tent only on rare occasions. When he did come, he always displayed a special affection toward her for reasons he shared with no one. She herself may very well have known these reasons but she played along, always eager to do whatever he asked of her. Had he known what she was scheming, his punishment would have been no less than execution!

'Abd al-Rahman, like all the inhabitants of the women's tent, believed that Maymuna was once a servant in the inner court of Lumbaja, the daughter of Duke Odo. That's why he made the decision to keep her in this tent and make use of her in his dealings with the duke and his military commanders. But he kept this secret, revealing nothing of it even to Hani. And so on that morning, when she sent word to see him, he came quickly in the hope of hearing some news from the likes of Odo. But when he saw her standing by the entry with such effusiveness, he thought to himself how much she was in love with him and devoted to serving him. That pleased him since it would make it all the easier for him to use her in achieving his goals. He smiled, walked into the room and sat down on a cushion. "What do you want from me, Maymuna?," he asked.

She attempted to sit next to him with the proper decorum. "I want many things from you, my lord, and I don't know where to begin," she said with a sigh. He noticed teardrops rolling down her cheek as she bowed her head, appearing as if she were much too shy to confess her love for him. He was taken in by that, but he responded abruptly. "You know very well what I pledged to God since I decided to commit to this war!"

Maymuna acted quickly to clarify what she meant to say and that she assumed the emir had misunderstood. "My lord should not think for one moment that I do not desire to see this war come to a happy ending. Perhaps I was mistaken in my presumption of having what I do not deserve. There are dozens of women in my lord's tent who wouldn't dare speak to you in such a way. I just don't know what got into me. Did my heart tell me this was the right thing to do, or did my heart deceive me? I don't know. Whatever the case may be, I only want my lord to know what deep affection I bear for him in my heart. But I don't want to impose this or any part of it onto you, since love should not be forced." When she finished, she gulped and grew silent.

'Abd al-Rahman had figured she was in love with him but had never heard anything like this from her before. It occurred to him that she was doing this out of jealousy of Maryam, and jealousy makes people do strange things. To be sure, he asked. "By the way, have you seen our new guest?"

Maymuna was happy that 'Abd al-Rahman was the first to mention her name. "How could I have not seen her? I've put myself at her service ever since she arrived, knowing that that would please my emir. I didn't leave her side for a moment, except for the time she spent in the matron's room with Commander Hani." She spoke these words feigning an innocence that betrayed no ulterior motives. She then mustered all her strength to scrutinize the emir and see how he would react to this bit of news.

For his part, he felt a pang of jealousy especially as he recalled how her mother promised Maryam for him. Now, thinking about Hani alone with Maryam, he arrived at the inevitable conclusion that they were in love. His mind told him to intervene and stop this love affair, but his affection for Hani and his desire to preserve his loyalty to him until the end of the war, to which they both were equally committed, got the better of his personal feelings. And so he decided to wait until the end of the war. If they emerged triumphant and if Hani performed with the valor he had committed himself to, then he would help him win Maryam. With that resolved, he took heart and responded to Maymuna as if he were indifferent to what she told him. "Hani just left her, and I now saw her with the matron. I'm delighted she's comfortable here, and I hope you'll help me keep it that way."

Maymuna was dumbfounded by what she just heard, and she bemoaned that her little ploy had thus far come to naught. But she was determined to see it work, and so she went a step further in feigning ignorance and innocence. "My lord should trust that I do whatever he asks. No doubt this young girl is a rare creature of beauty, intelligence, and poise. She's a gentle spirit and anyone who spends time with her cannot help but fall in love with her. If I don't welcome her as a way to pay tribute to my lord, then I do so out of my own affection for her. It would be no surprise if the emir loved her above all others, since she is most worthy of him."

'Abd al-Rahman worried that if he remained engaged in conversation too long, he might reveal the secret he wanted so much to conceal. So he cut her short. "Enough of this! Tell me, why did you ask me to come here?"

Maymuna quickly assumed a serious tone. "I've asked you here concerning an urgent matter I'd like to discuss, and perhaps you'll find in it sufficient proof of my sincerity in serving my lord. With regard to that matter, I learned from some of my sources—whom I instructed to monitor the enemy following the fall of Bordeaux—that Count Odo and his men are lying in wait for you at the Strait of Dardun. It's not far from here on the way to the Loire River."

'Abd al-Rahman was not unaware of this piece of news since his spies were spread out in every direction. Many of them were from the local populations, especially the Jews, who assisted the Muslims to exact their revenge against the Christians and gain a share of the spoils of war. Nor was Maymuna unaware that he knew, but she feigned ignorance to make a display of revealing a vital piece of information, thereby justifying her summoning him and giving her the opportunity to divulge Hani's love for Maryam. She hoped by this to sow the seeds of jealousy between the two of them. On the other hand, had she been certain that he was ignorant of the information concerning the enemy's plans of ambush, she would have gone to great lengths to conceal it.

'Abd al-Rahman for his part played along, appearing delighted with this secret information. "God bless you, Maymuna, and I plead with you to keep your eyes and ears open."

Maymuna was disappointed that her ploy didn't succeed, and so she decided to try it out on Hani. After all he was a young man with no patience for secrets. Her goal was, after all, to drive a wedge between the two leaders so that their army would fail in its mission. So when she heard 'Abd al-Rahman acknowledging her loyal service to him, she flashed him a smile tinged with playful and affectionate reproach. Were it not for his composure and determination this smile would have ripped his chest open and penetrated his heart, igniting the flames of passion and making him forget the army and warfare.

☆ ☆ ☆

'Abd al-Rahman assumed that Maymuna's look of reproach came because he fell short in lavishing his praises on her. Her attempts at seducing him nonetheless pleased him especially since he wanted to exploit her to the benefit of his army. He returned the smile as a way to encourage her to continue her wholehearted devotion to serving him. When he stood up to leave, she also arose. "Were it not for my knowledge of all the missions that await my lord, I would beseech you to remain just a little longer. Are you compelled to leave at this very moment to confront the enemy nearby? And if you go, do you intend to abandon me here alone?"

'Abd al-Rahman read in this that she was still flirting with him. He smiled again and headed toward his horse intending a swift return to the camp. She followed him out and hardly had he reached the exit of the tent than she heard him say. "Welcome, Commander Hani! You're still here? Why didn't you come into the tent?" Maymuna was perplexed by the greeting. Meanwhile, Hani came forward as he wrapped his tunic around his torso. There wasn't the slightest trace of fear or embarrassment on his face. He thought it repugnant to sneak back to the camp like a fugitive after 'Abd al-Rahman had seen his horse at the women's tent. So when the emir's servant summoned him back to the camp, he stopped, one foot in the horse's stirrup, not saying a word nor budging an inch. The thought occurred to him that Maryam may have been looking on and watching his every move. He remained for several moments just standing there, then suddenly turned away from the horse and walked toward the opening of the tent to face 'Abd al-Rahman. But when he did not see anyone in sight and discovered he was alone, he stood by and waited for the emir to come out of the tent.

After 'Abd al-Rahman left, Maryam's thoughts drifted back to Hani and the way he departed. She was eager to learn more about him, so she made her way to the edge of the tent and found a small opening from which she could see what was going on outside. She watched him pacing about, with his cloak and sword dragging behind him. He was fingering his beard and mustache, and her heart nearly jumped for joy at the sight of him. She longed to speak to him but was afraid of the matron. Thus she remained content to merely feast her eyes on him and scrutinize his every move. Moments later she heard a commotion from inside the tent and learned that 'Abd al-Rahman was outside. She wondered what he would do when he encountered Hani. As the matron and other members of the household were busy bidding the emir farewell, she positioned herself in a spot from where she could see them without being seen. Then she saw Hani walk toward 'Abd al-Rahman until they came face to face. She could hear the emir addressing Hani in a paternal tone, scolding him for being late, but nonetheless receiving him warmly. Hani responded like an obedient and loving son. "They told me you were asking for me."

'Abd al-Rahman drew closer and put his hand on Hani's shoulder. "Does a man ask for anyone other than his brother or his beloved?" He said this with a smile as the occupants of the tent listened, none more delighted with these words than Maryam, and none more furious than Maymuna. Then the two disappeared, side by side, making their way back to the camp, accompanied by an entourage of servants and staff. Maymuna and Maryam watched as they rode off, each one in her own corner, with her own private thoughts. Maymuna went to her room and began to concoct a new scheme, bitterly regretting that the first plot had failed miserably. Maryam also withdrew to be alone, her feelings of love aflame in passion. She sat in her room to reflect on all that transpired between her and her beloved, basking in the warmth of his image in her mind, but at the same time anxious that she may have said or done something she would later regret. She retreated into her innermost thoughts where she remained for quite some time before suddenly awakening to the vial she was still gripping. She looked at it closely and opened it. She whiffed its fragrance and took great pleasure in the scent because it was Hani's gift. She poured a tiny bit of the perfume on her palm and rubbed it on her head, face and hands. Its scent filled the tent.

While Maryam was deep in thought, Maymuna entered, smiling with the smile of a lover. Maryam responded in kind and took comfort in her arrival. She had the urge to speak about her love for Hani which was overwhelming her thoughts, but she held back in fear this would anger her. She arose to embrace Maymuna who was quick to speak. "I see you returned from the matron's quarters," she teased, "and put on some fresh perfume!" Maryam was still holding the vial, but she quickly slipped it into her pocket as she smiled with a blush of embarrassment without responding. Maymuna suddenly realized there must be a connection between Hani and this little bottle of perfume. She was determined to pry the secret from her. "You seem to be embarrassed, sweetheart. Could it be that this perfume is from your visitor, the valiant prince Hani? I certainly hope it's from none other. I trust that were you to chose a lover from all the men in the world, your choice would fall on him!"

Maryam knew at once that Maymuna was on to her secret but she continued to play dumb. "How can you make such a judgment before having any proof? How could you possibly be certain of this?"

Maymuna broke into laughter and drew closer to Maryam. "I learned from a reliable source, not to mention the series of connected events. And even if you utter words to deny it, your expression says otherwise. I don't blame you for hiding it. After all love is best when concealed. It would be more appropriate for me to pretend to believe your denial, but I don't do so out of pity and affection for you."

Maryam, surprised and confused by the mention of pity, looked up at her. "I don't understand why you would pity me. Is there something that could warrant that? Please explain."

"I will not say anything further until you assure me of your trust in my affection for you and my concern for your best interests."

"You know full well," Maryam responded, "that I've taken a strong liking for you and put my trust in you the moment I met you. I'm totally convinced of your affections for me, so there is no need for further proof."

"You're right, my dear, and I feel your sincerity. But I'm afraid of telling you something lest you take it the wrong way. However, I will do as you ask out of devotion. It's nothing to worry about. It's just that I've had my experiences with these Arabs and I've come to know all about their temperaments, especially their raging jealousy. I'm sure you realize that you're in the tent of Emir 'Abd al-Rahman, and that all of the women in it belong to him. It would behoove you to be cautious and not flaunt your affections for Hani in front of him. I'm quite certain Hani himself would want it this way. However I'm telling you this not because of a rumor I heard. I'm fully aware of Emir 'Abd al-Rahman's love for Hani and his desire to keep him by his side—so much so that he would never deny him what he wants, especially since he's so dependent on him in this war. Hani is his right hand in waging this battle. But I want to alert you to what Hani expects from you, even if he doesn't show it out of pride. I've learned a lot about the habits and ways of these men concerning these matters. You may even have heard about my status with 'Abd al-Rahman. I'm the closest woman to him and he relies on me in many serious matters. But you can be sure he does only what he pleases."

Maryam accepted this advice in good faith. With her trust in Maymuna stronger, she found it easier to confide in her. "I thank you, my lady, and I will conduct myself with your advice in mind. I have no doubt you're most knowledgeable about these matters. You're the most insightful and gracious woman in this tent."

Assured by these words, Maymuna, moved on to another subject." I asked about the perfume, but you still didn't answer me. Where is the vial?"

Maryam took the vial out of her pocket and held it out. Maymuna took hold of it, opened it and whiffed the scent. "I've never smelled anything like this in my life! It's a special fragrance, and nobody here has anything like it."

When Maymuna held out the vial to give it back, Maryam offered that she try it. "Take a bit for yourself, you deserve it."

Maymuna declined the offer. "No one should wear this perfume other than yourself. It's a special present given to you." She gave it back making a strong show in refusing it. Maryam, impressed by this gesture, became all the more trustful of her and her affections, and she began to open up, enjoying her company and basking in her confidence and affection. Maymuna, meanwhile, was thinking of ways to manipulate these feelings to her benefit.

✡ ✡ ✡

'Abd al-Rahman and Hani arrived at the camp surrounded by members of their cavalry, as each man's thoughts lingered on Maryam. Hani played over and over again in his mind the words he exchanged with his beloved while gloating in the praise 'Abd al-Rahman lavished on him when he had only expected rebuke. 'Abd al-Rahman himself could not keep his mind off Salma and her words to him concerning Maryam. He recalled her hinting that when the war was over she might reveal to him the secret she had yet to divulge. He remembered how awestruck he was when he first laid eyes on the girl's ravishing beauty and dignified manners. But suddenly the image of mutual love between Hani and Maryam flashed across his mind and he was seized by a pang of intense jealousy. But he pushed this feeling quickly out of his mind. As his thoughts turned to the impending war, he realized how much defeating the enemy depended upon he and Hani fighting side by side. He realized that this victory could only happen if Hani was content, and that the only way he could be content was to win Maryam. As all this became crystal clear to him he regained his sense of devotion and magnanimity—and understood how easy it would be to please Hani. But fearing that his silence might lead to suspicion, he resumed the conversation. "Have you not praised God for our victory thus far in this war, Hani?"

"I have offered to God many prayers of thanks. I credit our victory also to our Emir 'Abd al-Rahman for his bravery and wise leadership," he replied.

"The credit goes to our commander Hani, the captain of our cavalry. I see our success also as the result of our fighting side by side, and I hope this continues until the end."

"This is my fervent hope as well," Hani added. "If we achieve victory it will be for the glory of all Arabs, for we will have conquered a vast amount of territory for their benefit. The Arabs will then rule over many peoples, prosper from the fruits of their labor, and spread the word of Islam throughout their lands."

"It seems to me that the conquest of Bordeaux has given you pleasure far greater than all the other territories we conquered and have yet to conquer!" The emir said this with a smirk on his face and Hani knew instantly that he was alluding to Maryam. He was delighted and let his feelings be known. "I can't deny it, Emir, she is all I can think about."

"Whatever makes you happy makes me happy as well," said 'Abd al-Rahman. "Believe me when I tell you that I will help you achieve all that you desire. But you should know that I made a solemn vow to God to abstain from women until this war is over, or at least until I cross the Loire River. Do you share my sentiments?"

"I do, and I too have made the same vow," replied Hani, understanding full well what the emir was trying to tell him. From that instant Hani felt that a heavy load had been lifted from his chest. He also felt a strong urge to share with Maryam this conversation with 'Abd al-Rahman. Of course, this was natural between sweethearts who delight in telling each other intimate details of other people—especially in matters that may concern them directly. They also delight in talking about their hopes and dreams—the more so if one of them is sworn to secrecy about something but is willing to share it with the beloved as a sign of complete trust.

The two rode on in silence until they reached the camp. The officers had completed the division of the booty and the soldiers were celebrating their winnings, especially the Berbers. When they reached the emir's pavilion, the two men went inside. 'Abd al-Rahman clapped his hands and several servants appeared instantly. "Go and summon the officers to come at once." When the servants left the pavilion, the emir turned to Hani. "I've been informed by our spies as well as other informants that the tyrant of Aquitaine, Count Odo, is camping with his army at the Strait of Dardun which is only a few hours from here. We must launch a preemptive strike before they're able to mount an offense. If we beat them and take out their commander then we will have won half the battle, or maybe even all of it.

There'll be no one left to stand in our way toward the Loire River. What do you think?"

"I think we should begin fighting. The troops are energized and fired up for victory."

"We'll ask the officers for their advice when they arrive. I think they'll agree only to a slow ground attack. We'll march with the infantry and leave the tents where they are with some guards to protect the loot. And if we defeat the Franks, God willing, we'll send for the women, children, and booty and march on to Tours by the Loire River. "

Nearly a dozen officers arrived, Berbers and Arabs, Egyptians, Syrians, Nabateans, and others. Bustam was among them. 'Abd al-Rahman presented his plan to them and Hani echoed his support. They agreed to march the following morning on condition that they leave their womenfolk there in the tents. "You all understand that we're moving forward to fight the Franks on their turf," 'Abd al-Rahman said to them. "It's nearby but they're well-fortified in the mountains. So we'll have to launch our attack lightly equipped. I don't need to remind you what happened to our soldiers during the battles we fought since leaving Andalusia. They were encumbered by the weight of their loot and that affected their fighting. How can we attack and run in those circumstances? So, I think we should leave these things behind with the women—and we'll place a guard in each tent. And if we succeed in doing to our enemy what we aspire to do, we'll replenish our coffers substantially." 'Abd al-Rahman made this last remark anticipating opposition from some of the men who only joined this war out of greed for riches. Hani picked up on this. "The emir is right on the mark on this, and I don't think any of us officers would disagree with him. We all fear that if our soldiers embark on fighting encumbered by the weight of their possessions, it will hinder their ability on the battle field, and the result will be failure."

'Abd al-Rahman was particularly worried about Bustam's opposition. While Hani was speaking he scrutinized the faces of the men, and he detected a look of reluctance on the Berber chieftain's face. He resumed his speech. "My solution is that we entrust the safeguarding of the booty to Bustam and to whomever he chooses among his troops to assist him." This was met with unanimous approval among the officers. After voicing their agreement, they left the pavilion and went back to prepare their troops to march the following morning.

Hani returned to his tent but couldn't go to sleep that night, his thoughts fixated on Maryam and what 'Abd al-Rahman had said about her. He told himself he should go and see her immediately that very night and tell her about the conversation between him and the emir, and that they had decided to depart the following morning to fight the Franks. H would ask her to be patient until they returned. His desire to join her was overpowering for he dreaded the thought of leaving without saying good-bye.

Chapter 6

A New Plot

The Muslim troops arose early the following morning for prayers. Then the bugle sounded and they prepared for battle. They folded up all the tents except those designated to store the booty. Bustam stayed behind with some of his men and a few from the other tribes. The army marched with the archers and lancers in tow, while Hani rode at the head of the cavalry. Several hours into the march, they arrived at the strait behind which Odo and his army were lying in wait, having been informed by their spies. The Muslims alighted on a flat stretch of land not far from the strait. The cavalry dismounted and unbridled their horses to graze and rest until the fighting commenced. They stationed guards around the camp and dispatched expeditions to scout the enemy's strategic positions from where they could launch an attack. Hani retreated to his tent to rest.

Reports poured in that evening confirming that the Franks were ensconced in the mountains, in large numbers, and well-fortified. However, there were no signs of movement to be detected. The Muslim high command convened to discuss how to proceed and decided to stake out various positions to monitor the enemy troops.

Hani spent the night mulling over all the concerns that clouded his mind. He thought again about leaving the camp for a few hours, especially since there would be no danger to the army during his brief absence. However, the fear of being discovered and shamed in the eyes of 'Abd al-Rahman deterred him. On the following morning, he awoke still preoccupied with the same concerns, still obsessing over his situation with Maryam as much as over his troops. He walked through a field past the camp and noticed a man dressed in Arab garb coming toward him from a distance, waving to him. He stopped, and when the man drew closer Hani studied him carefully. The man's face was completely covered, and Hani called out to him. The man then inserted his hand into his pocket and took out a handkerchief and handed it to Hani. He took it and instantly recognized the scent of Maryam's perfume.

"Who are you?" he shouted at the man, "and what news do you have for me?"

"This handkerchief should tell you who I am. Its owner is in need of you right away." No sooner had he said this than he turned around and quickly fled away. Hani was caught off-guard but then took hold of his senses. He yelled out to the man to come back but he didn't even turn around. He stood frozen for a few moments wondering what could be the reason for this summons. He rushed back to his tent, mounted his stallion, and wrapped his tunic around himself tightly. Without telling a soul he was leaving—certain he would be back by the end of the day—he galloped at full speed, not looking left or right, until he reached the tent. According to the position of the sun it was high noon, and both he and his horse were drenched in sweat. He dismounted and went immediately into the women's tent. He called out to the matron. She came out slowly wobbling on her haunches. When she noticed it was Hani, she shouted. "Where's Maryam?"

He was stunned by her question. "You're asking me about Maryam? I've come here to ask you the same question!"

"She's with you. Didn't you send for her this morning?"

"Me, send for her? Where is she? Tell me! This is no time for joking!"

She stood in shock as the color faded from her face. "I thought it was you who was joking. Did you not send your messenger for her this morning? He had your horse, your tunic and your helmet."

His blood boiled and he shouted at her. "I didn't send a soul. Here's my horse and my tunic. Do you realize what you're saying? Tell me the truth, or I'll cut your head off with this sword!" He gripped the hilt of the sword as he spoke.

The matron, bewildered, trembled in fear. "Calm down, my son, and I'll tell you the whole story. A man came this morning and I thought he was one of your troops. He arrived on horseback along with another black stallion which I was sure was yours. He was wearing a tunic and helmet. He told me you had sent him to bring her to 'Abd al-Rahman because of a private matter concerning her mother. He gave me this purse." She reached into her pocket and pulled out a purse with money in it. "At first I refused to take it, but he insisted. He showed me the stallion and tunic. He repeated that you needed Maryam for an urgent mission connected to the war. He said you sent along your stallion so that she could ride it to him. He revealed a secret code which no one knows except us, that is, the bottle of perfume. He mentioned it as proof that he was telling the truth, that he knew you had met with Maryam in my tent and gave it to her. How could I not believe him? Besides, he uttered a password from the Emir 'Abd al-Rahman that only I know. I've done everything I could to keep her safe, despite all of this. So I sent with her the most favored of 'Abd al-Rahman's women, and I entrusted her with Maryam's safety"

Hani listened to the matron's account as he trembled in anger. When he realized that Maryam was gone, he asked. "Who did you send with her?"

"Maymuna, the Frankish woman," she answered. "I believe you know her."

"I do know her. Where did they go?"

"When I was convinced he was telling me the truth, and when I saw how willing Maryam was to go with him, I gave her permission to do so. She mounted the black stallion and Maymuna the other horse and they all headed out toward the camp."

Hani trembled with rage as the matron stood before him with her heart racing in fear. She tried to calm him down. "Don't worry about her, my son. Maymuna is quite taken with her, and I know she'll watch over her carefully. Take a seat and calm down. She'll be fine."

Hani paid no attention at all to her attempts to reassure him. He was thinking about what she said about Maryam's departure. Then he remembered that the matron mentioned Maryam's mother. He reckoned that her leaving had something to do with the mother's secret. He began to imagine that Salma had devised this scheme to get her daughter back, but when he thought about the vial of perfume he dismissed the idea. He didn't know what to say. At a loss to make sense of what was happening, he decided to go back to the camp to look for her. But he remembered that Bustam was there. It occurred to him that he could be the culprit behind all this, plotting to snatch Maryam away from him, still clinging to the hope of possessing her which began the moment he captured her. Hani turned toward the matron. "You say they headed toward the camp," he asked pointing in the direction where they alighted the day before.

"Yes, my lord," she replied.

Hani went to his horse, swung up on the saddle, whispered to his stallion and took off like the wind. He swore to himself that he would kill Bustam if he found him with Maryam. As he drew near he noticed the tents where the booty was stored, and Bustam's soldiers who were guarding them. When he arrived, he saw an exchange of blows amidst a loud din of shouting. Some soldiers noticing him were quick to seek his help.

"What's going on here?" he shouted.

One of the men responded. "We demand to lodge a complaint against Commander Bustam's abuses. He unleashed his men on us to pilfer our share of the booty. They came and seized parts of it from our men and added it to theirs. When we tried to protest he wouldn't listen."

Hani, seething in anger, shouted. "Where is Bustam? Where is he?"

Hardly had he finished his question when Bustam came out from his tent, walking carelessly and stumbling as if he were drunk. Hani, seeing him this way, roared at him. "How dare you tamper with the property of the Muslim troops? Didn't the emir entrust you with protecting the booty, and here you are pouncing on it and hoarding it for yourselves. I guess they're right when they say you're not a Muslim!"

Bustam chortled as he wiped away the crumbs of food that had fallen on his beard. "What do you care about the booty? Hasn't that Christian girl kept your mind off it? Put the war aside and go back to the tent. You're better off in the company of women, but soon enough you'll see where your little infatuation gets you!"

Bustam's ridicule enraged Hani. Unable to control himself, he pulled out his sword and charged toward Bustam with every intention to chop off his head. Bustam was able to jump aside and save himself from the assault. Hani, nearly falling off his horse, grew all the angrier and swooped down on him like a bolt of lightning. Several soldiers rushed forward and stood between the two men but Hani paid no heed. Bustam would have been annihilated had he not ran off and hid in one of the tents. Hani was about to jump off his horse and follow him but some of his men surrounded him and pleaded with him to put away his sword to avoid shedding Muslim blood. Still mounted and stunned by his own reaction, he came to his senses, as if the mention of Islam had appeased his anger and calmed him down. He imagined what could have happened among the rival battalions of the army had he killed Bustam. He gave up on the idea of chasing Bustam, satisfied that he forced him to run away. He turned his attention to the matter that brought him there in the first place, that is, to look for Maryam. He scoured the fields that surrounded the tents but found neither black horse nor any women. He asked several soldiers who were standing by the tents, and whom he trusted, what was inside the tents. They assured him there was only the booty.

"Did any horsemen accompanied by women come to this area?" he asked.

"None at all. We've been here since yesterday, and we haven't seen anybody of the sort," one of them replied.

Hani stood bewildered, as all his fearful premonitions about Maryam's disappearance returned. He turned around to gaze at the flat stretch of land that surrounded him, and he could see that most of it was flat and empty, save a few hills that were dotted with grapevines and olive trees. There wasn't a soul in sight. He grew even more confused. His heart told him to go back to Dardun, where he might find Maryam.

The high noon sun was now tilted toward the west and his stallion began to show signs of fatigue. Hani was afraid to race it to shorten the trip. Yet if he didn't spur it on, he wouldn't arrive at the camp before dusk. He realized that he had to go. Gripping its bridle tightly, he set out for Dardun.

✫ ✫ ✫

Maryam had set out that morning with Maymuna by her side. She mounted the black horse, wrapped her cloak securely around her, and tied a helmet to the saddle. She trotted behind the messenger as Maymuna rode the horse next to her, looking as if she were totally perplexed by this urgent summons, and pretending to reassure her that she was coming along to be of service and to protect her from any harm. As Maryam was spurring her horse along, her thoughts ran in every direction, the figure of Hani flashing in every image that came to her mind.

An hour into the journey, the riders spotted a new camp toward their left. Maryam assumed that it was their intended destination, having no idea that the army had moved to Dardun. When she saw the small number of tents, she asked the messenger about the army headquarters, and where they were going.

"The army moved on to Dardun, where they'll fight the Franks," he replied. "We ourselves are marching toward a place close to Dardun. Our commander the emir has ordered me to take you to him. Either he'll be there when we arrive or soon thereafter."

Maryam believed everything the messenger told her. Her heart raced faster than her horse in anticipation of meeting her beloved. They continued on their journey leaving behind them the city of Bordeaux and rode on until they reached an isolated building with collapsed walls surrounding it. The messenger went ahead of them and entered the building from the gate of the wall that lead into a garden in disarray. It was clear to anyone who looked at it closely that it had once belonged to a family of means, and that it had been abandoned only a very short time ago. The two women dismounted and walked into the garden. Maymuna addressed the messenger, affecting concern for Maryam.

"Where are you taking us? We're close to Dardun by my estimation. Whose house is this we've entered? Don't you lie to me."

"I'm not lying, my lady," the messenger responded politely. "We're at the castle of a prince of Aquitaine, who abandoned it when he fled from the Muslim army. There are many estates throughout these farmlands that were abandoned by their owners, and they're now part of the Muslim spoils of war."

"Where is Commander Hani?" Maymuna asked.

"Apparently he hasn't arrived, nor have I seen a trace of him. But he's sure to be here soon." He took hold of their hands and walked them into the building through a large opened door. The only things they found inside were several large chairs that obviously could not be carried away at the time of the owner's escape. There was absolute silence save the sound of their foot-steps and the soft neighing of the horses. Not seeing Hani or finding any trace of him aroused deep suspicion in Maryam's mind, but she patiently held her tongue. She took comfort in Maymuna's presence and obvious concern, as well as in her superior knowledge of these parts, not to mention the ways of the Muslim army. Maymuna could well guess what was going on in Maryam's mind, and she feigned surprise and confusion. She persisted in asking the messenger question after question until they reached a large hall-like room that contained only two chairs. Maymuna took a seat and invited Maryam to sit next to her. They looked around them, inspecting the room, in wonder and annoyance. They sat for a short while without exchanging a word. Every so often Maryam would look out the window onto the garden, expecting Hani to arrive. The servant who brought them to the place left them alone and never returned.

Appearing to be frightened, Maymuna broke the silence. "My God, where are we, and what's happened? Where has that messenger gone? If only some of the Slav eunuchs from the tent had come with us!" She then clapped her hands in anticipation of someone coming to her, but only the echo could be heard.

Seeing Maymuna's fear, Maryam herself became frightened. "Have they tricked us?" she asked with a worried look on her face. "Where is the soldier? How can he leave us alone and take off just like that? Where has he gone?"

It was late afternoon, and they hadn't had a bite to eat, but Maryam was too distraught to give any thought to her hunger. While they sat in such a state, they suddenly heard the neighing of a horse and the crack of reins. Maryam looked out the window and noticed a horseman approaching. He was followed by two others whose heads and faces were covered. They were galloping at a fast pace before reaching the gate of the garden. The lead horseman dismounted, and for a split-second she thought it was Hani. Her heart pounded and she jumped up and went out to the gate of the garden, oblivious to the fact that both the clothing and horse of the rider were different from Hani's. As she drew closer to him she made out a stocky man staggering in his gait, with his sword dangling by his side and his cloak dragging from behind. When she got a better look, she recognized Bustam. She stood in shock as her knees knocked and the blood nearly froze in her veins. She turned to Maymuna and saw a look of surprise on her face. Maymuna went out to meet him.

"What do you want, Commander?"

"What concern is it of yours?" he replied, as he approached, all out of breath from fatigue, with the two men walking behind him.

"There are no soldiers around here, and nothing that would be of any interest to you," she said.

"We came looking for the woman. Isn't Maryam, the Christian girl, here?" As he said this snickering, he stretched out his hand to touch Maryam's face.

She stepped back quickly and turned away. Maymuna grabbed his hand.

"You shouldn't do what is unbefitting to men of your rank. Bear in mind that if you lay a hand on her you will incur the wrath of the Emir of the Muslim army."

Bustam shouted at her violently. "Who are you to advise and warn me? And what business is this of yours, as I'm not talking to you." He walked over to Maryam but Maymuna stood in his way and gripped his forearm. When he shoved her away she fell to the ground. He then turned to the two men. "Tie this one up and lock her in one of the rooms."

The two men immediately swooped down on Maymuna and bound her hands and feet. She yelled and screamed for help as she tried to fight off the two men and set herself free. Maryam made an attempt to help her but Bustam prevented her without laying a hand on her. "Don't be afraid, my pretty. We're not going to harm her. We just want to put her in her place."

When the two men finished tying her up, they began to drag her into a room. She turned around to Bustam. "You can do as you please with me, but I beg you not to lay a hand on this girl or defile her in any way."

The two men brought Maymuna inside the room and locked the door behind them. She whispered to them, "Where is Adlan?"

One of them drew close to her and removed his headscarf, exposing his face. He looked at her squint-eyed, as a lover beholds his beloved. "It is I, your servant, Adlan. I pray I carried out your mission just as you wanted!"

"God bless you," she replied with a smile. "And where is Hani now? What have you done with him?"

"I did as you ordered, most noble of ladies! And I hope you are pleased with the prisoner of your affections. Rest assured you will find no other more eager than I to obey your orders and carry out your every wish!"

She flashed him another smile and a nod of approval. "But where is Hani at this moment?"

"I figure he's still wandering through the desert searching for his beloved."

"And how did you manage to get the handkerchief to him?" she asked.

"After I brought you the black horse yesterday and entrusted it to this fellow," pointing to his companion, "I explained to him how to trick the old matron just as you instructed me. Then I took the handkerchief to the Muslim camp. I arrived in the morning, and fortunately for my lady, I saw him walking around the grounds. I rushed to him and, with my head and face covered, I gave him the handkerchief. He asked me about my mission, and I informed him that the owner of the handkerchief wished to see him at once. Then I left him alone and went and hid in a place where I could see him but not be seen. I watched him jump on his horse and dash off to the tent. When I was certain that he was clearly out of sight, I took another road and headed to the camp of my lord, Count Odo. I informed him of the matter, as you commanded. After prodding him, they launched a surprise attack on the Muslims who must have been frightened and pulled back, and so the Franks took control of their camp."

Adlan spoke with gleeful animation while Maymuna kept her eyes fixed on him. After each sentence she smiled at him approvingly and when he finished she inquired. "And what happened with Bustam?"

"I went to him at the old camp and pretended that I was obediently performing a service which he would most certainly approve of. Then I told him that Maryam left the tent and went to a place where I could take him, and that he could do with her whatever he pleased on condition that he assured your protection. He heaped praises on me and gave me an expensive present. I was expecting that Hani would show up at any moment and that they would fight until one of them killed the other, and your good fortune would be complete and your revenge against this army fulfilled. But Hani arrived right after Bustam departed, and not finding Maryam there, he came to the conclusion that Bustam had kidnapped her. When he found him at the booty tents, they started to quarrel. Hani was set to chop his head off, but Bustam escaped and hid in another tent, where he remained until Hani left. Then I coaxed him to come here quickly, and I came with him. On the way, we met up with this fellow here who was sent to warn us to hurry. We exchanged robes and together we accompanied Bustam here."

"Blessings on you, my loyal servant," she said. "And when our hopes of crushing the Arab army are realized, I will dub you with another title." She spoke to him fluttering her eyelashes in a flirtatious manner. His face radiated as he stared into her eyes and his heart leapt with joy as he imagined her amorous rewards.

When Maryam saw Maymuna being dragged into the room with her hands and feet bound and warning Bustam against harming Maryam, she was more convinced than ever of her sincerity. However she grew more worried about her own safety and what Bustam might do to her, especially since he reeked of alcohol. Besides, he had a belligerent look in his eye, and all the blood had faded from his face. He was girded with a thick belt to which a large dagger was attached. He cupped his right hand over the hilt, and with his left hand he held his sword. To Maryam he looked like the devil incarnate. She prayed to God for His protection against him and secretly begged Him to spare her life from this wicked man. She was still wrapped in the red cloak she believed to be Hani's that covered her long black dress, and was still wearing a black headscarf that covered her forehead to the tip of her eyebrows and which she tied tightly under her chin. This gave her face a round shape from which her eyes glowed. Her gloomy expression added dignity to them. Yet despite all the terrifying things she witnessed, her resolve did not weaken. It may well have been that she was no longer as frightened of Bustam as when she first set eyes on him, even though he kept Maymuna shackled and locked up in a room and was alone with her in this huge house.

Bustam gaped at her with lewd pleasure. He then invited her to take a seat as if he were seeking to engage her in polite conversation. She sat on one chair and he on another. He wrapped his cloak around him, concealing his dagger and sword. He began to speak to her in Arabic with a strong Berber accent. "You have nothing to fear, Maryam. I wish you no harm since I have strong feelings of affection for you. It seems you've been duped by this Arab servant-boy, and that you've been taken in by his charm. The fact remains that you're my share of the spoils of this war—mine and mine alone! If I wanted to prevent him from getting at you, I could have done so from the beginning. But I chose to be kind to you and treat you courteously. But now that you have fallen into my hands, you should comply with my wishes!"

Maryam trembled as she listened to him say these words, wondering whether he had come there as part of a plan or purely by coincidence. She wanted to keep him at arms length by engaging him in conversation until Hani arrived, which she truly believed he would. "You should put all that aside for now, Commander. Everything in good time. You're now engaged in a war, and when it's finished, each man will get his just deserts."

"Do not dawdle with me with talk about the impossible. Hani won't get a single strand of your hair. You're now in my grip and no one will wrest you from it. You'd better submit to me willingly, or I'll take you by force."

Hearing his threat made her realize the danger she was in. But again she decided to continue stalling him in conversation until Hani arrived. "I see no cause for threats, commander. Threatening a young girl does not befit a man who considers himself a great leader and takes pride in his bravery and skill in battle, especially one such as yourself who has pledged himself to the jihad."

Bustam bellowed a sarcastic laugh. "It's true, I am a brave commander, and the battlefield bears witness to that. If it weren't for me, the name of that slave boy wouldn't fly from the lips of our soldiers, nor would those

Arabs have a flag to wave in these parts. So if you realize that, utter no name but mine."

When she heard him mention Hani and the Arabs, she knew that her civil manner with him would be of no avail, and so she decided to attack his pride. "Enough of this name calling and insinuation. You're not at the level of Hani, and if he were here at this very moment, you wouldn't dare speak in this manner."

Stunned, Bustam looked at her with daggers coming out of his eyes. He grabbed her arm forcefully to scare her, but was surprised by the firmness of her muscles as she managed to free herself from his grip. She stood up. "I'm warning you not to touch me. My patience is at an end."

Her persistence and the strength of her body filled him with rage. "Do not indulge yourself in false hopes. One simple blow with this sword of mine will end your life in an instant. You're nothing more than a captive who can be bartered for a few dirhams. I was mistaken in treating you kindly, since you take my kindness as weakness. You know there are dozens like you in my tent who would be only too happy to bend to my will."

Chapter 7

The Two Hanis

After being subjected to Bustam's threats to kill her, Maryam was on the verge of responding when she suddenly heard a loud noise coming from the garden. She detected the voice of a man saying, "Commander Hani is here." She was startled by this and wanted to know what was happening. She sprinted toward the door with Bustam on her heels. She saw a group of Arab horsemen surrounding the black stallion, asking themselves if it was not Hani's stallion, and wondering where he could be. Bustam shouted out to them, "Hani isn't here. What brings you here?"

One of them stepped forward, with a concerned look on his face, covered in dust and dirt, and dripping sweat from his forehead. "We were attacked by the Franks, Commander. The fighting was fierce. Commander Hani has been missing since this morning. Our cavalry hasn't been very successful, and the tide is turning against us. We've come to search for him. If he doesn't come back to us we don't stand a chance. When we saw this black stallion, we thought he must be here."

"That isn't his stallion," Bustam replied as he looked back to the inside of the house. "Maybe he went off to save his own neck. Why don't you go and look for him somewhere else?" The man and his companions drew back, inspected the horse closely, and having decided that it wasn't Hani's, turned around and went away.

The Arab army lost much of its strength without Hani. They were attacked with their guard down while they were resting in their tents. The Emir 'Abd al-Rahman had been held up in his tent since the early morning, preoccupied with a number of urgent matters, and expecting Hani to come and review the battle plans for the day. When Hani failed to show up at the appointed time, he thought of dispatching a scout to search the area for him. All of a sudden some of the soldiers came rushing in to announce that the Frankish army had descended upon them like a violent storm. A deafening clamor then erupted among the troops, and the emir exited his tent and headed for his horse. He ordered the scout to find Hani and informed the other commanders to mobilize their troops and prepare for battle. Hardly had he finished his orders than a torrent of arrows rained down on his tent. When he gazed out to the battlefield he saw the Franks charging toward them, raising thick, dark billows of dust on the battlefield. The emir jumped on his horse and called out orders to his men, waiting and hoping that Hani would arrive and take charge of the cavalry. The scout returned a short while later only to announce that no trace of Hani or his stallion were to be found.

'Abd al-Rahman was baffled. The more so because he had grown so heavily dependent on Hani to lead the attack as commander of the cavalry, the most powerful branch of the Arab army. Furious with the difficult position in which his army now found itself, he took it upon himself to lead the horsemen into battle, except that he found himself at a loss as to how to arrange the battalions, since he was not familiar with their ways nor they with his. But time ran out, and the two armies clashed. The Arabs wavered and stumbled at first, but 'Abd al-Rahman's exceptional courage and his quick thinking in the tightest of spots pulled the troops together. He kept his composure and inspired his soldiers to carry on with valor, as he plunged forth and penetrated the front lines of the enemy, resistant to the swarm of arrows pouring down over his head.

The midday sun had since changed direction and Hani had still not returned. 'Abd al-Rahman pulled back momentarily to dispatch a large scouting expedition to search for him. He himself remained in charge of the battle, comforting and urging on the soldiers. But the sun was about to set and the Franks were on the verge of defeating the Arabs. The cavalry, nonetheless, continued their valiant fight as their eyes darted from time to time across the horizons in anticipation of seeing their commander or hearing the slightest piece of news of his whereabouts. Wherever two or three of them came close together on the battlefield they wondered among themselves where Hani could be and why he was absent. They realized more than ever that their need for him far exceeded what they had imagined.

For all the magnanimity and deep affection which he unabashedly displayed toward Hani, 'Abd al-Rahman was best known for his unwavering sense of duty. The thought occurred to him that infatuation had taken Hani away from the battlefield to be with his beloved. He made a vow to himself that, if this were indeed the case, he would forbid Hani from seeing Maryam. These thoughts flashed through his mind along with the dreaded realization of the impending danger he and his army were facing. His eyes roamed in every direction hoping he would catch sight of Hani arriving to join them. But what he was witnessing only increased the unsettling fear he felt in the pit of his stomach at the specter of his army falling apart, especially the cavalry, as the enemy forces drew closer to his tent.

Falling deeper and deeper into the throes of despair, Emir 'Abd al-Rahman glanced toward his left and, in a split-second, detected from the distance the shadowy figure of a lone horseman through the billows of dust and under the thick downpour of arrows. As he drew nearer, he could detect the rider mounted on a black stallion and draped in a red 'abaya and helmet, with his sword prominently dangling from his side. The rider was giving free rein to his horse as it raced with such dazzling speed that its head stood erect, its mane flapped with the wind, its tail raised upright, and the muscles of its legs fully flexed. Its barrel was firmly erect, and its hooves ran through the dust clouds rising above him, looking as though the stallion was racing with the wind while the dust clouds struggled in a vain attempt to keep pace. The horseman remained firmly seated on its back as though oblivious to the torrent of arrows and the charging enemy. When 'Abd al-Rahman could see more clearly, his heart beat with joy, thinking it was Hani. He rode his horse toward him expecting him to alight, but the horseman remained on his stallion to attack the enemy, shouting to the troops. "Hani has arrived, so you will not fail. Fear not the enemy troops, for they will be your captives by the end of the day."

'Abd al-Rahman, convinced it was Hani, asked one of his men to go and fetch him. But the horseman rode his stallion toward the enemy to an area from which he knew the enemy would never think the Arabs would be attacking. The resolve of the Muslim battalions, especially the cavalry, intensified, and they followed him like lions on the prowl. The Franks, taken by surprise, decided to redirect their forces to the area from which the horseman lead the attack, when all of a sudden there appeared another horseman, also donned in a red 'abaya and helmet and mounted on a black stallion. Unsheathing his sword he attacked from the other side, shouting, "Hani has arrived!" The rest of the cavalry followed him, and the Muslims recovered their steadfastness and courage. By the time night had fallen the Franks had fled to the last man, and their campsite fell as booty into the hands of the Muslims, who scoured every tent and pillaged all their supplies, weapons, and possessions.

Emir 'Abd al-Rahman witnessed the attack of the second horseman from the other side, able to see that he resembled Hani and that he also rode a black stallion like Hani's. When the Franks retreated, he went back to his tent expecting to find Hani among the other officers, supervising the distribution of the loot, as was the custom. He arrived at the same moment one of the two horsemen on the black stallions arrived, and it was indeed Hani himself. The emir welcomed him, and Hani spoke. "Those Franks thought they would defeat us with deception and trickery, but God destroyed them. Had I known they intended to attack, I never would have left the camp for even one second."

Dismounting from his horse and seemingly occupied with removing the stirrups, 'Abd al-Rahman replied. "We were all worried about your disappearance, and we thank God for your return." He then turned and faced Hani. "Who was that other horseman who preceded you and referred to himself by your name?"

"There was no one else with me," Hani answered.

"But I saw a horseman on a black stallion like yours, and wearing an 'abaya like the one you're wearing. I saw him with my own eyes in the middle of the battlefield, just before you arrived, and I heard him referring to himself as Hani," he insisted as he turned toward the rest of the officers. "Where is that other horseman who was riding the black stallion?"

"We saw him attack from the front lines," answered one of the officers, "and then he vanished. Maybe he'll show up again soon."

"Go find him and bring him back to me," ordered the emir. He and Hani then turned and went into the tent followed by several of the commanders.

They sat to discuss the extraordinary events of the day and what dangers lay ahead. They all recalled the other 'Hani' with wonder and amazement, but it didn't take long before they turned their attention to the division of the spoils of war. There were no women and children to divide since the Franks never brought them to the battle sites. Their soldiers all managed to escape along with their leader Count Odo, the duke of Aquitaine, and the members of their high command.

The Muslim officers discussed the booty, tents, arms, ammunition, and all they were able to seize. They entrusted the army's scribe to divide and distribute it all, setting aside the portion which goes into the communal coffins. Since there was a relatively small amount, they completed the task quickly. As they sat in consultation and review, they talked about that horseman until it was time for them to disperse and go back to their own tents. Only Hani remained with the emir. He then told him his story, holding back nothing. When he came to the part about Bustam and his raiding the booty, Emir 'Abd al-Rahman shook his head. "To God we belong and to God we return! This matter with the Berbers saddens me, and I fear the consequences of their actions if we go too far in appeasing them. I'm also worried that if we punish them it'll destroy all that we're striving for."

When Hani mentioned the black stallion that was sent to Maryam he suddenly remembered what the matron had told him about the messenger who was sent to fetch her. He recalled she had said he was wearing a red 'abaya and helmet similar to his own. It then occurred to him that there may be a connection between this messenger and the horseman who referred to himself by Hani's name. At that very moment the men who went out to look for the horseman returned and announced that they searched both camps but found no trace of him whatsoever. Hani returned to his private thoughts, and the more he thought, the more perplexed he became. He thought about Maryam and feared that some harm may have befallen her. Emir 'Abd al-Rahman, himself thinking about what Hani had told him about Maryam and her departure from the women's tent, suddenly remembered her mother and the mission she was undertaking. Doubt crept into his mind and he grew suspicious that she may have been pretending to be held captive as a ruse to escape. But in mulling over his conversation with her and what she said and how earnest she appeared, he dismissed these misgivings and decided she was telling the truth.

Both men remained silent for several moments deep in thought about Maryam and the mysterious horseman until they heard the galloping of hooves toward the tent. A young servant rushed into the tent. "Two horsemen at the gate are requesting entry," he announced.

"Let them in," replied Emir 'Abd al-Rahman.

The servant went out and quickly returned with a man following in his footsteps, wearing a helmet and a red 'abaya. As soon as they laid eyes on him, they knew it was the horseman who called himself 'Hani.' Hani, noticing a black garment underneath the 'abaya, was the first to speak: "Welcome to the horseman who calls himself Hani!" The horseman remained silent, peering out from behind his face scarf.

'Abd al-Rahman then addressed him. "You have indeed distinguished yourself with this army. Why don't you lift your scarf and make yourself known to us?"

The horseman raised his hand and removed his helmet, revealing from underneath it a black headscarf. He then took off the 'abaya under which he was wearing a black robe. Hani immediately recognized it as Maryam's robe. "Maryam!" he yelled out, "Maryam!"

The horseman raised his hand and removed the headscarf and there underneath was the face of Maryam beaming with vigor and beauty. The face scarf had kept her warm, making her cheeks flush crimson and her eyes sparkle. The bravery Maryam displayed, so rare among women, amazed Hani, and hardly able to contain himself, he blurted out, "Maryam, my darling, these feats were yours? We hold you in awe for your grace and beauty, and never did we imagine how skillful you are in battle. Tell me, my love, what happened? Where were you and how did this come to be?"

"I stand before you and before Emir 'Abd al-Rahman, having done nothing worth making such a fuss about. Whatever I did was only in the name of Commander Hani to whom all credit is due." She spoke with her familiar lisp, and there shone on her face something beyond bravery and pride which only lovers can detect. Then, remembering she was in the presence of the emir, she was overwhelmed with deference and lowered her head.

"God bless you and God bless Hani, for your equally remarkable feats today. Were it not for both of you, this army would have suffered a setback with unimaginable consequences. Please, my daughter, take a seat and tell us all that happened. What possessed you to undertake such a dangerous attack? I heard from my brother Hani that you were tricked into leaving the tent this morning. And that he set out to find you, and had not returned before you came back, fretting he would never find you. So, tell us what happened."

"I beg you," she pleaded, "that before I begin to tell you my story you welcome kindly my friend and companion, Maymuna, who suffered greatly on my behalf. She's right outside this pavilion," pointing her finger to the outside. The two commanders knew the two women were missing and were not surprised to hear this. The emir clapped his hands and when the servant entered he ordered him to bring in the woman waiting outside. Seconds later, Maymuna entered affecting a humble and demure manner. 'Abd al-Rahman beckoned her to take a seat on one of the carpets, smiling at her as though he approved of her good deeds. He then motioned to Hani, still standing, to sit next to him. Both commanders, side by side, were all ears as they awaited Maryam's story.

She began with the messenger's arrival requesting that she go with him to Commander Hani. She recounted how Maymuna offered herself in her service, and how she accompanied her and helped her along the way until they arrived at the abandoned castle. She next told them about Bustam's arrival and how roughly he had treated them, and how Maymuna had stood in the way to protect her. The men turned toward Maymuna, who bowed her head in embarrassment. Hani felt a surge of jealous rage shoot through his body when he heard Bustam's name. Leaning toward the emir he whispered in his ear, "I should have killed him when I had the chance this morning."

Maryam continued. "When Bustam saw my friend trying to protect me he ordered his men to bound her hands and feet. When they locked her in a room she screamed for help. I lost all hope of rescuing her, and so I begged that filthy beast to be gentle with her and with me, but his evil soul was intent on destroying me in that abandoned castle. I tried to persuade him to leave us alone when some cavalrymen came looking for Hani. That's when I learned that the Franks had attacked and that Hani was missing. The Arabs were in dire straights because of that but Bustam was not in the least bit fazed by the news. He chided me and suggested that the Commander," and here she pointed to Hani, "was a coward who ran away from the battlefield fearing for his own life. He told me that Hani was nothing more than a worthless servant-boy, even though everyone thought the army couldn't succeed without him."

Hani turned away, visibly embarrassed by this last sentence.

Maryam continued with her story. "My reply to Bustam's comment hit him like a ton of bricks. When he jumped up at me with his hand on his sword ready to strike me, I screamed at him. 'Shame on you, you despicable man! Men like you have no right to call themselves commanders. Instead of raising your sword at a woman, go and help your brethren in their time of need. If Hani were with them they wouldn't find themselves in such trouble.' Showing no sign of shame, Bustam only grew all the more furious by these words. He continued in his aggressive behavior with his fist clutching the hilt of his sword. 'If Hani were a real man,' he replied, 'he wouldn't have fled the battlefield like he did today. He's a coward!' Then he unsheathed his sword. He pointed it at me, with rage in his eyes ready to strike. At that moment, I forgot all the talk about the weakness of women. I imagined myself killing him, not only to save my own neck, but to be able to come back and join your army, since its failure would cause me grave harm, as you well know. But I got hold of myself and spoke to him calmly. 'Don't threaten me with your sword, and don't think for one minute that I'm a little girl intimidated by swords. Take my advice: stop bullying me, and leave me alone.' I took hold of his forearm and shook it. Disdainful of my advice he pulled his arm away and raised his sword to chop my head off, but I quickly stepped back to avoid the blow. He rushed forward continuing his attack. I couldn't help but scream at him. 'I warned you, Bustam, so heed my words.' He then grabbed hold of my robe thinking I was about to escape. I threw myself at him, grabbed his right hand with my left hand, and with the other hand I reached for his belt, removed his dagger and plunged it into his chest. 'I will rest only when you are murdered,' I shrieked, 'even if my hand is stained with your blood.' With the dagger firmly lodged in his heart, he staggered for a moment and his sword dropped from his hand. Then he fell to the ground dead. I seized his sword, and I rushed out to the black stallion. I put on the 'abaya, placed the helmet on my head, and rode off to the battlefield as quickly as I could. I pretended to be Hani in order to motivate the troops. If my deeds were successful, it was only because of his glorious name."

✼ ✼ ✼

When Maryam ended her story with how she stabbed Bustam, Emir ʻAbd al-Rahman shouted in disbelief: "Did you really kill Bustam?"

"I did indeed kill him, and I explained to you the reason why. Whether you forgive me or punish me because of it, I leave that up to you," she replied.

Hani echoed her response: "He's been asking for it for several days now. If you hadn't killed him, I would have. So, if the emir wishes to punish someone let it be me."

"I have no intention to avenge his murder, but I do fear how it might affect our army. When you find out from…" Suddenly he was conscious of Maymuna's presence and decided not to finish what he was about to say, changing the subject. "We'll continue with that subject later, but tell us, Maryam, what took you so long to come back here since the battle ended several hours ago?"

"I was busy with my friend, here" she said pointing to Maymuna, "whom I left tied up in that abandoned castle before rushing off to the battlefield. After the battle was over, relieved by the army's victory, I went back to save her the same way she tried so hard to protect me. I found her as I left her all tied up. Seeing that the two guards had departed, I unfastened the ropes that shackled her hands and feet and brought her back on horseback. Had I not been able to rescue her my life would have been ruined, since she suffered so much on my behalf. When I returned, night had already fallen, and I was guided here to your camp by the moon and stars. I recognized the emir's tent from the banner hanging outside the door."

As Maryam spoke there was a serene dignity on her face and an echo of truth in every word she uttered. While the emir marveled at her, Hani brimmed with so much love that he couldn't contain himself. "May God bless the womb that bore you. You're a harbinger of glad tidings and our army's lucky star."

Maymuna at that moment stood up from her seat, appearing diffident and grateful. "No wonder Commander Hani is so smitten with her, such vigor and in the prime of youth. Even all of us women have fallen in love with her. I myself have never, in this or any other land, laid eyes on such a young maiden like my sweetheart here, who combines the grace of women and the courage of men, a ruler's esteem and a mother's compassion, not to mention her honesty and high-mindedness. She's worthy of both your admiration. At first I considered her my friend and companion, but after what she did to rescue me, I now look up to her as being above my station."

Maryam was overcome with embarrassment, as beads of sweat poured from her forehead and trickled down her cheeks. 'Abd al-Rahman was quick to notice this. Wishing to change the subject, he interjected. "Maryam deserves this and more, but for now, the time has come for her to go and rest after such a trying day." He clapped his hands to summon the servant. "Prepare a tent for these two women and bring them everything they need. Then, retire the two horses to the stable."

The servant made a gesture of compliance and left the tent with Maryam and Maymuna in tow. Hani followed Maryam with his eyes, his passion burning inside him. His thoughts vacillated between his pledge to marry her after crossing the Loire River and his plans to attack the Franks along the way. 'Abd al-Rahman could see the expression of love on Hani's face and was pleased to see how attached he had grown to her. He made peace with how the two lovers bonded in courage, passion, and pride. His thoughts abruptly shifted to Bustam's murder. He was sure that his followers would rise up and demand revenge. If they were to find out it was Maryam who killed him, they might seek to harm her which would affect Hani, causing even greater dissension among the ranks. He sat frozen in his seat, lost in these thoughts, with his head lowered. Hani sat equally lost in his thoughts, solely focused on Maryam and the Franks and fortresses that might stand in their way.

When 'Abd al-Rahman snapped out of his stupor, he noticed Hani sitting with his head bowed down. He sensed immediately that he was thinking about Maryam and her valor. "May God bless you and give you happiness with this young girl, for you are most deserving of her. But I need to know what you think about Bustam's murder. He certainly deserves what he got, but don't forget how much we needed him, and how we depended on the might of his sword and the loyalty of his tribesmen. You know how these Berbers are with us, especially his men. They've helped us only in their greed for profit, and they've been following our orders begrudgingly since they're convinced that we lord our power and wealth over them. So when they find out about the murder of their leader, they may very well disobey orders and break ranks, especially now that we're desperately in need of unity. So what do you think?"

Hani responded with an answer that appeared to have been rehearsed for days. "Nothing is more important than appeasing the Berbers. If they're not helping us in this war out of loyalty to Islam, they're supporting us for a share of the loot. They only obeyed Bustam to such an extent because he was the middleman between them and us. As long as they profit, they'll remain obedient. Also, we can persuade them that his death will increase their share of the booty given how greedy he was in claiming so much for himself. We can give bonuses to their officers and let them select their own commander to replace him. If you entrust this matter to me, I can guarantee you success."

'Abd al-Rahman was impressed with such wise counsel and put Hani in charge of carrying out the plan he had suggested. On the following morning the officers convened and agreed to move the tents and the booty left behind in the old camp to their new campsite. Hani completed his mission as planned, while the army began its preparations to advance toward the Loire River after Salma returned from her mission. 'Abd al-Rahman was pinning his hopes on the success of her mission. He knew full well that the unity of his army was brittle given its various factions and the conflicting interests among his officers. If he didn't find a way to hold the army together, the outcome would be dire. Besides, he was also hoping that Salma's mission would spare much bloodshed and ease the conquest.

Maymuna for her part was distressed by her failed plot to defeat the Muslims. But she was full of cunning and deceit—and she had a well-prepared back-up plan. She acted as if she were held captive because of Maryam, and rejoiced in Bustam's murder because he was on to some of her secrets. Right after Maryam had ridden off on the black stallion earlier that day, she dispatched the two men to follow her. When they returned with the news of the defeat of the Franks, she ordered them to flee, as she remained at the abandoned palace tied up, hoping that Maryam would send someone to rescue her.

Chapter 8

Salma in Bordeaux

When we last left Salma, she was mounting a horse and departing the Muslim camp on her way to Bordeaux with her elderly servant Hassan by her side. When they reached the outskirts of the city she turned to him. "Did you ever think we would be lucky enough to finally reach the Emir 'Abd al-Rahman as stipulated by the will?"

"No, I didn't think so," he replied. "But now that you mention the will, what possessed you to take it from the place where I had hidden it, far from anyone's sight? And where is it now?"

"Are you asking why I was holding it when we left the other captives? I took it out when I feared for my life. I thought these Arabs were going to kill us. I was determined to keep it close to my body and inhale the fragrance of its owner one more time before I died. Then, I was going to entrust it to you or someone else to deliver it to the commander of this army. But now it's safely hidden underneath my robes, and the only thing that worries me at the moment is that Maryam is alone in the Arab camp."

"She'll be fine, my lady. The Arabs take very good care of their guests. Besides, Maryam is in the care of their leader, and I noticed how much attention and affection they lavished on her, especially Maymuna. Her eunuch slaves told me how fond she's grown of Maryam," Hassan reassured Salma as he trotted beside her.

Salma pulled on the rein of her horse to slow it down. "I must tell you, the only thing that worries me about Maryam is that woman."

Hassan, looking down, careful to avoid the stones and bristles on the ground, was surprised by what Salma said. "What makes you so afraid of her, my lady?"

"I've met this woman who calls herself Maymuna before, and she's real trouble. But what I fear most is that she recognized me as well. The longer she remains in that camp, the more dangerous she will become, no doubt. That's why I'm determined to see this mission through, and to expose the truth about her to the emir so that she doesn't dupe him and cause all their plans to fall apart. Her loyalties lie with the Franks, and she's only interested in their victory. I'm shocked that she's made her way into the emir's pavilion, and I won't rest until she leaves these lands."

Hassan himself was intrigued by these sentiments and was eager to hear more about her. "Do I know this woman, as well?" he asked.

"I'm sure you do," she responded, "but let's put that aside for now." With that, he said no more.

As they approached the walls of Bordeaux, they noticed throngs of people, waiting in groups or standing alone outside the gates. They came to ransom their captured loved ones, and they appeared relieved no doubt by the civility with which they were treated. Only the Jews were upset with this kind treatment, especially those who had already purchased captives. They were about to bring them to auction when an edict was issued ordering them to free the captives, which they did grudgingly.

Seeing the crowds congregating by one of the gates, Salma decided to avoid the commotion and enter through another gate. She proceeded directly to meet the archbishop of Bordeaux at the Qalaya, the gate of the bishop's residence, and left Hassan seated on his horse by the entrance. Once inside the walls, she saw priests and monks scurrying anxiously about. Their faces were beaming with joy at the return of the church vessels, which Hani had supervised the night before, along with the order to free the captives. Most of the priests recognized Salma, and they greeted her warmly and shared with her the good news of the returned loot. She congratulated them and immediately asked for an audience with the archbishop. When permission was granted, she entered his quarters. He welcomed her warmly and deferentially. Although he wasn't aware of the nature of her mission, he nonetheless held her in high esteem for her intelligence and strength of conviction. He blessed her with the sign of the cross and a short prayer and invited her to sit next to him. He inquired about her news and she told him all that had happened to her from the moment she was taken captive. She reminded him of the Arabs' custom of gentle treatment toward all those under their protection, including the captives and prisoners. She went on to explain that wherever their sovereignty extends, east and west, all people, regardless of their faiths, enjoy freedom of religion and civil treatment not customary in the Frankish lands. She also informed him that the pillaging of the Cathedral of Bordeaux was carried out by non-Arab Muslim troops.

The archbishop sat and listened to her, recalling how often she extolled the virtues of the Arabs, but he remained unconvinced. He assumed that she was merely obsessed with them the way she was obsessed with teaching her daughter Arabic while she was living in the Frankish realm. But now that he himself had finally seen something of the kind treatment and justice from the Arab armies, he was open to persuasion. Sensing this, she seized the occasion and turned to explain the reasons for her mission.

"I still remember, Your Excellency, how you rebuffed me when I spoke in laudable terms about the Arabs, but now you yourself have seen proof of this, even at a distance. If you had the opportunity to deal with them and live among them, as I have had, you would grow more at ease with them. I'm still at a loss as to why so many inhabitants of these lands continue to fear and resist them."

"I believe what you're saying, my daughter" he replied. "I've heard accounts of their fairness, but I have also seen such ferocity from some that scares the daylights out of our children. Besides, it's been practically proven that they worship idols instead of God."

Salma smiled incredulously. "Worshipping idols? This is no more than a false accusation hurled against them by their enemies. They worship only the one and true God. They respect the Christian faith and revere Jesus Christ as well. It's inconceivable that idolatry be attributed to them especially since their prophet struggled to rid the Arabs of the idols they worshipped before his time. He destroyed all the images and statues in Mecca. He dissuaded his followers from these idolatrous rituals and forbade them from drawing icons and sculpting statues. So anything you hear of this nature is only meant to vilify them. On the other hand, I won't deny that there does exist among some of them crude and voracious behavior, but that doesn't warrant generalization any more than condemning all the bishops for the religious violations of a few priests. Also, don't forget that the Arabs treat the people of these regions more kindly than the Franks who descended upon them in droves and governed them with a heavy hand. It was the Franks who turned them into personal slaves, burdening them with hard labor, and they never once appointed any one of them to hold a position of authority. It was the Franks who seized control and monopolized all the resources of the land. The Gallic peoples were reduced to peasant slaves working the fields. Have you seen any Gaul appointed to a high position? Has any one of them seen a moment's rest since the Franks descended on them? Whenever the Arabs conquer a land, on the other hand, they leave the people free to maintain their own beliefs and follow their own customs. They even allow them to rule themselves and operate their own courts, limiting their jurisdiction over them to military matters and defense. They only take from them the poll tax, what they call 'jizya,' which is a small amount in comparison to the exorbitant taxes the Franks extract from them. Such is the freedom these people enjoy under Arab rule. And I needn't remind you that the current conditions under Frankish rule are even worse than what they were in the old days of the Roman rulers. Most people live like chattel. It's true that Arabs have slaves and indentured servants, but they are given more humane treatment. Slavery, although legal, is frowned upon in Islam, and Islamic law advocates its abolishment. Had the Christians of both east and west not seen the benevolence and justice of the Arabs, they would not have preferred them over the Persians and Byzantines. I've gone to great lengths to remind you of all of this since my goal is to stop all the bloodshed. Will you help me? There is no doubt that the Arabs will conquer these lands. Let their conquest be based on treaties that guarantee safety to people and their property, instead of forced capture, spilt blood, and demolished homes and fortresses. Your Excellency's efforts to help achieve this goal will be more effective than the efforts of someone like me."

Salma spoke with an earnest serious expression on her face, enunciating each word with a fervent urgency. The archbishop listened with acute interest, astonished by her extensive knowledge of the Arabs. It was as if she had lived among them for many years. Some of the things she said far exceeded the common knowledge of the inhabitants of his lands. He found himself, above all, inclined to being persuaded that it was, in fact, his duty to prevent unnecessary bloodshed.

"May God grant you eternal reward for all your efforts in fostering harmony among His children. We pray to Him and to our lord and saviour Jesus Christ that all will end in peace," he intoned.

Reassured, Salma went on to finish the story of her mission. "I am not asking Your Excellency to command our Christian Brethren to hand over the lands to the Muslims passively, nor to assist them in taking the country by force. I think it best to leave the matter in the hands of whoever triumphs in the end. If the Franks win the battle, then they will remain in power, and the country will remain under their rule. But if the Muslims win, then this will not do us any harm at all, since their rule will be better for us than the Franks."

The archbishop was comforted by these words, especially being a man of Roman origins who witnessed Frankish injustices seeping into his own circles and curbing his influence. "I would like my brother bishops from the other parishes to hear this advice, but my fear is that if the Frankish governors get wind of it, then matters will only worsen for us."

"I, myself, can inform whomever you so wish. But I do request that you send a message to the bishop of Poitiers and assure him of your trust in my sincerity. If you should meet with him, inform him of my views on this matter, and please be sure to send word to the members of your inner circle as well. I'm quite sure there isn't a single person in all of Bordeaux who hasn't witnessed or heard of the Arabs returning captives and vessels pillaged from the churches."

"What you say is correct, my daughter, and we won't deny these noble deeds," the archbishop added.

"I also hope that you will contact the ruler of the realm. Count Odo has sent word to him requesting his help to stop the Arab campaign. I recently learned that the Count is camped at the Straits of Dardun, but I will leave these matters in your hands. I myself will be going to Poitiers soon. Do I have your permission to contact the bishop there?" she asked.

The bishop agreed and rose. He scribbled a short message on a small piece of silk cloth and handed it to her. She took hold of it and kissed his hand, asking God to bless him. As she was preparing to take her leave, she thought about the distance between Bordeaux and Poitiers—about one hundred miles—which could not be traveled in less than three or four days. She also figured that Hassan would not be able to make such a journey on foot. So she asked the archbishop for another horse and he readily complied. She thanked him and departed. During all this time the inhabitants of the monastery were whispering among themselves about what was going on and wondering about the reasons for her visit. When Salma exited the abbey, she saw Hassan and the two horses. She mounted one, he the other, and they left Bordeaux and headed for Poitiers.

✵ ✵ ✵

Hassan was familiar with several roads that lead to Poitiers. He chose the easiest and safest. He planned the trip with the goal of arriving by sunset at a monastery where they could spend the night before resuming the trip the following day. On the road that first day, Salma spoke very little—her mind was occupied with the ponderous mission that lay ahead. As night was falling they came upon a small monastery at the foot of a mountain and close to a river whose waters flowed most of the year. Vineyards and olive groves dotted the landscape, as well as lemon trees and small apple orchards. Like most of the monasteries of the times, a high wall encircled the solitary building and there was only one gate. When they arrived at the door Hassan pulled the rope that rang the bell. A monk's head appeared from above. He peered out of a small window and asked them to identify themselves.

"We are strangers passing through these parts and seeking a room to spend the night. Will this be possible?" Hassan pleaded. He spoke in the local language but clearly with a foreign accent. When the monk descended and opened the door, Salma entered, leaving Hassan behind to help the stable hands tend to the horses before joining her inside. When the monk got a good look at Salma, he was relieved by her dignified appearance and conservative dress. He then dashed off to his superior to inform him of their arrival. Granted permission to allow her entry, he scuttled back to Salma.

"Please come in, and meet the abbot," he announced, "so that he can settle you in a room of your choosing."

Salma followed him through the courtyard. She was surprised to see it crowded with men, women, and children, most of whom seemed to be residents of Bordeaux and its adjacent villages. It dawned on her they were seeking refuge in the monastery, in fear of the impending Arab invasion. When she reached the abbot's office, he stood up to welcome her. He then ordered that food be brought to her before asking her about the nature of her visit. At first she replied only that she was coming from Bordeaux on her way to Poitiers.

"Perhaps you're fleeing Bordeaux as a result of the pillaging of churches and the killing of prisoners of war," the abbot suggested.

Salma was quick to respond. "It was a mistake for those to flee because of the pillages. That was an atrocity committed by a small unit of Berbers attached to the Arab army. When the Muslim commander got word of it, he immediately ordered that all the stolen goods be returned. He allowed the families to redeem the prisoners at very low cost, and he treated the citizens of Bordeaux with compassion."

With a shocked look on his face, the abbot responded. "What do those Arabs know about compassion? What stops them from killing since they have no religion nor any sense of shame?"

"Have you even met any of them, Your Reverence?"

"No, but I've heard much said about them," he replied.

Salma was about to respond to these accusations with facts when, at that very moment, an uproar erupted from the courtyard. The abbot stood up, clapped his hands, and a monk came rushing in. "What's all that commotion," he asked angrily.

"It's Datus," the monk replied with a sheepish smile on his face.

"How can that be?" asked the abbot. "I ordered him to keep away and not talk to anyone. I told him he could come for food only when absolutely necessary."

"Apparently, he's run amok," the monk answered. "We saw him attack the lady's servant," he continued, pointing to Salma, "throwing punches and slapping him, shouting: 'Mama, mama!' He would have killed him if we hadn't stopped him."

Hearing this, Salma suddenly remembered her servant. "Where's Hassan?" she cried out. "What's happened to him? Is he alright?"

"He's safe and sound," the monk reassured her. "But we weren't there in time to prevent Datus from attacking him. After we pulled him off the first time, he came back and attacked him with a club in his hand. When we finally got hold of him, he threw the club at the servant and fell to the ground, delirious with anger. We left him on the ground writhing convulsively, calling out to his mother."

The abbot shook his head as though seeking divine protection from some impending evil. He went out to see for himself what was happening. Salma followed, still in shock over what she had just heard and dreading that this person was stark raving mad. When they reached the courtyard, Hassan had already been taken to his room to have his wounds dressed. Her eyes immediately fell on a young man in the prime of his youth, handsome, with big eyes, a fair complexion and blond hair, lying on the ground with his cap blown off his head and his hair disheveled. She saw him struggling to get on his feet, appearing drunk. He was turning his head right and left as if he were looking for something he misplaced. The abbot ordered the monks to keep Hassan away, safe from Datus' view. He then reached out and took the young man's hand, blessed him, and spoke kindly to him. He instructed him to go to his room. The young man went off, casting his gaze in every direction.

Salma assumed that the young man had gone mad or was possessed by the devil, as people of that era were wont to believe. But she wanted to be sure. When the abbot returned to his office, she went with him. She noticed that the expression on his face had changed, which aroused her curiosity. She no longer thought of going to look for Hassan. She held back from asking until he began speaking to her in a low voice.

"Do you wish to continue debating about the Arabs and about how they are a people of faith and civility?"

"I don't understand, Father, what connection there is between this incident and the Arabs and Muslims. Did that young Frank attack my servant and nearly kill him because he's an Arab?"

The abbot closed the door and beckoned to Salma to sit on a cushion set down on a carpet. He sat on another and began to speak. "If you knew the story of this young man and why he was so enraged and belligerent, you would be persuaded by what I'm saying about the Arabs and cease to speak well of them."

"What is his story?" Salma asked, taken aback.

"You should know, my daughter, that this young man is a Frank who was conscripted to fight the Arabs when they began their assault on our lands. He had a mother who was the only person in his life, and he the only person in her life. He left home and went off to fight. During his absence, the Arabs entered his town, pillaged his home, and carted off his mother to their citadel where they keep all their captives. When the young man returned from the battlefield and discovered what had happened to his mother, he rode off to the citadel taking along with him a group of his companions. They arrived and found the citadel bolted shut. Then, they saw several Muslims peering down from above the wall, and heard them asking who they were and what they wanted. The young man's answer was that he came to take back his mother, who had been taken captive. One of the Muslims responded that he would turn her in exchange for the stallion he was riding, and if not, then his mother would be slaughtered before his very eyes. Datus flew into a rage of anger and told him he wouldn't give up his horse, and that the Muslims could do whatever they liked. He said that thinking they were only threatening him and would never act upon their threat and actually kill his mother. Moments later he saw them waving her head before throwing it down to him. Datus' blood boiled in his veins and he lost his mind. When he realized he couldn't climb the wall to reach the murderers he began to strike his face, wail in agony, and kick his own horse like a deranged madman. He left his companions and came immediately to us. It was when he told me what happened that I realized the Arabs were a cruel and violent people with no morals or compassion. Datus hasn't spoken a word or kept company with a single soul since the horrible incident that happened a couple of years ago. Perhaps seeing your servant and guessing from the color of his skin or the accent in his speech that he was an Arab, he flew into a rage, and remembering his mother, did what he did."

Salma, dumbfounded by this story, felt as though any attempt to defend the Arabs would be feeble and useless. But she tried nonetheless. "Surely, you understand that these atrocities occur in all wars and by soldiers from all armies—Arabs, Franks and others—but what's at issue here is the conduct and intentions of the conquering army."

The abbot interrupted. "What good is it to consider their intentions when we saw for ourselves the actions they committed during their conquest, which do not require any further evidence? Did they not pillage the monasteries and loot the sacred vessels? Did they not take the monks in Spain prisoners and sell them off in droves like slaves?"

Salma seized the moment to say what she came to say. "Yes, some Arabs did pillage churches and monasteries, but this was not sanctioned by their commanders. Often they return stolen goods and release prisoners, especially members of the clergy, because their Prophet instructed them to do so. The most recent crimes were perpetrated by Berber battalions connected to the Arab army who pillaged the cathedral in Bordeaux. When the emir learned of this, he immediately ordered all the loot to be returned, and he issued an official apology. He warned his soldiers not to repeat such actions. Arabs are people of civility and justice, and I believe they are better for the inhabitants of these lands than the Franks. I say this before you on condition that it be protected by the code of the secrecy of confession, not to be revealed to a living soul, that the truth of what I am saying..."

The abbot cut her off before she could finish her sentence. "That the Arabs prevail? God save us!"

"God will grant victory to whomever He wishes," she said stunned. She then remained silent thinking that the abbot was among those impossible to convince. It also occurred to her that expressing her support for the Arabs openly might cause her some harm, but she took comfort when she recalled that her conversation with him would not go any further since he was bound by the seal of confession.

✡ ✡ ✡

When she left the abbot's office, Salma went to the room they prepared for her to spend the night. She awoke the following morning determined to resume her journey. When she called for Hassan, she was told he was unable to travel due to a severe head wound. She went to see him immediately and found him in bed, his head bandaged and his eyes heavy with exhaustion. She asked him how he felt.

"That young man struck me and intended to kill me with that club," he answered. "Were it not for God's mercy, I would surely have succumbed. For the life of me, I have no idea why he attacked me."

Salma never kept anything from Hassan, since he was the repository of all her secrets. She told him the story of the young man and then went on to tell him all about her conversation with the abbot.

"But now we must hurry and proceed first to Poitiers and then to Tours so that our mission won't fail," she said with urgency. "The Muslims are anxiously waiting for us."

"Even if I could stand up," he replied. "I wouldn't have the strength to make the trip. If you wish to travel by yourself, I'll wait until I'm able to leave and catch up with you later. Go with God's blessings."

Salma lowered her head to ponder whether to wait a few days while he convalesced or to set out immediately on her own. She decided on a compromise. "I'll stay here and wait for you to recover until tomorrow. If you're not ready by then, I'll head out alone."

Hassan praised her strength and wisdom. "If by tomorrow it looks as if the wound is healing and if I no longer have a fever, then we'll know that my recovery will soon follow, God willing."

She was gravely concerned about his wound and wanted to nurse him back to health not only because she appreciated his many years of loyal service to her but also because she desperately needed him on this trip. She went to the abbot and asked him to call a doctor to tend to his wound. He summoned a monk who studied medicine and to whom many of the residents of the monastery went for cures. When he arrived, the abbot asked him to look at Hassan, and Salma lead him to his room. As soon as he saw the wound he pursed his lips and raised his eyebrows. Salma was quick to notice it and her heart raced out of fear for her servant. But she didn't let on and waited to see what the doctor would say. He turned to another monk who was there to assist him and instructed him to fetch 'the bottle.' He left and soon came back with a bottle and cup. The monk physician shaved the hair from Hassan's head, much of it matted in dry sticky blood, and reeking with the putrid odor of infection. The monk poured out a liquid that looked and smelled like wine. He asked the attending monk to wash the wound, which Salma now noticed as long and deep. She grew more frightened but maintained her composure and waited to hear what the doctor had to say. The monk re-bandaged the wound and asked Hassan to stay in bed until morning when he would return and examine the wound. When the three of them were out of the room, Salma asked the monk for his prognosis. "We're late in treating the wound. It would have been far better had we done so right after the blow. The only thing we can do now is wait until tomorrow," he replied.

Salma offered a prayer to God for his recovery and maintained her composure throughout the night. On the following day she awoke at the crack of dawn and went to see Hassan. She found him still sleeping. She called out his name but he didn't respond. She held out her hand to feel his forehead. He was hot, and she guessed that he had passed out from the fever. She called for the monk-physician. He came quickly, examined him, and told her he was in a coma, in a very serious condition.

"When will he come out of it?" she asked.

"We'll need to wait a day or two. Only God can cure him now."

Salma stood bewildered and frightened. She feared the worst. She passed the entire day on pins and needles, praying to God and beseeching His assistance in Hassan's cure. She spent another night confused, not knowing whether to remain by his side or to resume her journey. In the end she decided that her remaining would not do him any good, and that he was in good hands at the monastery. So, on the advice of the abbot and monk-physician, she made preparations to leave.

The following day, she went straight to Hassan's room and found the physician and his attendant by his side. He was still unconscious. She asked them about his condition. "I see that he's broken into a slight sweat, and that may be a good sign," the physician answered. She then went to the abbot and announced with regret that she had to depart urgently, entrusting

Hassan to his care. The abbot reassured her with lavish praise of the monk-physician's skills. Salma then requested that he allow one of his monks to accompany her to Poitiers. She took out of her pocket several dinars which she offered as a donation to the monastery. The abbot accepted her donation and granted her request for a monk to take her wherever she wished. When she finished preparing for her journey, she went back into Hassan's room to check in on him one last time. She found him in the same condition. The abbot escorted her to the gate of the monastery.

"If God should permit that he recover, then keep him here with you until I return," she pleaded. "I'll be back as soon as I can."

Again, he gave her every assurance, by now having formed a high opinion of her dignified manner, intelligence, and generosity. In the meantime, the servants in the monastery had prepared her horse and provided a mule for her traveling companion, equipped with a saddlebag filled with food and other provisions for the road. Salma wrapped herself in a black robe to make herself look like a nun traveling in the company of the monk. They rode off, with the monk leading the way.

Chapter 9

A Strange Apparition

It was mid-morning by the time Salma and the monk departed the monastery. They headed north on a road only part of which was paved. She was surprised to see so many abandoned houses and vineyards along the way. She knew that the inhabitants sought refuge in the big cities behind fortified walls in times of war, but what she was seeing appeared to be recent, as if the owners had left these lands only the day before. She thought to herself that something catastrophic must have occurred. She turned toward the monk riding next to her on the mule. "Why have these farms been so completely deserted?"

"I'm sure you're not unaware of all the hardship we're experiencing because of the Arab invasion of our country. The villagers don't have fortresses to protect them against all the robbing and pillage," he replied.

"But the Arabs are still far away from these villages, and it may be that they will never reach them. So why are the inhabitants deserting them?" she asked.

"It's not fear of the Arabs only that's driving these people away, my daughter," he explained. "They're also afraid of the Frankish soldiers who, whenever they pass, loot and subjugate the residents, and demolish their houses, and there's no one to stop them! It may be that the inhabitants of these villages heard they were approaching, and so they fled to God knows where. They may be hiding out in places remote from paved roads until the Franks leave."

Salma saw in what the monk was telling her a glimmer of hope that her mission would succeed. Her eye suddenly caught sight of a distant apparition of a horseman riding in their direction. When the monk noticed her watching him intently, he looked toward him and studied him closely. "I wonder who that horseman could be?" she asked.

"Judging by the garb, I'd say it was a Frankish soldier," he speculated. "But we can't be sure until we get a good look at his face, and it looks like he's coming toward us. If he gets close enough, we'll know or at least we'll ask."

The horseman rode towards them until they came face to face. He was wearing a face mask and only his eyes were exposed. The monk greeted him, but he didn't respond. He was scrutinizing Salma, her clothes, and horse. He then gripped the reins of his horse, turned around, and rode away. Salma was struck with panic and a thousand thoughts jumped into her head. But dreading most that the monk would take notice of her fear and think ill of her, she took control of herself and acted nonchalantly. "Perhaps our visitor was frightened by the sight of a nun's attire," she joked.

"I'm not sure it was fear, my daughter. But I don't like the way he rode off like that. He may have come to investigate us, or at least one of us. And when he found what he was looking for he went back to report on his mission."

Salma was no less convinced that this was the case but she stuck to her decision to appear unaffected. She opted for caution against falling into a trap they may be setting up for her. She abruptly changed the subject of the conversation. "Are we far from Poitiers?" she asked casually.

"If we continue at this pace, we should reach it by tomorrow morning," he responded.

"What would you say about traveling through the night, unless you're in a hurry to get back to the monastery? I myself would have no objection if we continue without stopping, as long as that wouldn't do us any harm."

"I'm not in any rush to get back, nor do I think that riding by night would be dangerous for us, especially since I know the people of these parts well, and they know me. Besides, there's a full moon. If we like, we can alight in the early evening at a monastery I know on the way, have something to eat, rest a while, and then be back on the road by midnight. That way, we'll arrive by early morning. I was ordered to be at your service wherever you go."

The monk's suggestion suited her very well, and she knew that when she arrived at Poitiers a bishop would be there to protect her from the treachery of spies because she was carrying a letter of introduction from the archbishop of Bordeaux. Once she set foot in his monastery, she thought, no one would dare to harm her. Considering the monk's idea to be the best solution, she agreed to travel through the night after stopping at the monastery he mentioned. As they rode along, she stole a peak every so often and looked backward, harboring the fear of soldiers coming to kidnap her. The monk, meanwhile, straddled on the back of his mule, chanted his prayers silently.

They rode throughout the day. The sun set before they reached the monastery. Although the light of day disappeared, the moon had yet to appear. They continued in silence with Salma guiding her horse on the heels of the monk's mule without seeing much of the road in the dark. There was silence all around, and the only sound to be heard was the tapping of hooves, at times over pebbles, at others over grass. By this time Salma's horse was weakening from fatigue, and the monk had to slow down his still active mule to keep pace. They trotted at a slow pace, with their eyes glancing every so often at the tops of the hills, when suddenly they caught sight of a light from above. Before Salma could ask what it was, the monk announced that they were approaching the monastery. Salma was relieved and for a moment forgot all her worries. They began their ascent up the hill with the mule leading the way in the darkness as though it were the light of day. The horse followed. Salma held tight on the reins, fearing the horse would slip and fall from exhaustion. After a slow, steady climb, they reached the plateau of the mountain. But the light they had seen was still far in the distance. Salma, hearing the patter of her horse's hooves, imagined horsemen following her. Fearing some evil that may befall her, she said a prayer to the Lord and made the sign of the cross. She became so scared that she dared not look back. The monk himself also resumed his prayers, when Salma caught sight of the light. Thinking they were close, she perked up and asked the monk if they had arrived.

"Rest assured, my daughter, we're here," he replied.

They reached a flat open stretch of land on the hill with a tall building Salma recognized immediately as the intended monastery. She found
herself riding toward the building until she was in front of the gate. The
light they had seen was no longer in view. The monk dismounted and
walked toward the monastery, still holding the reins of his mount, while
Salma remained on her horse. The monk pulled on the rope that rang the
bell. A doorman looked out from the peephole. Before they could hear
him call out, the monk shouted, "Open the door, and hurry!" He spoke
in Latin to identify himself more easily. The door opened and out came
a tall, emaciated monk, who spoke in Latin. When he invited them to
come in, Salma dismounted, and they stepped into a foyer. He greeted
them cordially and asked why they were arriving so late. They entered a
reception room, and the doorman left. He soon returned with a lit candle set in a wooden candle holder that carried the waxen traces of many
other candles. He set it down, went out once again, and returned with
some food. Salma sat down, having forgotten how hungry she was from
the long, exhausting day. The doorman-monk set before her a bowl full
of pieces of stewed chicken. She ate only a few pieces wanting to sleep
more than eat, and she drank a bit of wine. She reclined on a cushion
without asking the monk to awaken her the next morning, so tired she
was from the trip.

When the monk saw her fall asleep, he arose and went to the doorman's
room. They sat up for a while, talking of matters not connected to Salma.
By the end of the night, Salma's companion learned from his host the short-
est route to Poitiers. It just so happened that it was exactly the route they
had been following. He then went to sleep in a room they prepared for
him. Hardly had he put his head down when he felt the powerful wave of
exhaustion and fell into a deep sleep, not awakening until dawn. He rushed
up, awakened Salma, and dashed to the stables to prepare the mounts. They
were back on the road to Poitiers in no time.

The sun was shining and they passed some high mountain ranges
behind which nothing was visible. Salma felt lost. She feared they would
never find their way were it not for the monk's intimate knowledge of these
parts. By mid-morning they reached a hill from which they could see a
distant plain. To one side of it they saw a town with a high dome crowned
with a cross at the center. Salma recognized it as the Cathedral of Poitiers,

and, putting aside her fear and fatigue, she sighed with relief. "Isn't that Poitiers?" she asked seeking reassurance.

"It surely is, and we'll be there very shortly, God willing," the monk replied.

"From where do we enter? I see it has many walls and gates."

"We'll go in from the southern gate. It's the one you see with the large tree in front of it."

Salma silently rejoiced at their arrival, convinced now that no harm would come to her. But just when they were approaching the gate, she saw a platoon from the Frankish cavalry come out, donned with helmets and armor, their commander trailing behind them. They had long, pointed swords strapped to their leather belts at their sides, and they wore knee-length tunics beneath their armor. Their swords were sheathed in leather casings and leather arrow pouches swung from their shoulders. They wore screen netting over their faces, revealing only their eyes, nose, mouth and beards. Seeing their commander, Salma recognized the horseman who came to spy on them the day before, and she shuddered at the thought. Suddenly he rode toward her as the others quickly followed. Her heart sank, and she prayed to God. Then she moved her horse closer to the monk, as if she were seeking his protection or wanting to ask him something. Her face turned ashen white as the commander shouted an order to one of his men, pointing at her. "She's the one, seize her."

The horsemen surrounded her and her companion, who asked them what they wanted. "We've been ordered to arrest you and take you to Duke Odo," the commander replied.

"Why? We've got nothing to do with politics or war. I'm just a poor monk and she a woman. I think you must be mistaken," said the monk.

"We're not mistaken. Either you come with us willingly, or we'll take you by force," responded the commander.

Realizing the danger she was now in, and seeing that there was no escape from these men, Salma spoke up. "I think you mean to arrest me, and not this monk. Release him, and I will go with you wherever you wish."

Amazed by her courage and composure, the monk's first thought to himself was that he shouldn't try to save his own neck but remain by Salma's side. But concluding that his being there would be of no use, he held his tongue and waited to see what would happen. One of the horsemen then whispered to the commander, who ordered the monk to leave. The rest of the men surrounded Salma and escorted her away without looking back.

Finding herself in the clutch of the Franks with no way to escape from their grip, Salma remembered the letter she was carrying from the archbishop of Bordeaux to the bishop of Poitiers. She feared they may search her and find it, drawing their ire. She devised a way to hide it on her person in a place no one would see. Then she remembered the purse which bore all her secrets and her heart pounded lest it fall into their hands. These thoughts brought her to her daughter and how she left her at the Muslims' camp, and then to Maymuna and all her underhanded schemes. She was convinced that Maymuna was responsible for all the adversities she was facing: there wasn't a single soul in all of Aquitaine who knew her that thought ill of her the way Maymuna did. Taking control of her thoughts, she reminded herself that she embarked upon this mission in secret and that no one but Maryam knew when she had left. Absorbed in all these thoughts, she sat mounted on her horse surrounded by the Frankish soldiers and the masked spy at whom she stole a glance every so often to see if she could recognize him and figure out what was happening. Although he kept his mask firmly in place, she guessed from his body below the short tunic that he may not be a Frank even though he was dressed in their uniform. She noticed the dark skin tone of his legs—Franks usually had ruddy skin. She deduced that he was one of Maymuna's servant spies. At that moment she regretted not having exposed her true identity to the Arabs so that they could be spared from her devious schemes. She feared Maymuna might have lead them into a trap and spoiled all their hopes of victory. She thought of what may befall her only daughter, all alone, if the Muslims were defeated.

They continued their journey on horseback for several hours. Salma dreaded her encounter with Duke Odo, who might recognize her and accuse her of grave offenses against him. That would seal her fate.

Chapter 10

With Duke Odo

Late that afternoon, Salma arrived with the platoon of Frankish horsemen to a vineyard that overlooked a wide open plain. She saw in its midst a huge castle surrounded by tents teeming with soldiers. There was a flag flying from the top of the castle and she recognized it immediately as that of Duke Odo. She assumed that they had arrived at their destination, and she guessed that this castle had once belonged to a wealthy family who had since abandoned it.

The horsemen brought her to the door of the castle. When they dismounted, she followed suit. They handed her over to the guards, who kept watch by the door, and they took her inside the castle. Draped in her long black robe and veil, she followed the steady and firm pace of the guards. They passed through the castle courtyard and reached a large chamber. The guards stood at the entrance. One of them entered and then came out within seconds. He ordered Salma to enter. Inside, she noticed there were no carpets on the floor nor cushions to sit on, just the kind of mats soldiers take with them on the road. There was a single chair in the middle of the room on which sat a man, slim of body, pale in complexion, with graying blond hair. He had bulging blue eyes, a weak chin, and a long scraggly beard. He had prominent cheekbones above two sunken cheeks. He was wearing a purple cap-like crown, embroidered with gold, and in the middle above his forehead was a cross-shaped ornament encrusted with diamonds and rubies. His shoulders were draped with a blue brocaded cape, which covered his robe. Under the robe, he wore a short velvet tunic with a wide sash, weaved with gold stitching in the shape of birds. He also wore tinted leather leggings and his sandals were fastened to his feet with straps woven from sturdy camel hair. The chair he was sitting on had two large armrests on which he rested his forearms. Beneath the robe and around his neck hung a gold medallion in the shape of a cross. There was no doubt in Salma's mind that this was Count Odo, since she knew him very well, perhaps better than most of the officers gathered around him.

Odo had been partaking in rounds of wine with his guests. Having ordered that Salma be brought in, he set his goblet down on the table with the other goblets when she appeared. He wiped his beard with his hand and combed it with his fingertips. The instant he laid eyes on her, a look of surprise flashed on his face. Were it not for his naturally pale complexion, one would have detected the blood drain from his face. Salma was no less taken aback. But she maintained her composure and concealed her surprise. She stood before him, and the guards left the room. He motioned to his guests, and they all departed, leaving Odo and Salma by themselves. Finding herself alone with him, Salma grew anxious. He invited her to take a seat and she sat in a chair facing him, although she was prepared to remain standing.

Odo addressed her in French. "Has your anger reached this extent?"

"What anger are you talking about, sire?" she asked with feigned innocence.

"Do you think I've forgotten you, Ajila?" he asked.

She shuddered when she heard him utter the name no one had called her by for many years. But she kept her composure. "I believe, sire, that you take me for someone else."

"Even if my eyes were to deceive me, my heart does not," he replied laughing. "How could I possibly forget Ajila who broke my heart and undermined my authority, but who also did great harm to herself? Would it not have been prudent to refrain from such madness? Was it not a shame that you, a Christian, born into one of the best Christian families, champion the cause of a people without a religion and morals against your own people?"

"I do not understand, sire, what you're asking," she responded with her head bowed. "It's as if you're addressing another woman. The name you are calling me is not my name. My name is Salma."

Odo roared with a laughter that echoed throughout the entire castle. He then reached out, picked up his goblet and drank without taking his eyes off of her. He gulped down the wine and set the empty goblet back on the table, wiping his mouth.

"Let's put aside the bickering for the moment. So, tell me, Salma, as you call yourself, what brings you here? And what were you up to with the archbishop in Bordeaux?"

She realized that his spies had reported some of her actions to him. "What's so unusual about a Christian woman paying a visit to the bishop of her parish?"

"There's nothing unusual about the visit, but I'm asking you what transpired between the two of you. What actually brought you to go to him?"

"What transpired between us was a conversation about private matters that concern me alone and no one else. And you know very well that priests cannot violate confessional secrecy."

"I'm not asking you to tell me what you told him in confession. I want to know what you discussed about the Arabs and the Franks, about matters that pertain to war and peace."

With this clarification, Salma was now more than ever certain that he knew her secret. She felt there was little hope of being saved, but her despair emboldened her. "Since you seem to know what went on between us, why bother to ask me?"

"You dare to speak to Duke Odo in this manner?" he asked in staged anger. "You speak to the Duke of Aquitaine with such arrogance?"

Salma did not reply but flashed a smile which Odo understood more clearly than a direct response. He reciprocated the smile as if he regretted having threatened her. "There was a time back then when we wanted you to come back, but you refused, and as a result you've done harm to yourself and to your daughter, who is not to blame for any of this. But like yourself you wanted her to forsake her religion and church and to spend her life among the Muslims. But for the life of me, I haven't a clue about the secret behind this stubbornness of yours."

So certain Salma was that Odo knew her secret that she felt as if he had been present in the tent when she revealed it to 'Abd al-Rahman. She no longer saw any point in attempting to conceal or deny anything. "I see you're still speaking to me in riddles and innuendoes. Believe whatever you like, and do to me as you will," she answered.

"What I want to do, Ajila, you will see with your own eyes. Had you addressed me with such insolence in front of my ministers, I wouldn't have been able to overlook it and spare your life. But for now, I choose to be tolerant out of respect for our bygone love. I see that your love has turned into hatred and revenge. My revenge will be exacted in seeing you die in sorrow. Or, we could even kill you with the weapon of your choice," he retorted with a belligerent look in his eye and his beard shaking furiously. As much as he tried to conceal his emotions, his eyes were the windows to his raging soul, as articulated in the words of a famous poet:

Your eyes have revealed to my eyes things that had been concealed from me,

For, the eye knows from the eyes of the other who is an ally or an enemy.

Sensing the depths of Odo's wrath, and realizing that she was at this moment a captive in his grip, she thought it best to say nothing. The more so because she knew that Odo's burning desire for power over the Arabs was irrational, given that they had already defeated him in several battles. Watching her as she sat silent only increased his anger. "I see you still have nothing to say."

"What could I possibly say in response?" she asked, pretending composure and indifference, "to a commander surrounded by his officers and troops, with all the weapons of power threatening a woman alone and defenseless?"

Just as he was about to respond, they heard a violent knocking at the door. Duke Odo was stunned knowing that not a soul among his army would ever dare to interrupt him in a time such as this. He arose, clearly agitated, and dashed to the door with his long robe trailing behind him. Opening the door he roared in anger. "What is it that makes you knock so loudly?"

"Pardon Sire, but we have been asked to inform you of a messenger who has just returned from a mission. He's carrying an urgent letter, which he was ordered to deliver in person to his Excellency the Duke the moment he arrived at the camp, and even to awaken him in the event he found him asleep."

"Where is this messenger? Bring him in," he ordered.

A man wearing Frankish garb but with the look of a North African Berber entered. The instant she saw him, Salma knew he was a soldier from the Muslim army in disguise. Once inside, the man reached into his pocket and took out an envelope and handed it to Odo. The duke took it and returned to his seat. He tore open the envelope and pulled out a sheet of paper. He read the letter and then read it again, with a look of shock on his face. Salma pretended not to be paying any attention to Odo while exchanging furtive glances with the messenger who seemed to recognize her as well. She was certain he was a Berber, and he had an anxious look about him. She recalled having seen him at 'Abd al-Rahman's camp, and she figured the letter was from Maymuna. She wished to be spared from this captivity so she could be of service to the Arabs.

When Odo finished reading the letter he pretended to ponder its contents. At the same time, he stole glances at Salma to check any reaction or expression on her face, but he found her sitting silent and still. He wanted to probe further but he knew this letter called for immediate action. He beckoned to the messenger that he should depart immediately. He clapped his hands, and a servant entered with a lance in his hand. He stood up in a ceremonious manner and ordered the servant to take Salma to a room away from the castle and hold her there as a prisoner. "Since you insist on pleading ignorance, follow this servant. We will investigate your case further."

Salma arose and walked out without uttering a word. The guard walked her through the courtyard and into a long corridor until they reached a room that had only a mat and a small carpet. There was a tiny window that looked out onto the Frankish military camp. When the guard left the room, he locked the door behind him. Salma peered out the window and saw many foot soldiers walking about the pitched tents.

When she grew tired of standing she sat down on the carpet. She was worried about her incarceration and about the obstacles that lay before her. If only she could read the letter and discover what they were planning for her and the Arab army. But she wondered what good it would do her to know when there was no hope of her being released. She wallowed in these thoughts until sunset, not having eaten a morsel of food. So engrossed was she in mulling over her problems, she lost all sense of time. When the sun set and all that she could see was the dark of night, her thoughts turned to her daughter, to Maymuna and to 'Abd al-Rahman. Then she remembered the purse that she was concealing underneath her clothing, and wondered what use there would be in guarding it if she was cut off from the world with no one to rescue her. She lamented her separation from the loyal servant she left behind battling for dear life, and wondered if he had succumbed to his fever. If a person is dealt a catastrophe, he thinks it was intended for someone else but if by chance he encounters good fortune, then he imagines that fate is only favoring him. All these thoughts rumbled through Salma's mind while she trembled in fear of the commotion stirring outside the camp. The soldiers scurried in haste and rustled frantically in the tents when the bugle blew at sunrise summoning them to their morning meal.

Salma awoke to the clanging of the door's padlock and was startled. She looked up at the door and saw a light beneath the threshold. The door opened and a young man in a Frankish uniform entered, carrying a lit candle in one hand and a bowl covered with something that looked like bread in the other. They finally brought food, she thought, as she felt her acute hunger. Not able to restrain herself, she shouted: "Who are you?" The young man replied in a quiet voice. "I've brought you some food, my lady, on orders of my lord, the duke. He ordered me to make sure you eat it. It's from his private kitchen."

Salma was surprised by this hospitality, especially after what had happened between her and Odo. She sat silently waiting to see what the young man was going to do. He then set the bowl down on the carpet and lifted the bread. Underneath were small roasted chickens which emitted a most appetizing aroma, especially to one as hungry as she was. But she was hesitant to eat, as hungry as she was, fearing that the food may be poisoned. She studied the young man's face, trying to find a clue that might encourage her to eat or reject the food altogether. He stood holding the candle and its light shone on his face. She could see from it that he was different, and that the color of his skin was not like that of the local people even though he spoke in the Frankish tongue. She noticed his black twinkling eyes, his slight physique, olive complexion and a short sparse beard typical of young men. His features told her he wasn't a Frank, but that didn't surprise her since it was customary in many nations to employ foreign servants and slaves in castles. For some reason she saw no reason to fear him. Yet she wanted to be sure and encouraged him to speak. "What's your name, young man?"

"Roderic, my lady," he replied.

Her heart beat anxiously and the blood rushed to her face when she heard his name. But she kept her composure and looked into the bowl. She reached for the bread and began to shred it slowly into small pieces. The servant remained standing, having seen the stunned expression on her face without understanding why. He thought that maybe there was something she wanted but was too polite to ask. Then, he realized that he hadn't brought her anything to drink. "Perhaps you need some water?" he asked.

He set the candle down on the carpet and dashed out of the room with the door open. Salma knew that the water was close by and only a few split seconds passed before she heard the tapping of his sandals rushing back. He came in and set before her a cup of water, with a smile on his face. Her anxiety subsided somewhat. She looked into his face again and took comfort in his company. She thanked him for his thoughtfulness and expressed her wish that he be the only one to attend to her.

After setting down the cup of water, he left the room and gently closed the door as if he would be coming back after a short while. Salma ate the food and drank the water. She still kept thinking about this young man, so innocent and gentle-hearted. After finishing her meal she waited for him to return. She finally heard his footsteps. He came in with heavy blankets and pillows and set them on the carpet. "My lord the duke instructed me to bring you these to sleep on," he said.

"I thank you for your thoughtful care," she said, "and I hope, young man, that I could one day reciprocate the kindness. I also hope that you and no one else will assist me while I'm here, if that's possible," she repeated.

Roderic replied with a smile. "I also hope likewise. I wouldn't want anyone to wait on you who doesn't value your worth and fails to provide you with excellent care."

Salma figured that the young man knew something about her situation but she didn't let on. He picked up the bowl and cup and went toward the door. "I remain at your beck and call and will make every effort to serve you, so rest assured," he said, as he left the room and locked the door. Salma felt some relief from all her worries. She spread out a blanket to lie on and used another as a cover, and she rested her head on one of the pillows. She was exhausted from all the events of the past days. Overcome with a powerful drowsiness, she fell into a deep sleep. When she awoke the following morning, Roderic brought her breakfast and attended to all her needs. In the light of day, she got a better look at him and came to the conclusion that he looked more Arab than Frankish. But he spoke French like a native and his name was Frankish. She resolved to discover his true identity, all in good time.

Salma spent several days in captivity and used the time to study the residents of the castle. She was also hoping to find some way to escape. She observed the close attention and care she was given and the way they monitored her every move. She was all too aware of the fact that Odo was determined to keep her imprisoned. The longer she remained the more restless she grew, worrying about the Arab army, knowing they were awaiting her on tenterhooks. But in her heart she knew they would prevail and enter Poitiers victorious. She wasn't concerned for them out of fear of Odo and his army. They had defeated him on numerous occasions. What worried her was what might happen to Maryam in the company of Maymuna. She thought it most likely that the letter that the messenger had brought to Odo was from Maymuna, and she was determined to find out through Roderic.

That morning she awoke to an unusual commotion coming from the soldiers. She looked out her window and saw them folding the tents and preparing to depart. She grew unsettled with fear about this move, but then thought it might provide her with a chance to speak with Roderic. Perhaps he could tell her something she didn't know. When he brought her breakfast, she initiated a conversation. "I see you are preparing to depart. Are all of you leaving or might some of you stay here?"

"We're all going, and Duke Odo has ordered that you come with us," he replied.

"Where are we going?"

"To Tours, by way of the Loire River."

This took her by surprise, knowing that the Loire River is the northernmost border of Aquitaine and that what lies beyond it is under the sovereignty of Charles, Duke of Austrasia, whom she knew to be in fierce competition with Odo for power and influence. She wondered if Charles was more concerned with expelling Odo from his realm than with resisting the Arab conquest of Aquitaine. "Are you absolutely certain they're going to Tours?" she asked Roderic.

"Yes, my lady, I heard the orders loud and clear."

"Are you aware of the rivalry between the two dukes?" she ventured to ask.

"Of course, I am! Who is not?"

"Then whatever possesses Duke Odo to march to Tours? Doesn't he fear his enemy, Charles? "

Hearing this question, Roderic shifted his gaze toward the door, fearing there may be someone nearby who could hear. He then turned to Salma and responded in a hushed voice. "That's a secret only a few in this army are privy to. I'm afraid that if I divulge it, great harm will come to me."

She scrutinized his face for any sign of information, and hankering to hear more, she continued her questions. "What could you possibly fear of a poor imprisoned woman who is no more concerned about this matter than she would be about any trivial matter? I only asked because I enjoy your pleasant company. Furthermore I can't imagine you being so concerned about this army since you don't seem to be part of it." With that said, she again scrutinized his face in the hope of detecting there some clue. She detected a look of surprise and a change of expression.

"Your keen observation amazes me," he replied with a sigh. "You've discovered in only a few days what the most powerful and knowledgeable men of this army have yet to discover."

Gladdened by this subtle hint, she continued to probe. "It appears, then, that my observation is right on the mark, and that we're united in wanting the same thing. So, tell me, what made Odo decide to march on to Tours? Don't be afraid. I fervently hope all will end well for you."

"The reason for the transfer is that the Arabs fought us while we were close to Bordeaux, and they defeated us. And we've just been informed that they're not far behind in pursuing us here."

She cut him off. She was delighted to hear that her absence hadn't delayed their advance and certain they would find no significant resistance on the part of the local inhabitants. "Is the Frankish army using Tours as a place to flee from the Arabs?" she asked.

"It may very well be as you say. But I think they're going to use Tours as a position of defense, not as an escape."

"Defense against whom? They'll find harsher enemies there than they will in the Arabs."

"That's the way it was before Duke Odo found a new ally there," Roderic replied.

"How is that possible, when the rivalry between the two dukes is so fierce? Each one has been wanting to dominate the other ever since the fall of the Merovingian state, which used to unite them under one rule. Whoever among the two proves to be the stronger will dominate all the other duchies."

"That's actually what's happening. This division is what enabled the Muslims to take Aquitaine and get this far. If they cross the Loire River, then the lands of Austrasia will fall easily into their grip because the bishops hold a bitter grudge against Duke Charles, and they may even incite the masses to overthrow him. Should the Arabs appear at this time, they may very well find local support for their conquest."

Salma's heart raced with delight at the prospect of an Arab victory, but she knew well enough not to believe rumors and hearsay. "Why the resentment toward Charles from among the clergy when he's such a great leader?" she probed.

"The reason, my lady, is that he expropriated their property, seized the profits of their monasteries, and parceled them out to his troops. He insulted the bishops by punishing them, and by elevating some of the younger ones over their elders. And I needn't remind you what that will do."

Persuaded of the bishops' wrath toward Charles, Salma continued her probe as to why Odo was seeking Charles's assistance. "But I don't understand why Charles has agreed to an alliance with Odo. Has Charles done this out of fear of the bishops?"

"Not at all, my lady. It's just that when Duke Odo realized he couldn't repel the Arabs from entering his realm, he was compelled to seek his enemy Charles' help."

"But how did he ask for his help? And doesn't this mean that he will inevitably lose control of his country?"

"I don't think he's failed to consider that. But his hand was forced. He'd rather have his country ruled by a Christian rather than a stranger from another land and a different religion. I also think he sought Charles' help because he was pressured into it by some of his most trusted advisors."

"Who would dare to give him such advice?" she queried.

"I don't think the advice came from this camp. I learned about a letter that arrived the day you were imprisoned, and which urged Odo to seek Charles' help. I think it affected him greatly, because as soon as he read it he dispatched a delegation to negotiate an alliance with Charles, and a reply in the affirmative soon followed."

Chapter 11

Who is Roderic?

Salma was so sure it was Maymuna who wrote the letter that she pleaded to God for help. She concealed her anger so well that it could not be read on her face. She was now more resolved than ever to find out the truth about Roderic's identity. "You've talked to me about matters of great importance, Roderic. You must trust me a great deal," she said with a caring expression. "Please know that your trust in me is very well placed. Since you believe in my sincerity, rest assured that I will make every effort to reciprocate in kind. But I'm still struggling to know more about you since I don't see you as someone from these parts."

"There's no doubt I view you as sincere," he responded, "or else I wouldn't have revealed anything to you. What you desire from the depths of your heart I desire as well. That's what's given me the courage to share this information with you."

She knew from that moment on that he was one of her people, and she was determined to get to the truth. "Tell me about your life," she said, "so that we can work together to be saved, God willing."

"Before I do, will you permit me to ask you something I noticed when we first began to converse?" he asked.

"What is it?"

"When you first asked me my name, you had a look of shock when I said it was 'Roderic.' Was that because of the name alone, or was there something else that surprised you?"

Salma feigned a cool detachment. "I don't recall being surprised in the least."

He believed what she said and remained silent. Still waiting for him to respond to her first question, she noticed him peering at the window as if he were on the lookout. She herself turned and looked out the window, seeing only the soldiers packing their gear and preparing to depart. She looked back at Roderic, who was struggling to respond.

"Is there something you're afraid of?" she asked.

"Not at all, my lady," he replied. "It's just that I'm afraid that the time will come for us to leave before I get a chance to finish my story, which may be rather long."

"Can you summarize it for me? Do you know Arabic?"

"No," he responded.

Salma was disappointed, since she was sure from his features that he was an Arab. "Do you speak a language other than French?"

"I speak Bulgarian. It's the language of my youth."

"Ah, so you're a Bulgarian by birth? You don't seem so."

"I'm not myself Bulgarian, but I grew up in the household of a man from the tribe of the Bulgars," he explained.

"How is it that you speak French like a native?" she probed.

"I picked it up from experience. The Bulgarian who raised me later sold me to some Franks. Then I was traded to Duke Odo."

Salma, surprised that her questions were of little use, decided to make them brief and straightforward.

"Where were you born?" she asked.

"I was born in Seville."

"Then you're a Spaniard?"

"Not at all."

"Then, are you an Arab?"

He sat silent and a look of fear flashed over his face.

Who is Roderic?

✳ ✳ ✳

Salma realized he was reluctant to open up to her. Perhaps he couldn't totally trust her because she herself didn't look Arab. "Don't be afraid, my young man, you're talking to a woman who has only affection for Arabs. But what you're telling me is disturbing. How is it that you grew up in the lands of the Bulgars but were born in Seville? There's a vast distance between these two places. Are you only imagining what you're saying, or is it possible that whoever told you where you were born tricked you or lied to you?"

"No, I'm sure about that. I lived in Seville for the first few years of my life, and I still remember parts of it."

"You remember parts of Seville," she asked anxiously. "What exactly do you remember?"

"I remember a large palace with huge gardens. One of the gardens I remember especially well because I used to play there with my friends."

Had he noticed the look that suddenly flashed across her face, he would have known right away that she was caught by surprise at the mention of Seville and its palace, and that she was trying very hard to conceal her emotions.

"So, you were one of the children of the palace? What else do you remember?" she continued to probe.

"I remember only that palace. I was taken away from Seville when I was a small child. Were it not for the frightening events I witnessed at the time, its image would not have been engraved in my mind."

"What did you see that frightened you?"

"I saw the murder of the emir of Andalusia."

"Do you remember his name?"

"I didn't know his name at the time. But later I learned it was 'Abd al-Aziz ibn Musa ibn Nusayr, who conquered the lands of Andalusia for the Arabs."

She had to struggle with all her might to keep the look of shock from her face. She continued to press Roderic. "What do you remember about his murder?"

"I remember the year was 716 AD, and I was about five years old. I was playing in the garden with a girl who was a bit younger than I. She was the daughter of the emir, and we were raised together. While we were playing, I saw some commotion stirring among the servants, and then all of a sudden they stood in absolute attention. I rushed over to get a look, and the emir's daughter came with me. Then the emir came out, donning a cap and robe, followed by an entourage of turbaned notables. They passed through the garden. As they passed us, the emir patted me on the head playfully and said something I don't remember. I recall being very impressed since I had never seen him in such a formal procession. I later learned he was going to his prayers. I went back to playing, thinking no more of it, when all of a sudden I heard people shouting and screaming. Some of the servants rushed out and carried off the emir's daughter, leaving me there. I was terrified, being left all alone in the garden. I started to cry. I saw men running from the direction of the mosque. Then I saw a sight that many years have failed to erase from my memory, and thinking about it still makes me shake with convulsions. I saw a group of men dashing toward the palace. One of them was holding a severed head by the hair. It was dripping with blood. The man's hand and clothing were also drenched in blood. I got a good look at the head and knew right away it was Emir 'Abd al-Aziz. I burst into tears, but they were all too busy to notice me. I remember staying there until sunset without a soul paying any attention to me. My grandfather finally showed up and quickly took me into the palace to my mother. We remained in Seville only a few days after that event. I left with my father and mother to Syria..."

As Roderic was relating his story Salma sat with a fixed gaze, her eyes frozen and distant. A gamut of emotions could be read on her face, from shock to sadness and pain, as Roderic graphically described these events. When he finished he saw tears in her eyes but attributed them only to her being affected by the sadness of his story.

For her part, a wave of suppressed memories from the distant past came crashing through her mind. She now felt a desire to speak of them openly, but prudence and caution prevented her. She wanted Roderic to finish his story. "Your story is so strange and disturbing. Tell me, what happened after you went to Syria? And how did you come to the land of the Bulgars?"

"I assume you've heard about the Arab campaign to conquer Constantinople some ten years ago," he continued. "Having seen that city with all its fortresses and citadels, I wonder how the Arabs mustered the courage to launch a campaign against it."

Salma interrupted him. "Their goal was to reach these lands by that route. They hoped that the battalions that conquered Constantinople would join forces here with those that conquered Andalusia to complete the conquest of this continent, thereby opening the way for the Arabs to rule the world. Don't you see that having failed to conquer Constantinople, they kept trying again, hoping to conquer it through the European continent?"

Roderic was indeed impressed with Salma's knowledge and began to feel more comfortable with her. He continued his story. "I tell you my own story not necessarily based on the way it actually occurred, since I was only a child and didn't understand all that was happening, but from how I came to understand it later on. When we reached Damascus, we didn't find the caliph there nor did I know his name…"

"It was Sulayman ibn 'Abd al-Malik," Salma interjected. "He was a limping glutton who once devoured seventy pomegranates, an entire young goat, and six chickens in one meal. And he finished it off with several kilos of raisins! He would rather appoint himself caliph of the kitchens, not of the people, preferring to kill princes and shed blood!" She said all this with no attempt at all to conceal her disdain. Roderic went on with his story, leaving out minor details in fear of someone showing up unexpectedly. "We inquired about the caliph and were told he had just set out on an expedition to Qinnasrin,[8] and that he was also assembling a battalion to march on to Constantinople under the command of his brother, Maslama. The people pinned all their hopes on this conquest, and they were confident of victory. But I don't know what inspired this confidence."

"The Arabs' pride in the many kingdoms they had conquered got the better of them: they fervently believed that the entire world would be theirs," Salma responded. "Added to that was their confidence in Maslama,

---

8 Qinnasrin was a small garrison town located south of Aleppo, Syria, and is today a small village of ancient ruins. *Translator's Note*

one of the senior generals by whose command many lands fell into Arab hands."

Roderic continued his story. "You could say my father was among the most confident. When they asked him to join that expedition he agreed to go only if he could take my mother and me. He was convinced they would conquer Constantinople, where he hoped to settle. My father became one of Maslama's closest advisors because of his Greek, which he learned during his travels to Byzantium when he was young. Whenever Maslama would alight during a campaign, he had my father reside in his pavilion, while my mother and I would bunk in the women's tent. That fierce campaign was launched by both land and sea. The land forces, of which my father was a part, numbered twelve thousand five hundred soldiers. There were Arabs, Persians, and others, and most rode horses or camels. The naval forces, commanded by Maslama, comprised eighteen hundred ships coming from the shores of Egypt, Syria, and Andalusia. The ships carried the weapons and provisions. The land forces looked like a forest of men and beasts as they marched forward. We passed through Amoriyya, Tyana,[9] and Bergamus, conquering them all. Those Byzantines who didn't surrender fled. The Muslims seized their possessions and property as booty. The spirits and hopes of the troops were raised as long as the campaign advanced, especially since they conquered each town or village they crossed—that is, until we approached the border of Asia Minor at the Bosphorous, which was the only thing that separated us from Constantinople. The naval forces got there before we did, and so we used several of the ships to transport soldiers and equipment from the Asian side to the outskirts of Constantinople, to a place called Abydos.[10] This is the first time the Muslims crossed the Bosphorous. However, we suffered a horrible ordeal. I nearly drowned with my mother, but Providence chose to spare my life only to prolong my suffering."

Salma responded in a hushed voice. "On the contrary, Providence willed that you live to help the people you love." Roderic resumed his story. "We crossed the Bosphorous Strait with our horses, camels and equipment, and landed on the other side. We circled around until we approached

---

9 Bor in modern Turkey.

10 Abydos is the ancient city of Mysia in Asia Minor (modern Turkey) situated at Nagara Point on the Asiatic shore of the Hellespont. The town remained until late Byzantine times an important toll and customs station of the Hellespont.

Constantinople from the western side. There were troops waiting in a vast open plain. We dug a ditch around us and built a wall from mud. We entrenched ourselves for the blockade. We were near a major town where we found all the provisions and ammunition we needed. This was the first time I got a look at that awesome city. As a child I had no sense of what it truly meant to be 'grand.' The height of its walls overwhelmed me, not to mention the many implements of war they bore. I realized that from all the arrows, stones, and canon balls they hurled at us. It was there where I first witnessed the horrors of war. At first, I would scale our wall until I got a good look at the top of the city walls and watch the arrows lodge in its sides like the quills of a porcupine, with thousands more strewn on the plain between us and them. There were even times when, while playing in front of Maslama's pavilion, I would see the arrows pouring down all around me. I would then casually pick them up. I still saw war as a game until that one day when I saw something that made me stop wandering far from my mother's tent. I climbed the wall of our camp to have a look. I saw something flying toward us from one of the gates of the city. It looked like a torch on fire, like a shooting star, or a comet. It landed right outside the wall and exploded, lighting fires on large swathes of dry grass and emitting a powerful odor. I was terrified and ran back to my mother. I asked her about it, and she told me that they often shoot fires which burn whatever they hit. I no longer went anywhere near the wall. Later on, I learned that they call it 'Greek fire,' and that that was the reason they defeated us. They were able to burn our fleet by the sea, ironically after the wind helped us get into the port and anchor close to the city from the eastern side. The Byzantines panicked when they first saw our fleet. Some of the soldiers who were inside the city during the blockade told me that if they looked out to the sea, they could see our fleet as an endless forest whose trees were the sails and ship masts. When they looked toward land, they could see our camp which resembled a sea whose waves were the soldiers and riding animals, and whose ships were the tents and command posts."

"Fortune smiled on us, since the chains with which the Byzantine emperors used to restrict access to the city were broken. Our commanders talked about seizing the opportunity and entering the Golden Horn. However, they were advised by their informants to wait and avoid falling into a trap. When they got very close to the shore, they knew that the Byzantine fleet was approaching, and so they prepared to defend themselves.

But they started hurling fire as if it were shooting out from the windows of hell, and it destroyed most of our ships. Those who survived came back to us wailing in pain, and many of them succumbed as well."

"From that point on our fleet was of no use to us: so we turned our attention to our ground forces. Maslama had assumed that the inhabitants of Constantinople would be worn down by the blockade, and that with their supplies dwindling, they would be forced into surrender. What encouraged us to continue the blockade was that we knew that the Byzantines, after only a few months, sent a message to Maslama, offering to give him one dinar per head if he withdrew his forces. But Maslma was greedy and refused, insisting on conquering it by force or letting the people die of hunger. For our part, Maslama had prepared for all of our needs by planting and harvesting. We spent the winter and summer planting seeds and grazing animals, expecting the Byzantines to slowly starve. But we didn't see any sign of their growing weary even after a full year of our blockade. I later learned that the emperor at the time was 'Anastasius' or 'Artemius'. He held the reins of power despite not being from the royal family. He was shrewd and intelligent. When his ambassador returned from Damascus with the news of the war and the arrival of the Arabs at his doorstep, by land and by sea, he foresaw that the Arabs would set up a blockade. He announced to the inhabitants of Constantinople that whoever could not store three years of provisions should leave the city. They responded by stocking up on wheat and grains, reinforcing the city walls, and making all necessary preparations for the siege. And we were the ones to weaken before they did, having pinned our hopes on backup assistance from the caliph in Marj Dabiq who died, leaving us cut off from provisions…"

Salma interrupted him. "Do you know the reason for his death?"

"No," he replied.

"He died a victim of his own greed. He succumbed to indigestion. A Christian from Dabiq brought him two baskets filled with figs and eggs. He ordered the eggs to be peeled and he ate an egg and a fig, one after the other, until he finished the two baskets. Then he was brought marrow and a large amount of sugar and ate it. He became sick to his stomach and died."

Roderic resumed his story. "Despite the caliph's death, we were able to withstand the blockade another year. We learned how best to grow crops and familiarize ourselves with the climate. But then a severe winter hit us, and we could neither plant nor work. Our provisions dwindled and we were forced to eat the flesh and hides of our animals, as well as roots and leaves. What made matters worse was that the emperor, seeing how long the blockade was lasting and with the Arabs settled in, decided to bear down heavily on us. He dispatched envoys to the Bulgars, settled along the banks of the Danube, and urged them to come to the defense of his city, with promises of money and gifts. They descended on us by land, surrounded our camp, and restricted our movement. It got to the point that not a single soldier could venture off on his own lest one of these Barbarians hunt him down like an animal."

"The emperor announced to his citizens that the Franks were coming to Constantinople in massive fleets to protect Christianity. When word of this reached Maslama, he could not wait any longer. He resolved to withdraw. Using what was left of his fleet, he ordered that the camp be dismantled and preparations be made to set sail for the return to the Asian shores by sea. When the ships arrived, the troops loaded them with the tents and what remained of the horses and camels. As I mentioned, I had been staying in a tent with my mother, and when they came to disassemble it, each person was assigned a task. As my mother tended to hers, I went out to collect arrows left strewn over the grounds. I strayed far from the camp unaware. Suddenly two Bulgars pounced on me, like wolves on a hunt. I cried out for help to my father and mother, but there was no response. I looked over toward the Arabs' camp, while still in the clutches of one of the men, and saw my poor mother leaning over the wall and looking out, striking both sides of her face and screaming for help. One of the Bulgars then hid me behind a tree, from where I could no longer see anything. I began to cry as they alternately threatened me and tried to calm me down."

When Roderic came to this part of the story, Salma could no longer control the flow of tears that trickled down her cheeks and moistened the edges of her veil. As she looked at him, her eyes clearly expressed her shock and sorrow, which he read as her merely being affected by his story. He wanted to go on, but she cut him off. "Have you discovered what happened to your parents since then?"

"No, my lady," he replied. "I haven't seen them nor heard a word about them, nor have I seen anyone I knew back then. Since that time I was raised in the lands of the Bulgars in horrible conditions. I was charged with raising animals and fetching wood and grasses for kindling. I would roam the hills and valleys with my Bulgar mates, children and servants, and deliver whatever we could find to their huts. At nighttime, the family members would gather around a fire to keep warm. The fathers, mothers, and children were all better dressed than I. Some even wore clothing made of fur or wool. I just had a shirt and a flimsy cloak. In my hut, were it not for the mother's pity on me, I would surely have perished from the cold. One time she let me wear an old veil lined with leather, which belonged to one of her daughters. Another time she gave me a worn out garment that looked like a jubba made of goat skin which belonged to her husband. When I put it on, it covered all of me, from head to toe. When all is said and done, I don't think they did this out of sympathy, but more out of fear of losing the fruits of my labor if I were to die."

✵ ✵ ✵

"This was the way I lived for several years. During that time, I learned their language, their habits of eating and drinking, and their religious practices, forgetting my own language and religion. When I reached the age of twelve, I was taken away, along with a large number of young teens, girls and boys alike, whom they collected from the upper regions of the country. They were dressed only in skins and they had long flowing hair. They bound us together in ropes and marched us off, like herded sheep, to a place teeming with people and animals. It was a marketplace where people gathered from all parts to buy and sell, trade and haggle. They lead us into a kind of shed made of wood and stone. They untied our hands before locking us in. When we arrived at the marketplace I momentarily forgot all my troubles and grief, observing, mesmerized, all the different kinds of people and merchandise I had never seen before. We got there just before sunset, and later we spent the night in cold and darkness. I didn't say a word to the others because I didn't know their language."

"When we awoke the following morning, the sun was shining and we savored the warmth. Then we saw people buying and haggling, and we sat dreading our pending sale. Two men appeared, one short and the other tall, clad in robes of thick fur. They wrapped woolen scarves around their faces, and the tips of their beards dangled below the edges of the scarves. Their eyes were swollen red, either from the morning heat or from a night of heavy drinking. They followed our Bulgarian owners, who walked in a humble and respectful manner, into the shed, while the servants followed behind. The tall one stood near the entrance, while the short one came forward to inspect each and every one of us, picking out those he fancied. When he reached me, he stared into my face and began to speak to me in a language I didn't understand. I think he might have been a Visigoth or a Jew because I later learned he worked for Jewish traders. He stretched out his hand and took hold of mine and pulled me toward him. He then ordered me to open my mouth. He examined my teeth and tongue. He grabbed my shoulder and shook it. He checked my eyes and ears, hands and feet, then motioned for me to join those selected before me. After this first round of selection, they began to haggle. When the transactions were completed, our new owners lead us to their storerooms, having paid very paltry sums for us. They gave us some dry bread to eat and scraps of coarse burlap and goatskins to wear. They cut our hair and tidied us up a bit. I felt such joy for having been fed and clothed."

"Several days later, the merchants mounted us on donkeys. We were nearly a hundred people. We rode until we reached the lands of the Franks. They brought us to an inn, where they held us for several days. They divided us into groups. They selected a group of young beautiful boys to be castrated. I learned later on I wasn't selected because I was too old for that kind of procedure."

At this point in Roderic's story, the bugle was sounded for the troops to assemble. "I think I've gone on much too long. So to sum up, I was taken away and sold to a Frankish nobleman, and then later traded to Duke Odo. During my stay in this country, I've been hearing rumors of the Arab advance to conquer these parts. I even thought about fleeing to their side in order to search for my parents, since I hadn't heard a word from them from the time I was kidnapped. But I wasn't able to do that for reasons that would take too long to explain."

"I'm delighted to know my instincts were right about you," Salma said. "You're an Arab, and I am championing the Arab cause. Time doesn't allow me to explain, so let's leave that for another occasion. There are certain issues that connect me to your parents and your grandparents, which I will reveal to you later. But for the moment, keep to your work, and in the event they take me with you on this journey, I will do all that I can to protect you. So let's keep each other informed about ways to stay safe."

"I hear and obey," Roderic replied. He stood up, left the room and locked the door behind him. He nearly tripped over a man, not dressed in army uniform, squatting on the corridor floor close to the door, with his elbows wrapped around his knees and his head buried in his lap. Roderic panicked at the sight of him, fearing he may have heard what transpired between Salma and him. He tapped him with his foot as if to awaken him, but the man didn't budge. He tapped him again and shook him. Seemingly in a drowsy stupor, the man let out a loud yawn and stood up. He rubbed his eyes and looked around as though he had just awoken from a deep slumber. Roderic's fear abated thinking the man fell asleep there merely from exhaustion. He chided him and ordered him to go away. The man, appearing afraid, dashed away.

Salma was so pleased with Roderic that she rejoiced at the prospect of being saved with his help. Since he was entrusted to guard her at the castle, so she thought, he must enjoy the trust of Duke Odo. This made it all the more likely she would escape and rejoin the Arab camp to tell Emir 'Abd al-Rahman about Odo's appeal to Charles for help. She worried he might be deluded into thinking the Frankish troops had thinned out, only to be stunned by Charles's unexpected strong presence. If the Arabs were to lose just one battle, then all their efforts would come to naught. Her thoughts suddenly shifted to Hassan and how she had left him at the monastery. She fervently hoped he was still alive, at least long enough to see Roderic and recognize him. It was long passed midday as she stood by the window looking out at the soldiers as they folded up their tents and loaded their gear, hoping to find some clue as to where they might be heading.

Salma remained by the window for quite a while until she spotted Duke Odo riding in procession with his knights, seated on a saddle plated in silver. They wore uniforms shimmering in shades of green and purple, with Odo in the middle, mounted on a most magnificent stallion, and capped in a crown studded with jewels, which sparkled in the sunlight like little candles. Over his shoulders a squirrel gray cape was draped lined with gold and silver brocade that reached the sleeves. A gold chain, holding a solid gold cross encrusted with diamonds and rubies dangled from his neck. Salma noticed that his saddle and bridle were also bejeweled. The stallion beneath him was prancing playfully, looking haughtier than its rider, the duke, who obviously took exceptional care of it.

Despite all the pomp and ceremony, Salma detected a palpable tension in Odo, perhaps, she thought, because he regretted having sought help from his nemesis, Charles. Or, perhaps he was harboring the hope that Charles would refuse his appeal, or maybe he wished that something could have happened to prevent him from asking in the first place, leaving him thus by himself to face the Arabs. For, if he succeeded in repelling them, he alone would rule Aquitaine. And, even in the event they defeated him, he could make a pact with them thereby retaining control over his realm under their tutelage. But if he did emerge triumphant because of Charles, he would perhaps fail to prevent his new ally from claiming sole sovereignty over all the Franks, thereby forcing himself into oblivion—that is, unless one of Charles's sycophants didn't kill him first. In the end, being faced with the choice of siding with the Arabs or with Charles, Salma wondered why Odo did not prefer the Arabs, since it is human nature to harbor jealousy toward those closest to us rather than toward our enemies. Left to one's own instincts, one would more readily surrender to strangers than to one's own kin. For this reason, you see conquered peoples submit to the rules and regulations of their foreign conquerors more readily than they would to conquerors of their own kind, not to mention the resentment that often rages between the ruler and his subjects within a single realm. Jealousy develops more readily between two people over an attribute or a strength that only one of them is blessed with, but both are deserving of.

For that reason envy is at its sharpest when it arises among people who have similar characteristics.

No wonder, then, that Odo appeared to Salma as having regretted his decision to seek Charles's help. As he drew closer to the window of Salma's cell, he looked in her direction and set his gaze upon her for several moments, without a word or signal. She watched the battalions march by, in formation according to tribes. The commanders and sergeants donned coats of armor and helmets. Some hoisted banners of many shapes and colors. Others held the crucifix or images of the Blessed Virgin holding her infant. And then there were those who carried icons of angels, birds and other Christian and Roman symbols. A band of musicians marched before the duke in silence. When the marching stopped, Salma heard the rolling of drums, the clanging of cymbals, and the blowing of bugles. Her emotions stirred as she imagined the impending outbreak of war between the Arabs and the Franks for whom help was now on its way. The more she imagined the outcome and the possibility of a Frankish victory and an Arab defeat, the more she trembled inside and the more blood rushed to her face.

The army was now beyond the range of Salma's vision. Only a small unit of servants and back-up troops remained on the camp grounds. She grew anxious, especially since Roderic hadn't come to bring her food or to speak with her. His absence elicited the worst thoughts. She went back and forth to the door to listen if anyone was coming. She heard footsteps, but not from sandals, and not the sound of Roderic's steps to which she had become attuned. She wondered who it could be when, all of a sudden, the door flung open and a man entered, wearing something that resembled Arab garb. She examined him closely. He looked much like the messenger who brought Odo the letter while she was meeting with him. She silently said a prayer to God and maintained her composure. "What do you want?" she hastened to ask.

He glared at her. His eyes were far apart, he being severely cross-eyed, and they rolled around in their sockets. "I don't want anything," he replied. "It's just that the duke ordered me to be at your service." He adjusted his cape exposing the sword he was wearing beneath it. She remained calm, fearing the worst possible outcome, knowing that this cross-eyed man was one of Maymuna's most active spies. She was sure that he had had a hand in all her adversities. She didn't dare let on, and she decided that affecting ignorance as well as patience was her best strategy. "God bless you. May I assume you're from this camp?" she asked.

He smiled as if sneering at her ignorance. "No, I'm from another camp." Then he howled in laughter. "Is there anything I can do for you?"

Pretending to know nothing, she continued to act unfazed by his scornful tone. "I have everything I need for the moment, but do you know what happened to the young man who was attending to me before you?"

He answered as his lower lip curled in derision. "I don't know. Maybe he went on a mission to Toledo or Bulgaria. Or maybe he missed his grandparents and flew away to see them."

Hearing these things, she realizes that he had heard her conversation with Roderic. Salma's heart pounded furiously, but she kept a straight face. "Thank you just the same, but I don't need anything right now." She wanted him to leave and to be left alone to think things over. "You don't need anything at all?" he probed. "Aren't you pining for someone in Bordeaux or the Loire Valley?"

She understood he was mocking her and that he was on to her secrets. If she responded to him, she would have to listen to his painful taunts. "No, thank you, nothing at all," she replied.

"If you don't need anything, well, then, there are things I need," he replied.

She turned to him, trying to understand what he was getting at. He was chortling as he looked at her mockingly. "I need you, madam!"

Her brow arched and she grew angry, but she maintained her dignity and composure. "What do you need, servant?"

He reacted with an angry look. "Don't anger me, my good lady, I'm only asking what Duke Odo's ordered me to do."

"And what does he want?"

"He wants you to come along on this campaign. We'll spend the night wherever they pitch their tent."

She understood by the use of the plural that he intended to go with her. "Are we to leave at this moment?"

"Yes. I prepared a horse for you to ride."

"Well, I'm ready, since I didn't travel with any provisions."

"Let's go then," he replied, as he pointed to the door.

"You go first, and I'll follow you," she said. He went out of the cell as she asked. She wrapped her cloak around her, hiding her purse and the other items she was carrying. She went out into the corridor and then to the main hall, from where she peered out onto the courtyard. She saw a saddled horse and two horsemen armed to the teeth, carrying lances and covered in armor. Unfazed by this sight, she went to her horse, mounted it and trotted off as the two horsemen rode by her side. The cross-eyed servant followed them mounted on a donkey.

On the road, Salma drifted in a cloud of thoughts, thinking most of all about the turn of events after having nearly escaped from danger. She thought about Roderic and wondered whether they put him in chains or killed him, and whether she would suffer the same fate. She wasn't afraid of death as long as she was able to accomplish what she set out to accomplish first. She was one of those who value duty over personal comforts, who live their lives only to perform their obligations, and who believe that there is no difference between life and death when fulfilling one's obligations.

Salma rehashed these thoughts to the point of exhaustion as they rode to a destination that was unknown to her. At times, she could see the entire expedition forces in front of her and at other times they were by her side. After a while it became clear that they were riding north, and that they were heading to Tours, which was situated on the Loire River. Her heart pounded in her chest as she recalled the river, and she imagined all the pacts and treaties connected to it. She remembered many things that agitated her and added to her worries, and she nearly burst into tears.

At sunset the battalion reached a stretch of flat land, where they unloaded their gear to spend the night. They awoke at sunrise and continued their march. Not a soul spoke to Salma except on matters of immediate concern, such as food and the like. She observed the hills and mountain passes that dotted the roads, and at times she tried to eavesdrop on conversations among the soldiers, expecting to overhear information about the Arabs or their whereabouts. She carefully studied the road they were treading in hopes of catching sight of something that might reveal their destination. But she saw nothing of the sort and assumed they still had a distance to go. She did hear some of them talking about their journey from Bordeaux and making their way to Poitiers and the Loire River. She was sure they would encounter no serious resistance along the way. The great battle would be fought at that river, and whoever won would rule the land.

The army spent the third night and the fourth on the road, with Salma trailing behind it wedged between her two escort guards. They descended cliffs, climbed hills, and passed through stretches of flat land. On the late afternoon of their fourth day, they arrived at a small river, called the Cher, which snaked between two small mountain ranges covered with wild herbage and small orchards. They crossed the river from the left bank to the right one and ascended some hills that overlooked a vast plain extending to the city of Tours, beyond which they could see the Loire River. By this time, night had already fallen and Salma had yet to see much of anything because they were still far away from the city.

Several miles past the Cher River they picked a spot to rest. Salma was informed that they were to pitch tent for the night, and she waited to find out what they intended to do with her. The cross-eyed servant came with a couple of other servants, and they pitched a private tent for her close to Odo's pavilion, which she immediately recognized by its size and splendor. Being so close to him did not matter to her because she was already in such a state of despair. The men spent much of the night setting up the tents and fastening the pegs. When hers was ready, she went inside and saw that the servant had laid out some food. She ate, and feeling exhausted, lay down to sleep. She was still wondering about Roderic, since she hadn't seen him or heard a word about him along the way. Yet she dared not ask about him, lest suspicion toward him be raised.

On the following morning she awoke to an unfamiliar sound of a bugle. She arose and asked the guard what it was. He informed her that the duke had ordered the troops to assemble on the open field for a mass to be said in honor of Saint Martin, the patron saint of the Franks, who was buried in these parts. He explained to her that his grave had become a site for Christian pilgrims passing through Aquitaine and Austrasia. Salma knew that Saint Martin was a Christian patron of the Gauls in the fourth century of the Christian era, and that he was a bishop of Tours. When he died, he was buried in a small district outside the city, and a church and monastery were erected next to his grave. The area was named after him and he came to be venerated by pilgrims, who attributed miracles to him. When she saw the entire army assembled for mass, she stood by the door to pray with them. Then, Duke Odo came out of his tent in procession with his senior officers and advisors, all dressed in official garb. The priests, preceded by acolytes carrying a huge crucifix, were robed in liturgical vestments, bearing smaller crosses and chanting. They marched to the middle of the field and stood before a platform facing Saint Martin's Church, as the troops remained standing. A high mass was said, and their hearts were humbled and their spirits filled with the hope of victory against their enemy by the grace of God.

Although she participated in the mass, Salma's thoughts drifted to the ambitions of men and their weak natures. They devise laws forbidding murder and punishing those who kill, but then they lift their hands pleading to God, who inspired these laws, to help them kill their fellow men. Then they expect their prayers to be answered, believing that they are seeking truth and justice. If only they understood the real meaning of religion, Salma thought, they would strive to desist from bloodshed and stand shoulder to shoulder to preserve peace. But they don't act in this way, as if long ago they concluded, by instinct, that war is necessary for survival, and that if they did not kill each other, they would lose the world, or at least hunger and disease would kill them. War, Salma thought, will survive as long as there is self-love but that self-love is part of the very nature of man.

Salma emerged from these meditations by the voices of the choir and the scent of incense, and she felt deeply humbled. She thought about her life and all the horrors that filled it. She thought about 'Abd al-Rahman, and especially about her daughter, whom she left behind in his camp, and wondered what happened to her after the Arabs decamped and headed out to Tours. She thought about Maymuna and shivered in fear, agonizing over whether she would plot to harm Maryam. She felt the aching desire to inform the Arabs of all that she knew in order to put a stop to Maymuna's schemes and spare them her deceit. Then she thought about Hassan, imagining that had he been there with her at this moment, she would have sent him on that mission to warn them. She had these thoughts as the soldiers lifted their voices in prayer and the priests chanted their hymns. She couldn't help but cast her glance across the four corners of this campsite and imagine what lay beyond it—the fields that extend to the Loire River, the city of Tours lying on one bank, and the monastery of Saint Martin on the other. The only things she actually caught a glimpse of were the tips of their towering buildings at a distance. While all these images flashed through her mind, there suddenly loomed from the distant horizon two apparitions. First, their heads appeared, and gradually the bodies. They were two horsemen. She fixed her gaze on them and longed to know who they might be. She soon made out their black robes and skull caps in the fashion of monks. Her curiosity was somewhat assuaged—somewhat because many monks in these parts traveled to the big cities to buy provisions for their monasteries. As they drew closer, she saw them mix with the soldiers and join in on their prayers. She shifted her attention back to her inner thoughts. She remembered the young Roderic and longed to see him again.

The bells rang, announcing the end of the mass, and the troops dispersed to their tents. Odo returned to his pavilion with the members of his inner circle, and Salma went back inside her tent as three guards bearing lances hovered about. She noticed that the cross-eyed servant wasn't among them and realized she hadn't seen him since the morning. She spent the rest of the day with a premonition that something was about to happen, something that would free her from her bondage despite the fact that there was no cause for such hope and that everything around her indicated otherwise. But there is a kind of premonition, something like inspiration, in women of refined sensitivity, and a woman may intuit an event before it happens. She could even share it with her husband, but when asked, she would not be able to provide any evidence or basis for her intuition. But then the event suddenly happens. A man, on the other hand, sees only what his intellect guides him to see, through logical reasoning and palpable facts. So, when Salma felt her hopes rising, she felt a bit more at ease, while her intelligence struggled to push aside this fantasy, given all the adversities she was facing.

When night had fallen she sat on a carpet which they laid out in her tent. She felt anxious and unsettled and sought comfort in prayer, still affected by the mass earlier that day. When she finished her prayers she was tranquil. She lay down to sleep and with no lamp in her tent her mind returned to her earlier thoughts. But the commotion and bustle of the servants distracted her, and she looked up and fixed her gaze at beams of light flashing outside the tent. She heard a loud noise but couldn't make out what it was. She sat up and strained to listen, and the sounds grew clear. She overheard talking in the local dialect.

"You cannot stop me."

"I will prevent you unless Duke Odo orders otherwise."

"This is not a matter that calls for the duke's orders."

"But his orders are to be obeyed. This prisoner is involved in a case of grave concern. The duke has strictly forbidden anyone to meet or speak with her."

"Good heavens! Would you go so far as to stand in the way of administering the blessed sacraments?"

"I don't care! But what harm is there in our asking permission from the duke?"

"You all know full well that we devote our lives to hearing the confessions of criminals for their sins. We make the rounds to the prisons, and we visit the prisoners, preaching to them and guiding them to repent."

"That may very well be, but we've been strictly warned against allowing anyone to enter, except the custodian."

"Where is this custodian?"

"I don't know. He left this morning, after warning us emphatically not to let anyone enter."

"Send someone to get the duke's permission, then."

"I'm afraid he may have already retired for the night. Let the matter rest until tomorrow."

"We don't have the time to postpone this! We're leaving early tomorrow morning for Saint Martin's Monastery. Go and get the duke's permission, and let's not argue about it any further. I have never met anyone as insolent as you in all my life. If you don't comply, I'll go into the tent whether you like it or not, and tomorrow you'll have to face the consequences of your insolence."

Salma heard another voice come into the argument.

"Don't be angry, Reverend Father! My comrade is a young man unfamiliar with the rights of monks and priests. You may both enter, and no need for permission. We only ask that you keep us in your prayers."

"God bless you, my son. This is the way of those who will find salvation. May I ask that you stand at a distance from the tent lest you hear the confession? As you well know, confessions are sacred and must be held in the utmost secrecy."

"Of course, we understand completely. But we must ask your reverence to do it as quickly as possible, lest the matter reach Duke Odo and we be blamed for letting you enter without his permission."

Salma was stunned as she listened, while her heart beat a mile a minute. She tried her hardest to recognize the voice, but was unable to do so. However, it reminded her of the monk who accompanied her from the monastery to the outskirts of Poitiers.

She waited to see how the conversation would end. When it was over, she craned her neck to see who was coming in. A man entered carrying a lantern in the shape of a bird looking up toward the sky, emitting light from a wick that seemed to come from its beak. He held the lantern in one of his hands by its cross-shaped handle. With his other hand, he held his cane. When Salma saw him, she jumped up and looked into his face and rejoiced to find that it was that very monk. She kissed his hand and a crucifix he was carrying. She noticed another monk who had come in with him, and when she went to kiss his hand she was shocked to see that it was her servant, Hassan. She was so overjoyed that she was about to cry out his name but caught herself just in time. She regained her composure and motioned to the monk and Hassan to sit down. She herself sat, with the look of shock still clearly visible on her face and waiting anxiously for one of them to tell her what brought them there. The monk set the lantern on the floor and sat across from her. Hassan remained standing and she asked him to sit. He sat out of politeness and whispered, "I thank God for bringing me to you, my lady. I hope I've brought you some comfort."

Just as Salma was about to respond, she grew mindful not to say or do anything she may regret. She knew the abbot was fiercely supportive of the Franks and detested the Arabs, and she never expected this monk to come to her assistance. "What brings you here? Did the abbot from the monastery where we stayed and where you convalesced send you here?" she asked Hassan.

It was the monk who responded. "Certainly! And it is I who was accompanying you to Poitiers until they took you from me. I went back and told the abbot what happened, and had I not done that, it wouldn't have been possible to find you." He said nothing further that would explain why the two of them had come. She then looked over at Hassan and nearly laughed at the clerical robes he was wearing. "It looks like you joined the order of monks."

"I wore these clothes, my lady, as a pretext to get to you. Actually, the abbot suggested it. And the father here has joined me in bringing you a message he will tell you about."

Aching to know the content of the message, she blurted out, "Please, go ahead!"

✵ ✵ ✵

Just as the monk was about to speak she remembered what happened to her the last time she was with Roderic and how that cross-eyed servant eavesdropped on their conversation. So she asked him to speak softly and instructed Hassan to keep a watch for the guards. He peeked out from several openings in the tent until he spotted them several yards away, sitting and chatting. He came back, reassured Salma, and sat down. The monk began to speak in a whisper and Salma was all ears.

"It's no secret to my lady that we, a community of monks, just like all the clerical orders, have given our lives to the worship of God and to serve humanity and save souls. We do not accept payment or favors for our work. For this reason, kings and generals treat us with deference and assist us in our mission. In turn, we help them by assuring the people's loyalty and obedience. We're often instrumental in bringing them to power or even in deposing them. Monks, especially, have gained their trust and respect. Without us they cannot accomplish much since we give them our loyalty and service. Duke Odo has been our supporter and we have been his, except in a few cases. We've overlooked several of his lapses and missteps, attributing them to the weakness and folly of human nature, mindful of the fact that we're in a situation that calls for a united stand in this time of war. If we turned against him or showed our disapproval of him in public, his realm would cease to exist. The Gallic people, the indigenous population of these lands, harbor little affection for the Franks. They would love to rid themselves of them at the first opportunity. I suppose you discovered that when you spoke with our venerable abbot. But now Duke Odo has perpetrated an act that proves his weakness and cowardice, and we can no longer maintain our patience with him. I take it you knew this all along?"

Salma put her head down to ponder these words. The monk didn't wait for a response. "If Duke Odo acts upon his wishes, then his power will be destroyed, taking with it our standing among the people as well as the welfare of our monasteries. It will annihilate our religion, and people will live in chaos."

Salma immediately understood what he meant. "You mean, his seeking the help of Charles, the ruler of Austrasia?"

"That's precisely what I mean," he replied. "Charles is most ruthless toward the clergy. The clerics of Austrasia have already tasted the bitterness of his retribution. He pillaged the monasteries' property and distributed it to his army. He insulted the bishops and committed atrocities against them. Now, Odo is calling upon him for help, and if he defeats the Arabs, all of Aquitaine will fall under his claws, and our churches will be fodder for his ambitions. It's not the first time Odo thought of seeking his assistance, but we were able to stop him in the nick of time, pointing out the dangers for him as well as for us. But now that the horses and swords of the Arabs have struck the fear of God in him, he's called out to that man. The news struck the people of these lands like a thunderbolt, leaders and peasants alike, because they know how dreadful the outcome will be."

☆ ☆ ☆

Salma's heart was jumping for joy as she heard the monk utter these words. She recalled the hopeful thoughts she entertained earlier that day. She truly believed she inspired righteousness, and that from this moment on fate would turn against the Franks. But she sat tight-lipped to listen to the rest of his story. The monk, pausing to cough and wipe his beard with his handkerchief, continued to speak.

"Our abbot was the most irate of all because he was Odo's most loyal supporter and staunchest defender of his interests. When he got wind of the duke's actions, he was most anxious to stand in his way because he's convinced that if this alliance succeeds, then his people, government, and church will all fall under Charles's fist. It's evident that from what you had to say, he's considering the help of the Arabs, or perhaps he received a letter from the archbishop of Bordeaux to that effect. What I do know is that he sent for me the following morning and asked me what I thought. Although I informed him the day I returned of what had happened at the gate of Poitiers, he had an intense interest in discussing your case and asked about the men who snatched you away from me. When I told him they were Duke Odo's men, he shook his head and pursed his lips. He instructed me to go and fetch this gentleman, who by now had recovered from his wounds. But I hadn't yet told him about you for fear of upsetting him. When I went to fetch him, I told him and, as expected, he became very upset. I brought him to the abbot. When we arrived, he instructed me to close the door and then whispered to us in secret that I bring him to you. No doubt you'll be pleased to know he can help you achieve your goal. Shall I go on?"

"Do you need to ask? Please, pray tell."

"He handed me a letter he wrote himself and addressed to the abbot of Saint Martin's Monastery, whose contents I don't know. But there's no doubt in my mind that it expresses his firm resolve to block Charles and his army from defeating the Arabs, or at least that he not go to war with them. Our abbot has come to prefer Arab sovereignty over that of Charles and his band of hoodlums, in part because of the civil treatment the Arabs display toward their Christian subjects, and in part to protect the honor and safety of monasteries."

Salma smiled with great relief at hearing these words, oblivious, at least for the moment, to all her trials and tribulations, which, in the end, worked out for the best. She believed with all her heart that all these events happen according to the will of the Creator of the Universe. Such is the belief of people of all faiths, and mankind by nature is inclined to it, trusting that the world was created to serve him. When man sows and the heavens send their rain, men of faith believe the rains are his reward. If there is drought, then that is their punishment. And if a catastrophe befalls a man even though it is his fault, he blames someone else. And if he does not see the hand of the Creator in all of this, then he blames fate or time. Thus, Salma saw the early signs of her mission's success, and she smiled contently.

"Where is this letter?" she asked the monk.

He put his hand into his sleeve and took out a sealed envelope and handed it to her. She took it and put it into her pocket. "How do we get to Saint Martin's Monastery?" she asked. "We're surrounded by troops who stand guard day and night. Isn't there anyone who could deliver this letter instead of me?"

"No one else but you can do that," the monk replied, "because the letter is entrusted to you alone, and our abbot, may God keep him safe, instructed us to do all we could to get you out of this prison. And, so, what do you think?"

"I don't know what to say. I don't think the abbot realizes how tight the security is and how closely I'm being watched here. You see that for yourselves and you've heard what the guards said. Can you think of a way for me to escape?"

Hassan was speechless during this time, but when he saw how perplexed and at a loss they were, he spoke up. "Perhaps I have a solution."

The two looked at him somewhat skeptically, unable to imagine him capable of devising a way out.

"What's your plan?" Salma asked. "If you have one, now is the time to speak up."

"I've been plotting this for a while." Hassan stood up and adjusted the clerical robe he was wearing. He unfastened the rope tied around his waist, flung it around his neck, and began to remove the robe. "Wear this robe over your clothing, and put this cap on your head. Pull it down over your ears and cover your face. Take this cane, and walk out with the monk. No one will have cause to believe you're not the same two monks who came in. When you get well past the camp, do as you see fit."

The monk was pleasantly surprised by this crafty scheme, and impressed with Hassan's noble willingness to risk his own life for his mistress. Salma for her part wasn't the least bit surprised, but that didn't prevent her from lavishing praise on her faithful servant. "Your gallantry doesn't surprise me, for all too often you have acted with the utmost courage and daring. But I can't bear to lose you, especially after your latest brush with death. The time has come for me to reward you for all that you've done in my service over the years. Most of all I wanted to see you once again to give you news that will make you very happy—news I could only divulge to you in person. But now I'm afraid that if we part we'll never meet again."

Hassan stopped disrobing and leaned toward her. "Well, then tell me now before we depart," he implored.

"There are so many matters I wish to relate to you and to get your opinion on, but I need you to carry out some urgent business," she replied.

"Do you think my staying here will be dangerous for me? Rest assured and trust that no sooner will you leave this camp than I will catch up with you."

"I think that if I were to tell you what I want to say, you'd prefer to stay here several days longer."

Hassan could hold himself back no longer. He was dying to hear what was on her mind. "Pray tell, my lady, what you found out and wish for me to know. Or, at least tell me first what you need me to do, and then we can talk again before you leave about your instructions."

Salma trusted her instincts and decided against telling him to avoid distracting him or giving him an excuse to stay longer than necessary in this camp. The situation called for dispatching him without delay to 'Abd al-Rahman to pass on what she knew about Maymuna, about what was happening in the Frankish camp, and how Odo was attempting an alliance with Charles, not to mention a host of other matters that could be of assistance to the Arabs. But when she saw the worried look and gnawing curiosity on Hassan's face, she answered. "Time doesn't permit me to tell you at this time, Hassan. I think it best that I stay and you take a message from me to the emir. The situation is most urgent, and if you do not do this, an opportunity will have been lost and all our efforts will dissipate like dust in the wind. Please, carry out my instructions, and don't worry, I'll be fine here."

"Whatever you say, my lady, but I don't see anything more urgent than your release from this prison and meeting with the abbot of St. Martin's. You need to stop Duke Odo from joining forces with Charles. When this is achieved we can all go and bring the good news to Emir 'Abd al-Rahman. "

"But the matter I wish to bring to the emir's attention is far more important than the news about Charles," she retorted.

"Could there be anything more urgent than news of Charles and his tremendous army coming to the aid of Odo, bringing with them vast quantities of equipment and arms?" he asked. "Besides, you know all about Charles's legendary bravery and might."

"I fear that there's an enemy and spy living within the midst of the Arab army and one they consider a friend. I discovered the secret during my captivity there. I'm now sure that the appeal to Charles for help was masterminded by this enemy alone. If we don't seize the moment and divulge this secret, then all will be lost."

Chapter 12

The First Secret

Hassan was baffled. He looked Salma in the eye and leaned forward as he spoke. "Who is this enemy, my lady? You can tell me without fear in the presence of this monk. He's a friend and loyal to our cause. Or, if you must, speak to me in Arabic since he won't understand. Please, who is this enemy you speak of?"

"It's Maymuna. Or, to be more exact, that treacherous woman who calls herself Maymuna, but should be called Mal'una, the cursed."[11]

"This is not unknown to us, for we've had a chance to observe her many times. But what have you learned since you've been here?" Hassan probed.

"I also knew her true identity the instant I first laid eyes on her at 'Abd al-Rahman's campsite. But I decided against exposing her until my return from this mission. I was afraid that if I divulged her secret, she in turn could expose mine as well. And you know full well that we don't want that at this time, even though 'Abd al-Rahman would honor me all the more were he to discover who I really am. But I swore that I would not reveal my identity to a single soul before crossing this river," she said, pointing out in the direction of the Loire River. "But had I known what she was concocting behind my back, I wouldn't have held my tongue. So now I must expose her to 'Abd al-Rahman at once!"

---

11 Zaidan is using a pun. The name 'Maymuna' means 'auspicious,' whereas 'mal'una' means the opposite, 'cursed.' *Translator's Note*

"But what is she concocting, my lady? Can't you tell me even that?" Hassan spoke as he kneeled before Salma, craning his neck and looking her straight in the eye.

"Could I possibly keep a secret from you, the repository of all my secrets? You were the only one who knew my true identity until Count Odo recognized me and threatened me. For now, he's turned his attention away from me since he's so preoccupied with the war. Or maybe he's put off dealing with me, secure in the fact that I'm now his prisoner. Either way, the fact of the matter is that this woman, the so-called Maymuna, a favorite among 'Abd al-Rahman's harem for her beauty and cunning, is none other than Lumbaja, the daughter of Duke Odo, the commander of this army!"

Hassan, stunned upon hearing this new piece of information, stood up. "The daughter of Duke Odo, the commander of this army?" he asked in a low, hoarse voice.

"One and the same," Salma replied. "I think you know her, having seen her on numerous occasions with her now deceased husband. Do you remember Munaydhir, the African, who ruled the territory of the Pyrenees between Spain and Aquitaine?"

"Yes, I remember him, and I know that when Emir 'Abd al-Rahman al-Ghafiqi assembled an army to conquer these parts, he found out that this Munaydhir was collaborating with the Franks against the Arabs. And so he launched a surprise attack against him and killed him, pillaging his property and harem, and sending it back to the caliph in Damascus."

"Do you know what prompted him to collude with the Franks against the Arabs?" she asked. When he responded that he did not, she told him.

"Duke Odo knew about the bitter rivalries between the Arabs and Berbers of which you are well aware. When he learned that Munaydhir was influential among the Berber tribes, he thought that if he succeeded in gaining his confidence and approval, that it would help his case against the Arabs. And so he made contact with him, and Munaydhir agreed to a pact on condition that he give him his daughter Lumbaja's hand in marriage. Odo accepted to marry his daughter off to this Berber chieftain. His aim was that she take control and use her beauty and cunning to help him in his campaign to defeat the Arabs. Lumbaja stayed with Munaydhir for a while, to see through the plot she devised with her father. But when 'Abd al-Rahman got wind of the matter, he acted swiftly to free the Arabs from the impending danger, and he killed Munaydhir, foiling Laumbaja and her father's scheme."

"I heard something about this a while back. I also heard that this wife was taken among the spoils of war to Damascus as a prize for the caliph," Hassan added.

"But they staged all of this, fraudulently and deceptively. It appears that Lumbaja made one of her slave girls don her clothing and call herself by her name, while she pretended to be one of the slave girls, in order to remain at 'Abd al-Rahman's camp where she could be her father's eyes and ears and monitor the Arab army's movements. It turns out that it was she who sent word to her father urging him to seek Charles's help. Since he was not about to act on his own, most likely fearing shame in the eyes of his troops and subjects, she used all her considerable influence over him, and so he reached out to Charles. What scares me most about her is that 'Abd al-Rahman trusts her and seeks her advice. Is there anything more perilous for the Arabs than that?"

"No, my lady," replied Hassan. "I must bring this information at once to 'Abd al-Rahman. Will you write a message for me to take?"

"Above all else, we must get out of this prison. Once we're out, all these problems will be easier to solve."

While Salma and Hassan were hashing out these matters, the monk was pacing back and forth, peeking out every so often from the folds and slits of the tent. He turned to Salma and spoke. "We've spent a long time talking and the guards may be getting nervous. I see them hovering about and whispering among themselves, and this could spell trouble for us."

"You should put on this robe and leave the camp with the Father, my lady. I'll follow you a little later. We'll meet on the bank of the Cher River, under a large walnut tree where the Father and I sat yesterday." Salma agreed and put on the monk's robe and cap. He handed her the cane and motioned for her to leave quickly.

The monk cleared his throat, tapped the pillar of the tent with his cane, emitted a loud cough, and exited the tent with Salma behind him. When he passed the guards he pretended to be engrossed in prayer. Then he lifted his hand to bless them and they removed their caps and bowed their heads in veneration. Not a single guard dared to approach the two of them lest they disturb them in prayer. Salma's knees wobbled as she walked, less out of fear for her life than out of great discomfort at fleeing on the sly and masquerading in clerical garb. She looked all around as they were leaving the tent, hoping against all odds to catch sight of Hassan following them. She regretted leaving him behind in that tent, so certain she was that he would be more successful in carrying out this mission. It was pitch black and the only things they could make out in the dark were the shadows of the hills and trees.

After walking for some time, the monk turned to Salma. "We're not far from the walnut tree, my lady. It's right over there," he said as he pointed straight ahead. She looked in that direction but couldn't see a tree. What she saw were piles of branches against the horizon. She soon realized that the tree was on a slope and that what she was seeing were the top of branches. She then spotted a shadowy figure gradually drawing close to the tree, as if it were coming toward them from behind a hill. She stopped to look more closely, and all of a sudden it was in full view. First she detected the Frankish uniform. Her heart beat rapidly when she discovered it was Adlan, the cross-eyed. She offered a silent prayer to God to protect Hassan from any harm her scheming may bring him. Adlan walked passed them without greeting or exchanging words with them. Salma was relieved. After a short while they reached the top of the hill behind which she saw a giant tree overlooking a wide plain. They descended the hill toward the tree and sat down beneath it. In front of them a spring of water trickled down to a ravine that flowed into the Cher River. Salma was spent from all the walking and worrying. She sat down on a rock.

"I'm worried about Hassan," she told the monk. "I can't imagine he'll be able to escape from the camp."

"You needn't worry about him. If he hasn't escaped by now, he'll be able to sneak away in a couple of hours when the guards fall asleep," he replied, reassuring her.

"It's not the guards I'm worried about, but the man we just passed. He was the informant that led to my arrest. Had he not been away from the camp tonight, the guards wouldn't have been tricked by your ruse."

While they were engaged in this exchange, Salma was nervously counting the seconds and feeling as if every minute amounted to an entire day. Suddenly they heard the sound of rapid footsteps. They turned in its direction, and saw a shadowy figure racing toward them. Salma was convinced it was Hassan. When he drew near, she was seized with panic at the sight of him, bare chested, arms exposed, hatless, and disheveled hair falling over his face, fitting the image of a devil as they imagined in those days. But she suddenly heard him speak. "Don't be afraid my lady, it's me, Hassan." When he came right next to her, she screamed. "What happened to you? What did you do?"

"Were it not for my appearance, I wouldn't have escaped. I ruffled my hair and crawled out of the tent on my hands and knees, howling like a demon. The guards were frightened and ran off thinking I was some kind of evil demon. They came to their senses and realized it was a trick only when I was already outside the campsite. There I bumped into a man I think was Adlan, the cross-eyed Berber. He saw me but didn't recognize me. Did he see you here?"

"He did see us but didn't recognize us," Salma replied.

"We'll need to find another place," Hassan advised. "First, give me the robe."

When Salma removed it and handed it to him, he continued. "Let's leave here at once. As soon as that devious Berber reaches the camp and discovers your escape with the two monks, he'll be back here in no time with the army, and we'll be totally helpless."

"You're right about that," said the monk. "Why don't we make our way to St. Martin's Monastery? We may be able to get there by early morning and stay there safely. Then, you could dispatch Hassan on whatever mission you wish. Perhaps we can find someone to go with him to show him the way."

✵ ✵ ✵

Salma headed for the monastery with the monk in front of her and Hassan behind. They arrived at daybreak, utterly exhausted. They looked out from a hill onto a small town with a towering building in the middle and surrounded by high walls. It looked like all the other monasteries of the time, only more ornate. The outer wall was massive, and looking at its girth and height one would think it had been built to defend a major city. Saint Martin's was famous throughout all of Aquitaine and Austrasia, all of Europe, in fact, for its grandeur and wealth, and for its numerous icons and gold and silver vessels, not to mention the abundance of precious masterpieces and relics piled high in its storehouses. Although she had long heard of this monastery, Salma had never set foot inside it until now. It was up to the monk to decide how best to enter. He lead them to the main entrance which was a door much larger than most monastery doors, and he pulled on the rope and rang the bell with a secret-coded ring. A few moments later, a monk appeared on the balcony above the door, and Salma's companion addressed him in Latin. He quickly descended, opened the outer door, and welcomed the visitors. Salma and the monk followed him through another door and came to an expansive area that looked like a garden. In the middle was a large building, the monastery itself. Next to it was another building, and judging by the dome and cross on the top, they recognized it as Saint Martin's Church.

Hassan was behind them, still strangely dressed. Their companion, the monk, asked him to remain at the door. He advised the doorman to keep him there until they called for him. He stayed while Salma and her companion walked ahead. The two monks continued to speak in Latin, only scattered phrases of which Salma could understand. Then her companion switched to French. "My lady is carrying a letter to be delivered to his reverence, the abbot. Is he here at the moment?"

"I believe he's still across the river with the Duke of Austrasia, unless he entered the monastery from the back door, which opens to the bank of the river," he answered.

"When did he cross the river?"

"I believe the day before yesterday, but unbeknownst to all of us at the time."

"For what reason did he go?"

As they walked among the trees in the garden, the monk inspected the pathways as if he were searching for something he lost. By the time they reached this point in the conversation, they had arrived at a stone bench at the side of the church. He invited his visitors to take a seat. Morning was just about breaking, the birds were hovering above, a gentle wind was blowing, and the rustling of leaves chimed with the chirping of the birds. Salma found all this to be soothing, especially after the hardships she had endured over the past few days. She felt a strong desire to sleep but she mustered the strength to listen to the monks' conversation, hoping to learn why the abbot had left the monastery unexpectedly.

"Why did he go? The reason, my brother, is the occurrence of a new development. May God shield us from any adverse outcome."

"And what is this development, may God protect us?" Salma's companion asked.

"Have you not heard the news that Duke Charles of Austrasia is on his way with his massive army?"

"I heard he was coming, but has he actually arrived?"

"Yes, he has, brother, several days ago. He's currently on the left bank. As soon as he arrived, he sent for our abbot to meet him there at once. What could he do but obey?"

"What does he want with the abbot? Doesn't he have an army..."

"You seem to have no idea how this duke deals with the clergy, and with churches and monasteries!"

"I know a little bit."

"Then you must know something about his insatiable greed for church property and wealth. Have you not heard about the abuses he perpetrated against the clergy of Austrasia?"

"I heard something to that effect. And I fear he may do the same thing here with our churches."

They suddenly heard the bell ring and the host monk was startled. The others stood up thinking it was the call to prayers. But they noticed that all the doors remained tightly shut, and that monks were coming from a different direction and lining up along a passageway that wrapped around the garden and extended out toward the walls of the monastery facing the river. Salma and her companion stood up and waited to see what would happen. They soon saw a group of monks arriving, lead by one wearing a different robe and an elaborate hood. Salma deduced that this was the abbot who had come back from his meeting with Duke Charles. She found it surprising how quick and unexpected his return was. She examined him from afar, watching him closely as he stomped in with an angry look on his face, while the monks by his side remained deferentially silent.

The abbot was a man of middle age, with a thick black beard streaked with gray just below the chin, and a matching thick mustache. He had big, sparkling eyes with thick bushy eyebrows. On the whole he looked solemn and dignified, and the angry expression on his face made him look more so, such that all the monks maintained a stony silence. Salma read into his angry look an auspicious omen. As the abbot drew close to the monastery, Salma's companion went over to him, kissed his hand, genuflected, and removed his skullcap. Salma followed suit. The monks stepped back and the abbot went into the building, followed by the monks, who seemed baffled, whispering softly among themselves.

Salma and her companion waited for an opportunity to enter and speak with the abbot. Salma preferred that she go in alone with her letter. After several moments, the monk who had greeted them at the door of the outer gate came out. "The abbot has returned. He wishes to know what it is that you want," he announced abruptly.

"I would like an audience with him to present him with a letter I'm carrying," she replied.

"Where is the letter?" he inquired.

She put her hand into her inside pocket, took out the letter, and handed it to him. He took it, went back inside, and then returned, asking her to enter alone. Pleased with that, Salma proceeded, thinking about what she was going to say, fully aware of the fact that the abbot of St. Martin's enjoyed a higher rank and prestige than all the other abbots, given this monastery's vast wealth. They entered through a corridor that led to a courtyard, where she saw lots of monks passing through, in groups of two and three, as if they were busy at work. As they approached, the monks stepped aside to let her pass, until they reached the abbot's chambers. The monk pulled aside a curtain by the doorway with his left hand and motioned with his right one for Salma to go inside. She entered a large room furnished with carpets and wall hangings of magnificent paintings depicting momentous events in Christianity. A statue of St. Martin carved in stone was placed high above in the apse of the room, beneath which the abbot was seated. When she approached him, she genuflected, and just as she was about to kiss his hand, he raised it and asked for a chair for her to sit. He gave her a welcoming smile, but a glimmer of anger flashed in his eyes.

Salma took a seat. Her long veil which covered her head and robe added to her poise and dignity. She remained silent in deference to the abbot. The abbot went back to the letter and examined it as if he were reading it a second time.

"Who is this letter from?" he asked.

"The author's insignia is on it," she replied.

"I don't see any insignia, but I recognized it from the handwriting. Are you Salma?"

"Yes, my lord. I am your humble servant, Salma."

"Please, my sister, we are all God's servants. What do you want from me at this time?"

"I only want what you want. And I believe it is you who knows best."

The abbot forced a smile. "There's no need for flattery or sweet talk. You've come here on account of a grave matter. My brother abbot writes that it is of the utmost concern to me and to him, and that the future of the Church in Aquitaine depends on it. So, explain to me what is this matter."

"Forgive me, I'm at fault and unworthy of your attention. But I discussed with the writer of this letter a matter which he at first disagreed with and dismissed. But when he heard that Charles was coming to these territories, he came to accept my views. Does the duke's arrival sit well with you? Please forgive my boldness in asking, but what I will say depends on your response."

"You're correct, my daughter. None of my monks would dare ask me such a question, but you've come at a particularly trying time. What my brother abbot writes in this letter brings me no comfort. I reply to your question by stating that I see in Duke Charles a danger to the Church in Aquitaine."

"The abbot shares this view," she replied. "That's why he wanted me to intercede in raising a matter I hope will in the end reflect well on the Church and its flock of believers."

"What are you proposing?" the abbot inquired.

"Do you actually consider Charles a true Christian?" she probed.

"He claims to be one, but if that were the case, then why does he sanction what the church condemns? We heard such outrageous things about him, which we could hardly believe, until we heard them from his own mouth." He spoke these words seething in anger. "We heard reports about how he had robbed money from the monasteries and abused the clergy. At first, I was skeptical, until he summoned me yesterday. Instead of hearing kind words about how much he needed us, I heard only warnings and threats."

Salma was relieved to hear these complaints and grew optimistic that her goals would be achieved. "Warnings and threats," she repeated. "Why? Have you disobeyed him?"

"Not at all, my daughter. But he gave me an order I could not possibly obey. He commanded me to hand over immediately all the assets from this monastery because he needed them for the war. He told me how much he esteemed us at this critical time, and that he would defend us against the Arabs. May God forgive Duke Odo for exposing us to the greatest of perils in seeking the help of this perfidious man!"

"It is true that the greater danger comes from Duke Odo. He compromised his own independence and put the Church at grave risk. How does Your Reverence view these Arabs?" she prodded.

"They are our enemies, and the enemies of our religion," he replied.

Salma smiled politely. "Allow me, Your Reverence, to respond to this charge. Have you met any Arabs or befriended them?" "No, but I've heard quite a lot about them. I've heard that they worship idols, and that whenever they descend upon a place, they pillage the churches, force the women into servitude and concubinage, and destroy homes."

"Would you not take the word of a woman who has lived among them for many years?"

"Have you lived among them? Where? What's your connection to them? You seem to me to be from these parts."

"Allow me, Father, to answer these questions the best way I can. I've lived among the Arabs for many years, during which I learned that they have a religion like ours and that they worship the one God, like us. They are civilized and fair, abiding loyally by the rules and regulations. They conquered Spain and most of Aquitaine, and proved to be tolerant and just in victory. The Christians of Spain, Bordeaux and Poitiers, and in all the territories they conquered, enjoy religious freedom and fear not for their churches or property. Contrary to popular belief, Muslim soldiers do not plunder and pillage out of uncontrollable greed, but are alloted their lawful share of the booty by their commanders."

Salma went on to tell him the story of the Cathedral at Bordeaux, going to great lengths to explain what happened in all its details, knowing that if she succeeded in convincing the abbot of Saint Martin's, then it would make it all the easier to persuade the archbishop of Tours. And in the end, even if they didn't help the Arabs, then she would at least be content knowing that they didn't support the Franks.

The abbot listened attentively as he looked into her eyes, searching to discover the truth about this woman, as his instincts were not helping him much. He was taken aback by this woman's earnest sympathy for the Arabs, she not being one herself. But he deemed her praise of them at this difficult time a good thing, and he entertained the thought that this woman's arrival coming on the heels of his growing aversion and fear of Charles was something of a divine Providence. He was inclined to share Salma's view but thought it best not to make it known for the moment. He wanted to protect his religious standing, for he knew all too well that his siding with the Arabs could have a devastating impact on Christianity and wreak havoc in this country in the event they turned out not to be as Salma described them. Moreover, he was hoping that Charles would back down from his demands. If that happened, there would be no reason not to help him. He kept his head bowed, as he fingered the tip of his beard, then looked up at Salma.

"I thank you for all your efforts, but I ask that you give me some time to reflect on the matter and seek God's guidance and inspiration."

"Take whatever time you need to think it over, Father, but may I remind you that you are responsible in the eyes of God for the well-being of your flock. My goal is that your mission end in the best interests of the Church." With that said, Salma rose to her feet.

"You will stay with us, and let's wait and see what happens," he offered.

Salma realized the abbot wanted to keep her there as something of a hostage until he could ascertain the veracity of her claims. Relying on 'Abd al-Rahman's promises, she wasn't concerned with being held at St. Martin's. "I put myself in your hands," she replied to the abbot.

The abbot clapped his hands and a monk appeared. "Escort this woman to a private room and take very good care of her," he instructed.

The monk took Salma to an upstairs room in the corner of the monastery overlooking the Loire River. She took hold of the bedpost, overwhelmed with fatigue, lay down, and fell into a deep sleep. She awoke the following morning to the ringing of the bell summoning the monks to breakfast. She rose, dressed, and looked out the window, astonished to see ships anchored on the river and forming a line that made a bridge between the two banks. Many soldiers were crossing from one side to the other, bearing flags and banners of all shapes and sizes. She new immediately they were Charles' troops.

She followed the flow of the river as her thoughts drifted to Maryam and to all the ties that linked her to this river. She imagined all the possible outcomes of the clash between the two armies about to take place there. She was all too familiar with the conditions of the Franks, and she knew that Charles remained their lone strongman and last hope, and that if the tides turned against him, then the Muslims would attain full mastery over Europe with no effective obstacle lying in their path. If the Franks were to emerge victorious, on the other hand, then the Muslims would never again find a foothold on the continent. A more fatal consequence for her would be if the Arabs failed to cross the Loire River. Then she and her daughter would no longer have a life. As this thought crossed her mind, she put her hand into her pocket and searched for the purse that held all her secrets. She took it out and kissed it. The tears welled from her eyes as she thought about how much she missed Maryam after such a long separation. Not knowing what had happened to her, she comforted herself by thinking that no one would harm her because she was intelligent and resourceful, and because 'Abd al-Rahman was watching over her.

She continued to watch the soldiers crossing the river. The massive numbers on both sides caused her great alarm, and the sound of the drums, carried by the wind blowing from the northeast, pierced her ears, despite the distance. She stayed by the window for some time. The entire day would have passed in this manner had she not heard a knocking at the door. She went across the room, opened it, and found a monk and a servant carrying a tray of food. They handed it to her and left. Feeling her hunger, she sat down to eat. Hardly had she swallowed the first bite when she remembered Hassan and their monk companion. She clapped her hands, and when the servant arrived, she asked that Hassan be brought to her. He returned soon thereafter with Hassan dressed in a monk's robe, and his hair still disheveled. He stepped inside and she asked him to close the door and sit down. When he refused to sit, she scolded him affectionately.

"Let's leave the formalities aside. You are one of the dearest people to me. You sacrifice yourself to serve me. Sit down, and share this meal with me."

"I'll be happy to sit with you," he replied. "But I have already had breakfast with the doorman. I was also afraid that your efforts with this abbot may have failed."

"They haven't failed yet, thank God. But we must now let Emir 'Abd al-Rahman know what we've done so that he can proceed accordingly. Do you have any idea where the Arab army is at the moment?"

"I learned this morning from a conversation with some of the monks that it's close by, toward the west, and that Charles' army is advancing from the east. The two armies are expected to come face to face in an area just south of the monastery very soon."

Her facial expressions beamed with excitement. "Are you absolutely certain?"

"That's what I heard, and the reports seem to be consistent, so I believe they're true."

"Then we must get this message out to him at once. I wish I could go with you, but the abbot insists that I remain here for some unknown reason."

"It's better that you stay here at the monastery, away from danger. Besides, all the gates and towers are impenetrable and the monastery is off-limits to both armies. Leave this matter to me. I'll take care of it, not only as a service to you, but to me as well. A victory for the Arabs will be a victory for me, and their defeat will be my defeat."

Salma recalled her talks with Roderic, and how she decided not to mention him to Hassan. "I have news more urgent to you, personally, than all other matters."

"What is it, my lady?"

"Do you remember your grandson, Safiid?"

Hassan trembled at the mention of this name, especially after all these years, thinking he had departed from this world. "How can I not remember? May God rest his soul and the soul of his father."

"He did not die, Hassan."

"What? Safiid is alive? Where is he?"

"He's at Duke Odo's camp. He now goes by the name 'Roderic.'"

She went on to tell him some of the details of the story, while he kept his head bowed, as if he were dreaming. He then lifted his eyes toward her.

"Is he there now?"

"I'm not sure. He may be held prisoner there."

"I'm going to look for him after I deliver your message to Emir 'Abd al-Rahman."

Salma was awestruck by his readiness to put himself at her service regardless of his own interests and concern for his grandson. When she finished her breakfast, she instructed Hassan to bring her a pen. She took out a sheet and wrote a message to Emir 'Abd al-Rahman. She sealed it and handed it to Hassan. "Go with God's protection. If you need me for anything, I will be here. Before you go, I think you should don the monk's robe to protect you from the perils of the road. I believe our companion is returning to his monastery, so go with him and extend to him my wishes for his safety."

Chapter 13

On the Battlefield

Now we return to 'Abd al-Rahman's camp. Having followed Salma on her mission, we last left the Muslim forces at the outskirts of the Strait of Dardun after the Frankish retreat from the area. There, the Muslims remained waiting for Salma's return. During this time, Bustam was killed and Maymuna's scheme ended in failure. We also discovered her true identity as Lumbaja, the seductress daughter of Duke Odo, who passed herself off as a captive slave girl to be her father's spy. This ruse of hers worked successfully on 'Abd al-Rahman and his officers, and, were it not for Salma, her disguise would have remained forever concealed. Salma knew her true identity the moment she laid eyes on her in the women's tent, but, jealous to protect her own secret, she decided not to divulge Maymuna's. Thus, she decided to postpone revealing who Maymuna really was until she returned. But had she known exactly what Maymuna was up to, she would not have waited so long.

Maymuna remained in the camp after Salma's departure, with everyone still thinking she was Lumbaja's servant girl. She was thus free to use any means and spare no effort in preventing an Arab victory. After attempting to meddle in the Battle of Dardun but emerging without arousing anyone's suspicion, she turned to one of her demon spies and dispatched him with a message to her father, informing him of Salma's mission and the reason for her journey to Bordeaux and Poitiers. She goaded him into detaining her, arguing that doing so would be like detaining half the Muslim army. But this scheme only came to Salma's attention once she reached the gates of Poitiers. Maymuna, for her part, realized that her father was incapable of defending his duchy against the Arab forces, especially after witnessing the unity of the Muslim forces in the last two battles and her failure to sow discord between them. That's when she turned to her cross-eyed spy and sent him on the mission to her father. Much of her extraordinary cunning and strength relied on her intense influence over her father, and no sooner would she advise him on a matter than he would swiftly act upon it, so thoroughly convinced was he of her vast knowledge and sharp mind, not to mention all the information she possessed on Arab matters after having lived among them for so long. He was in the throes of despair and in a near state of panic when her letter arrived unexpectedly and lifted his spirits. That's when he contacted Charles, Duke of Austrasia. Charles accepted the invitation knowing that if they defeated the Muslims, he would then vanquish Odo, and rule supreme over all of France.

'Abd al-Rahman, for his part, grew restless with Salma's longer than expected absence and dispatched a scouting expedition to Bordeaux to find her. Through it, he learned that she had left there several days earlier. Maryam, despite her love for Hani and her emotional turmoil over it, was nonetheless most concerned about her mother. Meanwhile, Hani would steal away as much as he could to meet with her, either in the tent or out in the fields, where they would converse and cry on each other's shoulders far from the prying eyes of others. 'Abd al-Rahman turned a blind eye, conceding to their love and allowing it to grow. So absorbed did they become with one another, they might have forgotten all about the war, had their intended marriage not depended on its outcome and the success of the Arabs to traverse the land and cross the Loire River. For that reason Hani continued to goad 'Abd al-Rahman into battle before the enemy found time to shore up its forces and the opportunity slipped away while the emir was cautiously devising his strategy. The day the report arrived that Odo had contacted Charles for help, 'Abd al-Rahman summoned Hani and his council of advisors to share with them the news.

"This is what I feared," Hani proffered, "and that's why I've been urging the emir to strike quickly."

"I suggest we commence to march, immediately," 'Abd al-Rahman responded.

"This is my opinion, as well," Hani added.

'Abd al-Rahman paused to guess what the other officers were thinking. Since they included commanders of the Berber tribes, and not one of them spoke up, he was concerned. Hani instantly sensed the emir's discomfort with the silence. He knew all too well that the Berbers were driven only by their greed for booty and captives, and he also knew that when they heard that Aquitaine was joining forces with Austrasia, they would fear for themselves. And so he spoke up to entice them. "There's no need to prolong the discussion on this. God is bringing those two armies together as a boon to our booty. The money and treasures that these people possess are countless. If we defeat both armies in a single battle, we will control the whole continent, from the Latin west to the Byzantine east, completing our conquest of the world and spreading the word of Islam to all people. Your swords and your horses will deserve all the credit for that!" Hani chose his words carefully, combining the lure of the spoils of war with the sanctity of jihad, so that the seeker of loot need not be ashamed in responding to the emir's question. When he finished, the troops raised their voices in unison. "Saddle the horses and let's be on our way!"

'Abd al-Rahman responded. "May God bless you and Islam be strengthened by you." Then he ordered them to prepare for departure. When the officers left the tent, Hani remained alone with 'Abd al-Rahman. Hani sensed that the emir was disturbed.

"What's bothering you? Didn't they all agree to march?"

"You know Hani, that they are only in this fight for the profit. They've packed so much of their loot that they're burdened by all its weight. They can barely carry their food and equipment. How can they possibly fight?"

"You raise an important point, Emir. This Berber obsession with the spoils of war is a heavy burden on this army, not only because their greed comes at the expense of others, but also because it distracts them from fighting. If they take it all with them, it restricts their movement, and if they leave it behind, they leave their hearts with it. I think we need to devise a strategy to reassure them and keep them focused."

'Abd al-Rahman lowered his head in thought while Hani remained by his side. 'Abd al-Rahman adjusted his turban while Hani tightened the sash around his robe. The emir picked up his 'abaya and wrapped it around him.

"We should look into this. Leaving all this cumbersome booty behind and marching off to battle without it would be best for all of us, but who would dare tell the Berbers to forgo their loot? After all it was precisely that loot which persuaded them to fight."

Hani laughed. "I assume you understood that from my expression when I spoke to them. I was meaning to tempt them into moving quickly to Tours by mentioning one of the wealthiest Frankish monasteries, Saint Martin's, which is located there. But I held back in fear of putting only the loot in their minds and making them forget the war. Besides, it would only increase the resentment of the local people and leaders toward our army."

"You were wise in keeping quiet on that. I suggest that when we arrive on the battlefield, we make arrangements that will not anger anyone. We'll put all the booty in a designated safe area and put the owners' minds at rest. We'll create a place behind the tents."

"We'll take care of that when the time comes," replied Hani. The two men went out to prepare for the journey.

Meanwhile, Maryam sealed the bonds of friendship with Maymuna, who took advantage of every opportunity to win Maryam's heart with praise and flattery. In her sincerity and genuine affection, Maryam put her complete trust in her. This was not out of ignorance or folly, but simply the product of an open mind that trusts people and believes what they say. As part of Maymuna's wiles to win Maryam over, she concocted stories about her and 'Abd al-Rahman that she claimed could only be revealed to the most intimate of friends. She prodded Maryam into sharing secrets about her and Hani as well, while Maryam, extremely careful not to divulge the secret of their love, received a bouquet of compliments for her discretion and a show of respect for her privacy. Having succeeded in winning her over completely, and in full possession of her trust, Maymuna didn't leave her side, except for the times they slept or for those urgent occasions when she met with Hani.

The following morning the troops folded their tents and loaded their equipment onto the pack animals. They set out that day, the foot soldiers marching in tribal groups, led by a horseman bearing one or several tribal banners that flapped in the wind. Had someone seen this sight from a distance he would have thought that the flags were sails, its bearers ships, and the marching foot soldiers a sea of crashing waves. He would have thought that their white turbans and the tips of their spears were piercing the waves on the surface of the sea. The Berbers also marched in formations along tribal lines, with the client troops of non-Arab origin, like the Nabateans and Syrians, marching alongside the Arabs. Their uniforms differed slightly from those of the Arabs. The cavalry also rode in formation, one battalion following another, also each unit being led by the banners of its commanders. Hani's banner was the grandest of them all. Most of the horsemen donned heavy coats of mail and steel helmets. 'Abd al-Rahman rode beside Hani, ahead of the other commanders, and the captains of the tents rode with the women and children seated in howdahs. Maryam was one of two women not among them having chosen to ride on horseback like the rest of the cavalry. Maymuna was the other, insisting on riding beside her. They were followed by a detachment of soldiers and the pack animals carrying the gear. 'Abd al-Rahman and Hani, having reviewed the formations and inspected each unit carefully, were satisfied with the size of their army and confident of victory.

On the road, the Muslims passed by abandoned fields, replete with weapons left behind and empty houses, picking up what they wanted. When nighttime came upon them, they settled down to eat and sleep. On the following day they arrived at Poitiers and were met with no resistance to speak of. Odo's army had departed, by now far away and heading to Tours.

☆ ☆ ☆

The Muslims learned that day from their informants that Odo's army was close to the Loire River. They stopped to rest and reenergize, and then set out with 'Abd al-Rahman and Hani leading the way. About a mile into the march, they paused to review the enemy positions with their best scouts in order to determine where best to pitch camp. Late in the afternoon 'Abd al-Rahman and Hani rode to the top of a hill along the Cher River and looked out toward the east. The Loire River was on their left with the setting sun still fully visible behind them above the horizon.

They surveyed the area that lay before them on the east and caught sight of a wide open triangular-shaped field. Its base was the Loire River on the left and its furthest point extended to the south. They caught sight of tents and banners and were able to pinpoint the exact location where Duke Odo's army set up camp. Between that spot and the Loire River was another open field which looked to be about two miles away, and because it didn't appear to have any caves or other hiding places, they thought it to be suitable as a battlefield. They spotted several buildings at the edge of the triangular field that lay along the bank of the river, the closest of which were those of the city of Tours, specifically Saint Martin's Monastery which they recognized by the splendor of its church dome. From their lofty position, they detected motion and billows of dust rising above the banners and horses, confirming that the enemy camp was situated along the river. 'Abd al-Rahman ordered one of his guards to pass the word along to the troops to remain at the spot where they had paused and to await further instructions. Then, he turned to one of his informants, an Arabic-speaking Frank. "Isn't that Saint Martin's Monastery?" he asked for confirmation.

"It is indeed, my lord, the wealthiest of all the monasteries in this country."

"And what's that we see behind it?"

"It's the army of Duke Charles crossing the river from the northern to the southern bank. I learned just this morning from a man I ran into coming from the vicinity of the monastery that the duke began several days ago transporting his ships across the river to unload the massive amount of troops and equipment he brought with him."

"Do you know the exact number of his soldiers?"

"It's hard to say, but I have no doubt that he conscripted every able body he could pluck from the Frankish clans in Austrasia and beyond. He's fully aware of the Muslims' valor and strength, and he realizes that this war will bring him either total domination over all of France or the loss of control of Autrasia."

"May the latter happen, God willing," Hani interjected.

'Abd al-Rahman cut him off. "Isn't that Duke Odo's army on our left in the direction of the south? Isn't it moving away from the Straits of Dardun?"

The informant laughed. "Yes, my lord, and he himself is escaping as well. Because, whether 'Abd al-Rahman or Charles wins, Odo's control over Aquitaine will fall to you or Charles. Poor man, he loses either way."

That's all that 'Abd al-Rahman needed to hear. He looked out once again to decide where to set up camp.

"I don't see any place to camp better than the place where we are now," advised Hani. "We can cross this small Cher River and pitch tent right beyond it. We'll be at the same distance from both armies. Should they join forces we'll be directly in front of them, and the river will be directly behind us. In the event we're defeated, God forbid, we can cross the river and dig a ditch between us and them."

'Abd al-Rahman agreed with Hani's suggestion. "I think that's correct. Moreover, if we leave the women and all our gear here, and only have the fighting soldiers cross the river, then we'll be able to safeguard all our belongings. I also think we should leave behind the booty that's weighing down our soldiers, and let them go onto the battlefield lightly equipped. You know how much hauling this loot troubles me, and if we fail to convince the men, especially the Berbers, to set it aside on the day of the battle, then we could very well be defeated. We all know that the least encumbered fighter is the most effective."

"Let's call for a meeting of the officers and convince them to leave the booty behind. We'll explain to them why all this extra weight is dangerous. And then let's see what happens."

'Abd al-Rahman turned to the bugler who happened to be among the men riding with him. He asked him to go back to the camp and notify the commanders that they would be spending the night at that very spot, and then bring them up the hill to discuss the battle plans. The bugler sprinted off and in no time returned with the men galloping on their horses. 'Abd al-Rahman and Hani dismounted from their horses, and the commanders followed suit. They handed the bridles of their horses to their servants and stood on the hill overlooking a vast plain surrounded by the city of Tours and Saint Martin's Monastery to the north and west, and Odo's campsite to the south and east. 'Abd al-Rahman explained to them what he had in mind about the location for battle and the Cher River that lay behind it.

"I also seek your advice on a crucial matter that will be of great benefit to us all, that is, that only those of us who will be engaged in battle cross this river, and we leave the women, our loads, and all our possessions here with some men to guard them. What do you say to that?" he asked.

Two commanders from the Arabian Qays tribe spoke up at once. "The emir's opinion is correct." The other commanders followed their lead and agreed unanimously.

"There's another matter of grave concern that also worries me. As you know, God has rewarded our army with an abundance of riches in the way of booty: our men are so weighed down by hauling their shares that I am worried about how they'll be able to fight the enemy. The way I see it, we should leave our possessions in a safe place with the rest of the gear we'll be leaving behind. We can store them in one large tent and appoint only the most trustworthy of men to guard them, just as we did in Bordeaux."

'Abd al-Rahman could hardly finish his sentence when a young Berber chieftain spoke up. "We do not share this opinion. And you needn't remind us of what happened in Bordeaux. We were apportioned meager shares of the booty according to your orders, and, in the end, we lost our most powerful commander and the most courageous soldier in this army."

Hearing these words, which hinted at Bustam's murder and echoed the rancor and spite the Berbers harbored, 'Abd al-Rahman fretted that any response or reprimand could ignite an uprising, knowing all too well that the young man would say anything to defend his people. The emir replied with feigned innocence. "Indeed we suffered a serious loss in that incident. Commander Bustam was one of a kind and it will be difficult for us to replace him. But I don't see any connection between his murder and the booty."

He then turned to the rest of the commanders. "Let's all forget that incident and work for our greater cause. I have put forth to you my views, and if you have any other suggestions, speak up, since our goals and what we have to gain are all the same."

The commanders whispered among themselves before one of the Yemenis spoke up. "I believe that the emir is correct in saying that a soldier cannot engage in combat when he's encumbered by the weight of his loot. If a man loses his booty but wins in battle, then he stands to gain twofold."

While many of the commanders voiced their support of this view, Hani noticed that the Berbers remained silent. "I would like to add to what the commander said," Hani interjected, fearing the loss of their support. "If we emerge victorious from this battle, there's no telling how much booty we'll gain. Duke Charles, the commander of that army over there, has brought with him everything he could get his hands on from the monasteries, churches, and palaces of his realm. If we defeat him, we stand to take possession of all that wealth in addition to our pride and glory!"

The Berber chieftains were at a loss for how to respond. One of their senior commanders then spoke up. "There's no doubt that a soldier can only fight effectively if he's carrying a light load. But who among us can convince our soldiers to leave behind what they earned only through great duress. They don't seek military or political power, but merely their rightful share of the spoils of this war. I suggest we bring all the loot with us tomorrow morning and put it in a place close to where we will be fighting, instead of leaving it here. It would be easier for us to leave it close by than keeping it on the other side of the river."

'Abd al-Rahman had no choice but to concede. They returned to the campsite and retired for the night. On the following morning they commenced crossing the river on rafts they built on the spot. The Cher River was but a little stream in comparison to the great Loire River into which it flowed. 'Abd al-Rahman and Hani were the first to cross in order to designate the right place to disembark. They stood on a small hill from where they looked out onto the plain and chose the spot. The soldiers pitched their tents and set up their banners, working well into late afternoon. As Hani peered out onto the horizon, he caught sight of someone rushing toward them. He fixed his gaze closely and was surprised to see the figure garbed in clerical clothing. He then saw the man fall to the ground while pointing to Hani. Hani trotted his stallion toward him and, lo and behold, it was Hassan, Salma's servant, lying on his back, pressing one hand on his side as though suffering from pain, holding out something in his other hand and waving it to Hani. Hani got off his horse and stooped down to help Hassan sit up. The old man motioned to leave him be. When Hani asked him why he was there, Hassan replied in a stuttering, panting voice still pressing his side from the intense pain.

"My mistress Salma sent me with a message to Emir 'Abd al-Rahman… from St. Martin's Monastery…" he blurted, as he turned his eyes to the letter in his left hand. "I fled the monastery and when I saw your banners, I rushed to you as quickly as I could, but I was struck by the arrow of a traitor, whom I think was Adlan the cross-eyed. Certain I would die, I rushed ahead to deliver this most urgent message, but as you see, I fell before reaching you… Here is the letter."

His voice grew silent and his panting increased, his eyes closed, and his hand went limp. Hani called out to him but there was no response. 'Abd al-Rahman saw them and dashed over to see what was happening. Both men were deeply affected by Hassan's plight. Holding onto the hope he might still be alive, 'Abd al-Rahman asked Hani to fetch a physician. Hani mounted his stallion and sprinted to the campsite, shouting out for a physician. Moments later a Christian doctor from Andalusia, long in the service of the Arabs, appeared. When they reached Hassan, he tried to feel his pulse but not finding it, he pronounced him dead. He asked that he be washed and prepared for burial. They brought him back to a tent set up for these rituals.

'Abd al-Rahman took the letter, opened it, and read it out loud to Hani.

To Emir 'Abd al-Rahman al-Ghafiqi,

I write to you from Saint Martin's Monastery, where I arrived after many hardships, too numerous to explain at this time. When we meet again in the near future, God willing, I will tell you all. I rush to write this letter to inform you of an urgent matter I learned about during this journey. The woman who calls herself Maymuna is none other than Lumbaja, daughter of Duke Odo, and she has set up numerous pitfalls for me during this trip. She is also responsible for convincing her father to seek the assistance of Charles, duke of Austrasia, by way of a messenger, her crossed-eyed servant. Be warned, and do as you see fit. I also send you the good news that the abbot of this monastery is resentful of Charles, and he has promised to help me, and at the same time is holding me here for my own protection. I am safe and well treated, and I pray for your victory. I entrust to your loving and protective care my precious daughter, Maryam.

Farewell,

Salma

When he came to this last sentence 'Abd al-Rahman paused and looked up at Hani and then went back to the letter, deeply moved by its sentiments.

Hani responded. "I never saw any good in that cursed woman. Despite her ravishing beauty, I felt a deep repulsion for reasons I cannot explain. It's as though my heart was telling me something of her deception, and I was baffled by the excessive attention she was lavishing on Maryam…"

'Abd al-Rahman cut him short. "I pampered her but with much the same caution. I never completely trusted her, but I knew she could be of great benefit to us in reaching our goals, since she comes from these parts. But now things have changed, and we need to act swiftly. What do you suggest I do with her?"

"I suggest we kill her and rid ourselves of her once and for all," replied Hani.

"Once we get our troops into formation, I'll give it some more thought." With this, he mounted his horse and spurred it toward the campsite to prepare the soldiers for war. He lined them up along a third of one side of the triangular field that extended from the direction of Tours to Odo's campsite. He pitched his pavilion in the middle of the camp, facing the base, and Hani pitched his tent next to his. From these, the tents of the leaders of the tribes followed in succession, each clearly marked with the tribal flags flying over the entrance. A single tribe could have a number of commanders each with his own flag, according to the rank and size of the tribe. The tribes were arranged along kinship ties, the Mudariyya on the west side and the Yemenite tribes on the east. The Berber tribes settled in the south in a spot the emir let them choose. He ordered that a tent be constructed to house all the booty, and he chose a place to the south, in response to a request from the Berbers that the booty remain close to their quarters to prevent the Arabs from pillaging it. Finally, he set up makeshift stables for the horses on the back side of the camp leading out to the Cher River.

During the time they were pitching tents and settling down, Hani made the rounds throughout the camp to help 'Abd al-Rahman mobilize the combatants. But his thoughts were fixed on Salma's letter and the parts concerning Maymuna and Salma. It occurred to him that if Maryam knew her mother was being held at Saint Martin's, then perhaps she would request to go there, and he took comfort in that thought. Even if the Arabs were to suffer defeat, she at least would be safe and secure, or so he thought.

He spent the rest of that day and the next moving about and getting the troops into formation until the bank across the river was brimming with tents and stocked with weapons. In the late afternoon of the following day, 'Abd al-Rahman and Hani rode off secretly to the women's tent to interrogate Maymuna. For his part Hani saw no need for discussion. Were it up to him, he would cut her head off and be done with her. 'Abd al-Rahman, however, preferred to deal with her with prudence and caution. When they arrived, they went inside and 'Abd al-Rahman called out for the matron. She quickly appeared with her bracelets and anklets jangling with every step she took, looking as if she inhabited a sumptuous palace in Seville living in luxurious surroundings. When she saw 'Abd al-Rahman, she greeted him effusively.

"Where is Maymuna?" he inquired.

"I haven't seen her since last night," she replied, "but I think she's in her room with Maryam."

"Go and fetch her, and bring her back to us alone," he snapped.

She clapped her hands and a eunuch guard appeared immediately. "Go and tell Lady Maymuna that Emir 'Abd al-Rahman wishes to speak with her at once." She spoke in a broken, almost gibberish Arabic, the way foreign speakers do, like the Slavs who pick up words here and there after years of serving the Arabs. The eunuch bowed his head in obedience and left the room, while the others waited. Hani wanted to head straight to Maryam's room to reassure her of her mother's safety. Such is the pleasure of lovers who delight in bringing to their beloved good news of a loved one's safety after a long absence. Especially when it's a secret matter, a lover longs all the more to be the one to divulge it. The more confidential it is the more pleasure he takes in sharing it as a secret not to be divulged to anyone else. The pleasure grows even stronger when the bonds of trust are sealed by affection. When two people love each other, the bonds of trust are strongest, and they revel in the intimacy that lies between them.

However, he decided to stay with 'Abd al-Rahman until Maymuna arrived in order to goad him into having her executed. Considerable time elapsed after the eunuch went off to fetch Maymuna. The matron then ordered another eunuch to go after him. Minutes later, the first one returned. "I've searched every corner of the tent, but not a trace of her is to be found," he announced.

'Abd al-Rahman and Hani, knowing what they knew about this woman, were as stunned as the matron by her absence. "Where is she, my good woman?"

"Perhaps she went on an errand and will be back soon."

"I need to see her right away. Go and find her!"

"I haven't seen her since sunset yesterday," she said as she was about to leave. "No one knows her comings and goings better than Maryam." She waddled her way out of the room and was away for a long time. When she returned, Maryam was with her.

"I looked everywhere for her," she insisted, "but I couldn't find her. She's nowhere in these tents."

Maryam's perfume filled the air the instant she entered. 'Abd al-Rahman gave her a smile despite his anger toward Maymuna and his fear that she may have escaped. There was a glow about her and an expression on her face that would please anyone who cast his eyes on her. So just imagine how Hani felt, whose heart she had won and whose emotions she controlled. When she sat down, 'Abd al-Rahman began to question her about Maymuna. She explained to him that she hadn't seen her since the night before, and that she looked for her all that day, disappointed in the absence of her sole companion and her only consolation during her mother's absence.

"Can you think why she left?" he asked.

"I have no idea. But I did notice that she looked irritated late yesterday afternoon. I didn't think it was serious, and I didn't bother to ask her about it," she replied.

"Did you notice whether someone brought her a message yesterday morning?"

"Only the servants that usually attend to her."

"Was Adlan the cross-eyed among them?"

"Yes, as a matter of fact. I noticed because I hadn't seen him in a while."

When she answered this last question, 'Abd al-Rahman and Hani exchanged glances, and they realized Adlan had come back straight to Maymuna after shooting Hassan with the arrow. They deduced it was he who advised her to join her father because he feared her secret was going to be exposed.

Chapter 14

Hani and Maryam

Maryam looked to Hani for signs of good news. With the matron departed, she was left alone with the two commanders. Hani knew from the way she was staring at him that she was waiting for them to open up to her. Hani looked over to 'Abd al-Rahman and saw him lost in thought. "I suppose this treacherous woman found out she was about to be exposed, and so she fled to her father. But she won't be spared from the tip of my sword, God willing."

Maryam was stunned by these words, which contradicted everything she thought and felt about Maymuna. Her face blushed crimson, and her eyes flashed with shock. She turned to Hani, unable to contain herself. "What did this poor woman do to incur the wrath of the emir? I've come to know her as a most caring and kind-hearted person."

Hani turned to 'Abd al-Rahman. "May I please have the letter?"

Hani's sudden request for the letter took the emir by surprise. The emir intended not to show it to her to spare her undue worry about her mother. He didn't show any annoyance with Hani, but rather politely feigned ignorance of where he had placed it. This upset Maryam and made her think that they were hiding some awful news. She thought of her mother, as she shouted with her lisp. "What are you keeping from me? Did any ill befall my mother?" Then she burst into tears.

Hani was deeply moved and felt compelled to respond. "Rest assured, Maryam, your mother is safe and sound."

"Where is she?" she asked.

Pointing to Saint Martin's, he replied. "She's over there at that monastery."

"Why hasn't she come back? Is she sick, or is she being held against her will?"

'Abd al-Rahman staged some attempts to look for the letter, which he quickly found and handed to her. "Here is her letter, which will tell you all you need to know."

She took the letter, which at first she couldn't read because of the tears gushing from her eyes—tears of shock, fear, hope and joy, all at the same time. She wiped her eyes and read it, and when she reached the last sentence, *I entrust to your loving and protective care my precious daughter, Maryam,* she yelled out "Mama!" nearly choking on her tears. She reread the part about Maymuna, and a bewildered look flashed on her face. She looked up at 'Abd al-Rahman, her naturally angelic demeanor turning to anger. "May God punish this treacherous woman! Now I understand why she went off alone with that cross-eyed Berber last night. May God make her pay for her deceit!"

Maryam probed the emir about who actually delivered the letter to learn more about her mother's condition. When he told her it was Hassan and about how he died and was buried, she wept. Had she not been so preoccupied with Maymuna's deception and missing her mother, she would have felt the pain of his death more sharply—he had taken care of her since she was a child, forever devoted to securing her and her mother's comfort and safety. But her concern for her mother and her longing to see her were all-consuming. She looked at 'Abd al-Rahman with teary eyes and pleaded with him. "Will the emir allow me to go and see her, just to kiss her hand? I shall return immediately"

'Abd al-Rahman was deeply touched, and he could only comply with her request. "I shan't prevent you from going, but I intend to live up to her trust in me and keep you safe, as she asks at the end of her letter."

"You needn't worry about me, God willing. The road is easy and it's not very far. I can see the monastery from here, and I'll ride there very quickly."

"We're not worried that anything will befall you," Hani added in support, "especially after seeing the way you handled yourself at the Strait of Dardun. But I think it would be best for me to accompany you, at least until you reach the gates of the monastery."

'Abd al-Rahman agreed with Hani. "If you insist on going, I think you should leave now so that you arrive before sunset. I wonder, will Hani need a chaperone to prod him to a speedy return? There'll be no problem for Maryam to spend the night there. The monastery is a safe place."

Hani was delighted with this mission. He arose and ordered a horse to be prepared for Maryam. She fastened her robe and wrapped an 'abaya around her. Hani also put on his 'abaya and adjusted his turban, and the two trotted off on their horses. They crossed the Cher River on a bridge that the soldiers had erected the day before and galloped toward the monastery in the northeast direction. Halfway there, they dismounted and walked their horses, one beside the other. Finally being alone, Hani felt the urge to be playful with Maryam.

"Do you know what's behind those buildings?"

"The big ghiver," she replied with her funny 'r'.

"And do you know the name of the river?"

"The Loigh Ghiver," she answered, pronouncing both words with her funny "r." But hardly had she uttered these words when she remembered his promise of marriage, and she felt embarrassed. She turned her head in another direction and tried to change the subject. "I feel as though I can see Duke Charles' army coming toward us."

Hani cast his glance toward the billows of dust rising from behind the monastery.

"No doubt what you see is Charles' campsite. But the dust you see in the air is not the dust from their marching, but from pitching their tents and exercising their horses." He thought about the fierce battle that was going to take place on that field as he spoke these words. But he was confident of his own valor and full of optimism about victory.

The Battle of Poitiers

✵ ✵ ✵

While dwelling on these thoughts, Hani heard the sound of a ringing bell and pricked up his ears. Maryam explained that it was from the monastery and that they had drawn close. The sun was on the verge of setting, and had they looked up they would have seen its full form, still radiating much of its light and warmth. But they were distracted by the billows of dust rising from the south over the plain and close to Odo's camp. They figured that the horsemen were stirring it up with the hooves of their steeds.

They reached the gate of the monastery at sunset, and Hani rang the bell. The doorkeeper monk peered out from above, and Maryam addressed him in French, asking about a guest who was staying there. He came down, opened the door, and welcomed her. He was taken aback by the sight of Hani in his 'abaya and turban. He had never seen an Arab before, although he had heard the rumors that they were coming. Maryam dismounted, and Hani was about to bid her farewell, but his heart told him to stay. He remained seated on his horse by the entrance, and Maryam gave him a look that pierced through his armor and touched his heart. He dismounted and spoke. "I think I'll go in with you until you find your mother. That way, I'll be sure both she and you are safe. Then I'll go back." He then motioned to a servant of the monastery to take away the two horses. She smiled in relief and walked in with Hani by her side. They passed the inner door and were greeted by another monk, who inquired about the nature of their visit. "Do you have a guest here named Salma?" asked Maryam. The monk smiled and nodded and asked them to follow him. When they were inside the monastery, he escorted them up a flight of stairs and toward Salma's room.

Salma had been alone since Hassan departed, and she passed the time looking out the window or sitting on the cushion, thinking about how much she missed Maryam during this long separation. Her thoughts drifted back and forth, from one of her secrets to another, agonizing over how and when to reveal them. She fretted that maybe it would be too late, or perhaps her fortunes would turn for the worse and her efforts would vanish in the wind. She awoke early that morning in a state of despair and went to the chapel to pray. She begged God to protect her daughter, and returned to her room, thinking it was a prison, even though it was one of the most luxurious rooms in the monastery.

Her heart spoke to her and told her to look out onto the plain near Tours where perhaps she would catch sight of a messenger on his way, or perhaps inhale the fragrance of her daughter's perfume. She saw the Arabs' campsite, out in the distance. She dashed out onto a balcony overlooking the plain and was able to pinpoint accurately the locations of both the Arab and Frankish camps. Her heart pounded as she conjured images of the great battle that was going to take place there. She returned to her room, and her feelings of solitude grew stronger. The sun had gone down. Sunset is the most difficult time of the day for a free person, so you can imagine how it affects a prisoner. In her despair, she decided to go down to pray, but suddenly she heard footsteps on the terrace. Her heart began to pound more quickly as she looked out to see who was coming. When she heard footsteps coming toward her room, she became excited. She heard a knock on the door, and it seemed to her as if the knock was on her heart. She arose, her legs wobbling, opened the door, and the monk greeted her as he pointed to his two companions. She stepped out of the room and yelled out "Maryam!" when she saw her daughter. She threw herself on her and covered her with kisses as the tears rolled down her cheeks and she swooned with emotion. Maryam kissed her mother's cheeks and hands as she sobbed gently. The two women came inside the room as Hani waited by the door.

"Commander Hani brought me here to see you," Maryam said.

Salma welcomed him warmly and, showering blessings on him, she invited him to come in. "I must go back at once," he replied, "since we're now in a state of high alert. How are you? We received your letter, and we thank you for your good deeds and service to us."

"What have you done with that perfidious woman?" she asked.

"We couldn't find her at the camp, even though she was there last night. She may have found out about your letter and fled to her father."

Salma struck one hand with the other in disappointment. "So that evil woman escaped! Her cross-eyed demon servant must have gotten wind of our letter, and she ran away in fear of being exposed."

"May God punish the cross-eyed demon, since he's the source of so much wickedness. When you hear what that devil has done, you'll be heart-broken."

"What did he do?" Salma asked.

"He shot Hassan with an arrow on his way to us. It struck him in his side, but poor Hassan managed to reach the Arab camp on his last breath. He delivered the message and died," Hani explained.

"Died? Hassan died?" Salma screamed.

"Yes, mother, he died a most noble death. He died with honor and dignity, and they washed him and buried him properly. May God have mercy on his soul."

Salma bowed her head in silence, then spoke in a low voice as she shook her head. "Poor Hassan. He passed away without seeing his grandson, whom he recently learned was alive, nor will he ever see the outcome of this momentous battle to come."

They lit candles to brighten the room. Maryam withdrew into her private world as she thought about Hani, with whom she had fallen hopelessly in love unbeknownst to her mother. She knew that after bringing her to her mother, he would have to go back to the camp, and the thought of being separated from him was unbearable. She wanted so much to seek her mother's advice, even though she knew how tragic it would be if her mother didn't approve of their love. Hoping to draw her mother's attention away from Hassan, Maryam changed the subject.

"Don't you recognize Commander Hani, mama?"

"How can I not recognize him," she replied with a smile. "Isn't he the one who saved us from that Berber?"

"Yes, and he's the top commander in the Arab army after Emir 'Abd al-Rahman. The emir holds him in the highest esteem and cannot do without him. Hani leads the cavalry and he's the emir's right hand in commanding all the different battalions."

Hani blushed with embarrassment. He felt uncomfortable and did not want to hear any more compliments, but Maryam was not to be dissuaded from singing his praises. "He's fearless in executing his duties. I accompanied him on a mission to the archbishop of Bordeaux. Do you remember that?"

Maryam was relaxed and beaming with joy as she was about to elaborate on the details of that journey when suddenly, hearing a loud commotion, she stopped speaking. They all pricked up their ears. Hani caught the sound of his stallion neighing relentlessly as though it were craving the road. Hani stood up. "I see my stallion is summoning me to get back to camp at once." At the very second he finished his sentence they heard the sound of footsteps coming from the terrace. The door abruptly opened, and Hassan's monk-companion rushed in. Salma was surprised, since she thought he had already left the monastery with Hassan. She welcomed him and invited him to take a seat. Alarm clearly written on his face, he looked as though he wanted to say something but was at a loss for words. Interpreting this as shyness, Salma addressed him in French. "Speak up, Father. Tell us what's on your mind. There are no strangers among us."

"The abbot has instructed me to inform you of a matter, and it pains me to be the bearer of such news," he responded, stuttering.

Salma and Maryam both felt their hearts pounding furiously, while Hani, not knowing a word of French, understood that something was wrong by the expression on the women's faces.

"Please, do pray tell, Father," pleaded Salma.

"Duke Odo has sent a detachment of horsemen, armed to the teeth, with a message to the abbot ordering him to deliver you to him. Given what the abbot knows about my acquaintance with you, he asked me about the message and sought my advice on it. I advised him not to send for you, and he seems very much in agreement with that. On the other hand, he's afraid of the consequences, since he doesn't know who will emerge victorious in this next war. It's his duty to support the Franks. Then he suggested that I go along with you to beg Duke Odo to treat you respectfully. And if you wish, we may obtain from the abbot a letter of recommendation to that effect."

The monk spoke with a tied tongue, clearly affected in all his gestures by this order. Salma and Maryam were staring at him as if struck with paralysis. When the monk finished what he had come to say, Hani asked what was happening, and Maryam translated the message for him.

"And what does he want from her?" Hani asked.

"We have no idea," Maryam replied.

"She shouldn't go," he insisted.

Salma disagreed. "I think it's best that I go. If I refuse, they'll take me by force."

"By force? They take you by force while Hani is with you? That will never happen!" he shouted, as he clutched the hilt of his sword, seething with anger.

Maryam was enthralled by the protective care he displayed toward her mother and enthusiastically supported his position. "How can we permit them to take you prisoner, mother? We'll resist until our last breath even if they come by the thousands."

Salma disagreed. "I'm sure of that, but we have a war to fight and cannot expose the commander of the cavalry and one of the two most senior officers in the Arab army to the shenanigans of a gang of Franks. You could be struck down by an arrow the same way Hassan was yesterday. Better to let Hani return to the camp as soon as possible, since the Arab army relies on him so heavily to lead them and keep them unified. If we expose him to danger, we expose the entire army to danger. I beg you to do as I say, and fear not that something terrible will happen to me. I will be received there as an honored guest, and besides, the monk here will be with me. I will also be carrying a letter of introduction from the abbot, which will guarantee my safety. Moreover, it is my fervent hope that by being there I will render the Arabs a service far greater than I could if I were among them. There is no treachery in God's plan."

"You're attempting to do the impossible," Hani argued. "How could you be taken prisoner while I'm with you? That will never happen. I swear to God, I will raise my sword against them, even if there are thousands of them."

Salma cut him off. "If you don't do as I ask, you will upset me, and I know you don't want that. Duke Odo knows more about me than you do, and more than my own daughter knows. He's not summoning me with the intention of doing me harm. If he wanted to hurt me, he would have done so while I was being held as his prisoner. I ask you to swear on the honor of the Arabs and the glory of Islam to comply with my wishes. The time has come for me to tell you something I kept secret for many years." She then turned to the monk. "Please go and tell the abbot that I will be ready to depart in an hour or two. There's an urgent matter I need to discuss with my daughter before I leave."

The monk bowed his head and left the room.

✲ ✲ ✲

Salma arose from her cushion and adjusted her robe as a gesture of preparing to depart. She moved about in the room, then glanced out of the window toward the river without uttering a word. Hani and Maryam waited to see what she would do next, amazed at both her silence and her motions. She then turned to them with a changed expression on her face. Her eyebrows were arched, and her eyes gleamed with grave concern. Her natural look of serene composure transformed into a dour seriousness. Alarmed by this abrupt change, Hani turned to Maryam, who looked equally alarmed, and both of them sat dumbfounded.

"Do you know who your father is?" Salma asked her daughter as she looked her directly in the eye.

"No, mama," she replied as her cheeks flushed a deep crimson, shocked by this sudden question. Hani was no less shocked but remained dead silent.

"Do you know who your mother is?" she asked.

Maryam was all the more confused. "Yes, it's you."

Then, Salma addressed Hani. "You should know, my son, that I've been entrusted with this secret for nearly twenty years on condition that I reveal it to the leader of the Arab army who crosses this river. But the situation now compels me to divulge it, or at least part of it, at this time and to the second in command. We must do what we must. I'm no longer able to keep this secret to myself after all this time. I sought guidance from the spirit of the dearly departed, the owner of the secret, in revealing it now to my daughter and to you, Hani, on condition that you divulge it to no one until you deliver it to Emir 'Abd al-Rahman after this battle, and not a minute before. So, listen."

As Salma was speaking, Hani sat listening with burning curiosity while the blood in Maryam's veins ran cold, so affected was she by the unusually grave expression on her mother's face. Salma began her story by addressing her daughter.

"You know, Maryam, that your mother is Salma, but you don't know who this Salma actually is. I asked you if you knew who your father was and you answered that you did not, since he died when you were very young. I haven't mentioned him at all to you, and the only person who knew your true identity was poor old Hassan, who now has been killed. If I were to suffer the same fate, then the secret would vanish like dust in the wind for all time. That's the reason I must reveal it now. You should know, Maryam, that the mother who calls herself Salma is in fact Ajeela, the wife of Roderic, who was the king of Spain before the Arabs killed him in a battle at Fahs Sharis,[12] some twenty years ago, when Tariq Ibn Ziyad conquered Spain. Upon Roderic's death, Musa Ibn Nusayr appeared and continued the conquest until they reached Toledo, which was the capital city of Spain at that time. That's where I was living. I reconciled myself to the death of my husband and I continued to live peacefully in the lap of luxury and security as I had when he was alive. The Arabs came to call me Umm 'Aasim, and no one did me any harm. That's because Musa was a just and wise ruler. But he governed for only a few years before his detractors discredited him, causing the caliph to recall him. When he returned to Damascus, he was put in prison."

"Musa's goal after conquering the Iberian Peninsula was to expand the conquest beyond its borders until he reached Constantinople. His intention was to make it his base, from which he would return to Syria, taking every town that lay in his path, thus bringing every part of the Mediterranean basin under Muslim control. Given the vulnerability of these lands and the divisions and infighting among the rulers, this would have been an easy task at the time."

"When Musa was recalled to Damascus, his son 'Abd al-Aziz replaced him in Andalusia. The son was also fair and wise, and his father told him much about his resolve to conquer all of what the Arabs referred to as *al-Ard al-kabira*, the big continent. I was still in Toledo when 'Abd al-Aziz came to power. The first time we laid eyes on each other, we fell in love. He

---

12 Al-Maqqari, on the authority of Ibn Khaldun, cites this as Fahs Sharisha (Nafh al-Tib 1: 233). *Translator's Note*

asked me to marry him. I couldn't have wished for a more honorable and powerful husband. I accepted on condition that I be allowed to continue to practice my Christian faith. He agreed, but he also taught me about Islam, and I discovered how similar it was in many of its beliefs to the Arianism of our Visigoth forefathers."

"Later, we moved to Seville, where we resided for a number of years. All this time, he proved to be a model of intelligence and resolve. He confided in me many things he was determined to accomplish for the cause of Arabs and Islam, foremost of which was the conquest of the 'big continent.' This was an easy goal for him, since he treated his subjects with fairness and tolerance, and people of all faiths and classes grew to love him. His reputation spread to the far corners of the Christian world. As long as his stature remained elevated, he could conquer new lands with ease because people give their support to those who grant them their rights and freedom, not because they merely share the same faith or belief. 'Abd al-Aziz often expressed to me his ardent desire to complete this conquest, and I always encouraged him to continue to respect the citizens and treat them with generosity. He did this willingly, realizing the tremendous benefits to be gained. He also worked hard to keep together all Muslims, Arabs and Berbers especially, knowing full well that without this unity he would never attain his goals."

"But his aspirations were foiled when he was defamed by his jealous detractors, just as his father was. They accused him of being greedy for power and wealth, basing their accusations on his generosity toward his subjects. They claimed it was I who controlled his mind, and that I forced him to make the members of his government and all his subjects bow down when appearing before him, just as my husband, Roderic, used to do, or so they claimed. Among the rumors they spread was that I had him build a small door in his reception chamber so that I could be sure that everyone who entered bowed his head as though prostrating in prayer. God knows how many other lies they spread and how they failed to understand the truth of the matter. When these malicious rumors reached the caliph, they didn't just send him off packing like they did to his father; they plotted against him and had him killed while he was praying in the mosque. God have mercy on him!"

At this point in her story, Salma paused, choking back the tears. Hani and Maryam, feeling as if they were in a dream, dared not utter a word for fear of interrupting her. Struggling to produce a smile, Salma resumed her story turning to Maryam. "From him, I gave birth to you. He loved you more than all the other children born to him from his other wives and concubines. His greatest pleasure in life was to hug and kiss you every morning and every evening. Whenever he came back from a meeting with his advisors, he would play with you and do whatever he could to make you happy, at times forgetting my presence altogether. When he learned of the conspiracies against him and lost hope of remaining in power, he summoned me to his chambers the night before he went to pray at the mosque. When I arrived, you were in his arms. He placed you on his lap and kissed you, sobbing like a baby. I also began to cry because I loved him. I loved him for the purity of his heart, for his generosity and his noble intentions. Then he called out for Hassan and entrusted him with my care and yours. Then he turned to me. 'Those people are adamant in destroying all that I've achieved and in squandering all the riches I amassed for this country. My life will come to an end only by God's will and decree, and I will not beg them for it. Rather, I pity them for what they've lost and will stand to lose with my murder. I do not think they'll be fortunate enough to have a leader as fierce a guardian of Islam as I am, or one as well prepared to lead the conquest as I have. They won't find among themselves one who can satisfy the people and unite all the Muslim factions, nor carry out all those things that assure success.' Then, Maryam, he pointed to you. 'If this little sweetheart were a boy, I would entrust to you his upbringing.' That was his goal. 'I entrust you to raise our daughter with an Arabic education and to teach her horsemanship. Withhold from her the identity of her father, and do not let an Arab come close to her unless you clearly see in him the strength of resolve, as well as the qualities he needs to succeed. And if you find an Arab leader who answers to the cause of the conquest and who possesses all the qualities necessary to achieve that goal, then this little girl should be offered to him as a wife or daughter, whichever he so chooses.'

"When he finished this last sentence he handed me this purse, saying: 'If the Muslims arrive at a consensus on such a man as their leader, then he will conquer these lands most certainly. If he reaches the Loire River, tell him my story and convey to him my wishes, and entrust to him this little girl as a lucky charm to wear around his neck. Most of all, remind her to keep this purse with her at all times, because it contains something that will be of great benefit to him as well as to all the Muslims.'

"And so I took the purse and kept it safe with me ever since. It has stayed with me every hour of every day, and I still have no idea what it contains. After they brutally murdered him, I could no longer remain in Andalusia. I left and took Hassan with me, since he already knew all my secrets, and because he was such a loyal servant to Emir 'Abd al-Aziz.

"A number of emirs rose to power in Andalusia after 'Abd al-Aziz. Some of them made attempts to complete the conquest, but none succeeded because of their recklessness and greed. Then, I heard about 'Abd al-Rahman and all the things he did before embarking on this conquest—surveying the territories, establishing bonds with local rulers, getting rid of the weak and greedy, and treating the people with respect, not to mention his efforts at bringing unity to the Arabs and non-Arabs within the army ranks. I told myself that this was the man I was looking for. I waited patiently until he came to Bordeaux and conquered it. And you know what happened from then on."

At this point Salma turned to Hani. "I see now that Emir 'Abd al-Rahman is just the man 'Abd al-Aziz was speaking of, and so Maryam belongs to him, and I give her this purse which belongs to her, but only after the Loire River is crossed."

Maryam took the purse and tucked it inside her robe. Salma was dripping in sweat, with red eyes, and cheeks flushed with emotion as she recounted this story. Maryam, astonished, stood up and bent over to kiss her. "You're my mother and I thank God for that. I was frightened when you asked me if I knew who my mother was. So, my father is an Arab prince and my mother a Spanish queen..."

Hani, feeling a powerful surge of affection surging inside of him, interrupted. "There's now no doubt you're of pure Arab origin." Then he turned to Salma. "Your story, my lady, has been indelibly inscribed in my heart. I see now that you have surpassed the Arabs in the bonds of affection and loyalty to your commitments. You have been exemplary in the unwavering love for your husband, as well as in your support for our cause with your noble deeds and sacrifice. God bless you. I swear, if only we had ten men in our army like you and like this daughter of yours, we would conquer the whole world! But sadly, we're surrounded by many who join us only out of greed, and so very few of them grasp the real meanings of conquest and victory. They only see pillage and looting. We exhaust so much of our energy in our attempts to reconcile the tribes and factions, and if our leader were someone other than 'Abd al-Rahman, we would never have succeeded. God has granted that our leader bring us to the banks of this river and, if we cross it, the obstacles that lie before us will be lifted."

He then turned to Maryam and smiled. She immediately understood that he was alluding to their marriage, but the thought of being separated again from her mother overpowered her bashfulness. Salma, for her part, felt as though a massive burden had just been lifted off her chest by divulging her secret. But in realizing the enormity of turning over the purse, she cautioned her daughter. "I trust that you will hold on to this purse and guard it closely, and only give it to Emir 'Abd al-Rahman al-Ghafiqi once he crosses the Loire River."

"Are you still insistent on going to Duke Odo?" Maryam asked.

"Yes, but you needn't worry about me. He won't harm me, rest assured. And remember, I've made sure that you will remain in 'Abd al-Rahman's custody."

Maryam sighed, holding out little hope that she would see her mother after this next separation.

"It's time for me to obey the duke's orders." Salma stood up as she announced her departure. She embraced Maryam and kissed her repeatedly, as both mother and daughter wept holding on tightly, loathing to let go of each other. The sight of their embrace nearly moved Hani to tears. He stepped forward and gently pulled them apart. Salma's eyes were swollen from the tears, but she kept them fixed on her daughter with a smile.

"I know that I must let Hani go because the army needs him," Maryam said to her mother. "But what use am I to them? Why won't you let me go with you?"

"The army will only find its success with you among them," he interrupted.

Maryam understood that Hani said this only because he didn't want to part with her, while Salma realized for the first time that the two of them had fallen in love. But Maryam was by now so fully convinced of Hani's strength of character, and knowing how much 'Abd al-Rahman trusted him by letting him accompany her to the monastery. Salma didn't resist any longer. As Salma prepared to take her leave, she turned to Hani. "Take Maryam back before I leave, Commander."

"Forgive me, Your Gracious Majesty, but I am not moving until I see that your departure is carried out in respect and honor."

"Please trust that I will be treated respectfully, and that I will be honored as a guest when I arrive. You needn't worry since Odo knows my true identity, and I pray that my sojourn at his camp this time will bear fruit the way it did the last time. I have just discovered a secret that has protected both of us from great harm."

"This may very well be. However, I would indeed be ashamed of myself if I departed from this monastery while it is surrounded by a squadron of soldiers waiting for you. Since you do not allow me to prevent them from taking you, won't you at least allow me to wait and see that they take you peacefully?"

"Hani is right," Maryam exclaimed.

"I'll go then to bid farewell to the abbot. Wait for me in the garden."

Salma left the room, and they followed her. She headed toward the abbot's quarters while they went to the garden, which was now glowing in the light of the lanterns. Hani asked the doorman to bring them the two horses. He ordered a servant to go and fetch them. When they were brought to him, Hani handed the doorman a small purse containing some dinars and the doorman was delighted with the generous gesture. He then instructed the servant to take special care of the horses. The servant walked them around the garden, Hani's stallion standing out like a bride, adorned with jewel encrusted medallions and chains hanging from its neck, with the large pearl carved in the shape of a star that sat on its forehead, along with its gold bridle and silver spurs. The jet-black stallion looked like a star-studded night, as Hani stood next to it, alternating between looking at it and at Maryam. There wasn't a single monk passing through the garden who didn't stop and stare at the unusual sight of this magnificent stallion and the Arab horseman standing by its side. The horse, seeming to sense their admiration, preened before them, tapped the ground with its right hoof, and whinnied as though eager for battle, taunting the horses tied to the stables as if aware that they belonged to its owner's enemies.

Seconds later, they heard a ruckus coming from inside the monastery. Several servants soon came out carrying candles, followed by a group of monks escorting Salma and her companion. When they reached the outer wall, they walked by Hani and Maryam while Salma bid them farewell. The horses had been saddled for her and the monk, and they mounted immediately. The bugle was blown and the Frankish horsemen lined in formations around them as Hani and Maryam looked on. Maryam felt at that very moment that her mother had been plucked out from her heart, and she broke into tears. But quickly she pulled herself together and regained control of herself.

With Salma and her escorts out of sight, Hani mounted his horse and persuaded Maryam to mount hers. They left the monastery and headed back to the camp. There was a full moon, a clear sky, and a gentle breeze, as if Nature were in sympathy with the delicate state of their emotions. The two sweethearts rode in silence for some time, in awe of the natural beauty that surrounded them, trotting along the road as their feelings reflected all that they saw and heard that evening. The relationship between them now came to dominate their lives, and they exalted in the discovery that their lineage was closer and their bonds stronger than they had imagined. More than ever, Maryam felt it her duty to support the Arab cause because of her father's will. As they drew near the camp they spotted the faint light of its cressets which were barely visible from the distance against the light of the full moon. Hani was sorry that they were arriving before he had had the chance to tell her all that was in his heart. He pulled on the bridle of his horse to slow it down. Maryam followed suit, waiting for him to speak.

"You haven't said anything, Maryam," he said playfully. "Perhaps what you've learned tonight about your true origins has weakened your affections?" She stopped her horse and looked at him, trying to understand what he meant, but when she saw his smile, she realized he was toying with her. "I don't feel superior because of my heritage. A person gains honor only through the tip of his sword, just as Commander Hani has." With his emotions aroused, Hani attempted to slow down his stallion. "You're a woman of extraordinary honor, by birth and accomplishment. I witnessed you at the Battle of Dardun and saw you do what knights are incapable of. Praise be on He who instilled in you the courage of men and the grace of women."

"I did nothing special, Hani," she rushed to respond. "If fate favors me, I will continue to do all that I can to honor my father's memory and carry out his will. Courage is not a virtue in men only, but in women as well, and besides..." She stopped at this point, holding back something. Hani watched her as the moonlight shone over her black veil and its beams reflected on her face. He recalled the words of the poet who wrote about two moons looking into each other's eyes. But in fact the moon doesn't possess all the beguiling expressions you find on a lovely human face—like the beauty, dignity, and intelligence on the face of our young Arab heroine, the daughter of a king and queen, suddenly smitten by love and whose face was now glowing with a light which made her all the more desirable. She bowed her head as Hani continued to gaze at her, much too shy to express what was in her heart, and so she busied herself by untangling the hair of her horse's mane. Just as he was about to ask her what she was keeping back from him, a horseman galloping at tremendous speed from the direction of St. Martin's rode up to them. Hani took hold of the reins of his horse and looked closely at the rider. He could tell by his clothing and a white banner he was carrying that he was a Frank, and presumably a messenger of Charles. Hani took hold of the bridle and stepped forward, but not knowing French, Maryam shouted out, asking him who he was.

"I come bearing a message from Duke Charles to Emir 'Abd al-Rahman. Where is his tent?"

Maryam translated the response into Arabic. "It must be urgent, so it's best if we find out what it is," Hani suggested. She turned to the messenger. "We're going there right now. Follow us." They galloped away, worried that what the message bore could be a matter of life or death to the Arabs. Maryam suddenly recalled Hassan and how often he served as a messenger on missions like the one this horseman was undertaking. She couldn't help but cry out: "Poor Hassan!" Hani, riding on the edge of his saddle to be able to hear anything Maryam might say, was reminded, by the mention of Hassan, of something Salma had said earlier that day when she heard the news of his death.

"I heard your mother say that Hassan didn't live to see his grandson. Who was his grandson?" he asked.

"I recall a conversation between my mother and Hassan many years ago about his son who died in a war I don't remember. The son also had a young boy who vanished during the same war, and I suppose that was his grandson. Hassan grieved over this boy especially because he had no idea of his whereabouts. I later asked my mother about it, and she told me that she herself searched in Odo's camp for the boy who, by then a young man, was taken in by the Franks and renamed Roderic. But when she escaped from the camp, it was no longer possible for her to contact him."

When they returned to the camp, Hani took the bridle of his horse and turned toward Maryam. She understood by his look that he expected her to go immediately to the women's tent. "Shall I return to my tent?" she asked to be sure.

"Yes, my dear, it's better there where you'll be safe until God grants us victory. After that we'll go to the Loire River together. I hope that will be soon."

"If you don't mind, I prefer to stay here because of a matter I feel I may be responsible for. But if you insist, my duty is to obey. In the meantime, let's not forget the secret to which we are bound." She fiddled inside her clothing for the purse as she spoke.

"Shall I send you some guards?" he asked.

"No need for that as long as I walk in your shadow and you stay by my side wherever I go," she responded as she gestured her farewells and pointed her horse toward the tent. When she was out of sight, Hani turned to the horseman and brought him into the center of the camp. They were not stopped at checkpoints since all the guards recognized Hani and his stallion. When they reached the emir's pavilion Hani dismounted and asked the chamberlain if there was anyone with 'Abd al-Rahman.

"All the commanders were here," he replied, "but they've now gone."

Chapter 15

Charles' Messenger

Hani ordered the messenger to wait outside before entering. When 'Abd al-Rahman heard his voice, he shouted out to him like a father greeting a returning son. "What kept you so long Hani? We've been worried about you." Hani recounted to him all the events of the day after they reached St. Martin's Monastery—that Odo sent an army to take Salma back to his camp, and how Hani tried to stop them but was prevented by Salma. He didn't mention a word about the secret, although he did mention that Maryam returned with him and was now back in the women's tent.

"I brought with me a messenger from Duke Charles, the commander of the Frankish forces. He's waiting at the door as we speak. Shall I let him in?"

'Abd al-Rahman clapped his hands summoning the chamberlain. "Go find one of the translators and bring him in along with the messenger." The young servant dashed out of the tent and 'Abd al-Rahman sat in silence appearing as if he had just been struck with a piece of bad news. He took a deep breath inhaling the scent of battle and pondering the momentous event upon which he was about to embark. Hani felt the weight on the emir's shoulders and, awestruck, he stood also in silence. The chamberlain wasn't long in returning with a translator, a Jew from Seville who knew a number of languages and whom the Muslims trusted, as they did so many of the Jews of Andalusia who had supported them when they conquered the peninsula. The messenger followed them in and was immediately asked by 'Abd al-Rahman the nature of his mission. The horseman replied that he was bearing a message from Charles, Duke of Austrasia.

"Where is the letter?" 'Abd al-Rahman inquired.

The messenger put his hand inside his clothing and took out from under his arm a small container. He opened it and pulled out a scroll wrapped in red silk and tied in blue ribbon. 'Abd al-Rahman took hold of the letter and instructed the messenger to wait outside. He untied the ribbon and removed the silk covering and found a thin sheet of cardboard embossed in wax on which the message was etched in the tradition of letter-writing in Europe of those times. Since the Arabs used leather, papyrus or woven fabric for their writing, 'Abd al-Rahman immediately knew the message was in French and handed it to the translator, who commenced to read it out aloud:

In the Name of the Father, and of the Son, and of the Holy Spirit.

From Duke Charles, Commander of the Frankish army, Ruler of Austrasia to Emir 'Abd al-Rahman, Commander of the Arab army:

Greeting and Salutations:

> *My Brother Duke Odo, Ruler of Aquitaine has informed me of your intentions to invade his country without any provocation, which will lead to a war between you and us. You seek to conquer in your quest for profit. Your greed has been nourished by the weakness of those armies you have encountered until this day. I have heard much about your bravery, intelligence, and high-mindedness, so allow me to offer you my advice. Renounce these intentions of yours so that blood will be spared. I do not seek your surrender but rather your withdrawal from these lands. Refrain from seizing our properties and possessions. Return to the Spanish borders, for you do not stand a chance in confronting us. If you insist otherwise, then our meeting on the battlefield will take place very soon.*

> *Farewell!*

'Abd al-Rahman, visibly angered by the threatening tone of the letter, looked at Hani for his reaction. Hani responded by saying that he considered the duke arrogant and that the only response should be the sword. The emir smiled with satisfaction and summoned the chamberlain to bring the other commanders to his tent. Hani knew that 'Abd al-Rahman would only decide the matter by counsel to avoid any criticism or failure. After a while, the commanders appeared, and he read them the letter. After discussing the matter and proffering their advice, the emir dictated to the translator:

In the Name of God, the Most Compassionate and Merciful:

From 'Abd al-Rahman Al-Ghafiqi, Commander of the Muslim army in Aquitaine, to Duke Charles, Ruler of the Franks.

Greeting and Salutations:

> *I read your letter and was struck by your arrogance, which contradicts what I heard about your high mindedness and valor. Please know that we did not mobilize this army merely to conquer Aquitaine, but we have come together resolved to conquer the entire continent. Should you chose not to come here to face us, we will surely come to you in your own country, and then onto the entire Holy Roman Empire until we reach Constantinople. Then the whole world will yield to us, as our Prophet has promised. We advise that you think carefully about what happened to your Brother in Aquitaine, and should you fail to heed this advice, you have only yourself to blame.*

> *Farewell!*

✵ ✵ ✵

'Abd al-Rahman and Hani spent the entire following day preparing for war. In the late afternoon of the third day, while making an inspection tour of their troops, several of their scouts returned with reports of billows of dust rising on the horizon in the vicinity of St. Martin's Monastery. They immediately understood that Charles had advanced his forces and placed them in formation after his letter arrived. They rode up the hill and looked out to see for themselves, but also spotted the precise location of Odo's camp in the direction of the south. They were certain that the two armies had by now joined forces.

"The time has come to act," 'Abd al-Rahman said to Hani. "The Frankish forces are advancing. We must stay on high alert and be ready for any surprise attack they launch against us. At the same time, go to your cavalry units and prepare them for an offensive. I'll go and inform the other commanders." 'Abd al-Rahman marched off with Hani behind, barely able to curb his enthusiasm for battle.

However, the combined Frankish forces did not advance further toward the Arabs, but preferred instead to remain in their camp on the other side of the battlefield. 'Abd al-Rahman deduced that they would not launch an attack that day, and he sent word secretly to Hani of his assessment. After prayers that evening, the two men left the camp and headed toward a nearby hill that 'Abd al-Rahman had discovered the day before. They rode up and looked out in the distance. The moon was full, and its beams cast their light over the vast plain that lay before them, bringing into view the camps of Odo and Charles toward the east and south. 'Abd al-Rahman scrutinized the enormous array of pitched tents from both camps and tried to estimate their numbers. He was certain that they vastly outnumbered the Muslims but he wished to have someone who could give him precise information on the strength of their forces, the size of their arsenal, and other vital strategic matters. Hani happened to turn around and noticed the emir looking as though he had just caught sight of something new. He himself then suddenly saw the shadow of a man running toward them from the direction of Duke Charles's camp. He seemed to be in Frankish attire, but he wasn't carrying a banner nor did he look like a messenger from the looks of his robe.

"What do you make of this one who's rushing toward us, Emir?" Hani asked.

"I don't think he's a messenger, but he might be a spy or an ally." Hardly had 'Abd al-Rahman finished his response when the man came within ten yards of them. He then slowed down, and when he drew near he shouted out in broken Arabic. "Where is Emir 'Abd al-Rahman?"

"What is your business with him?" Hani inquired.

He pointed his finger at his tongue as if to say he didn't know Arabic, and then he gestured that he was coming from Duke Odo's camp concerning a private matter with Emir 'Abd al-Rahman.

'Abd al-Rahman whispered to Hani. "If we tell him I'm 'Abd al-Rahman he won't believe us. So let's point him in the direction of my tent.

Meanwhile, we'll sneak back into the tent from the back, and we'll make him think I was there all along." Hani pointed to 'Abd al-Rahman's pavilion and the fire in front of it, then headed back with the man following. 'Abd al-Rahman took a short cut and entered from behind. Hani entered, and moments later the chamberlain came to announce a young Frank waiting at the door to see the emir. 'Abd al-Rahman ordered that he be brought in and then called for the translator. 'Abd al-Rahman inspected the visitor and saw a young man in the prime of his youth, wearing Frankish clothing but having Arab features, with an olive complexion and a slight beard. When the translator arrived, 'Abd al-Rahman asked him to state the nature of his visit, but the young man insisted that he speak only with 'Abd al-Rahman in private, and that if he wasn't present he would speak only to commander Hani. Hearing his name Hani pricked up his ears. 'Abd al-Rahman then told him he was in the presence of both men, to which the young man replied that he was a messenger of Salma. Both men were heartened by the mention of her name.

"Where is she now, and who are you?" 'Abd al-Rahman probed.

"She's at Duke Odo's camp. I'm originally an Arab who ended up joining Duke Odo's army. Mine is a long story, which I told Salma only a short while ago. Odo had us arrested and imprisoned, but then Salma escaped and I remained in the camp. Then he had me released. He thought well enough of me and made me one of his servants. When Odo learned from Adlan the cross-eyed that she was at Saint Martin's, he dispatched a unit of horsemen to go and bring her back. I was one of them."

"Are you Roderic?" Hani asked.

The young man was shocked but he smiled at Hani as though he welcomed the question. "Yes, my lord, that is my name."

'Abd al-Rahman listened with great curiosity as he looked up at Hani for an explanation. Hani leaned forward and spoke in a low voice. "This poor fellow is Hassan's grandson. He's got a long history, which Maryam knows very well."

"Please, tell us why you're here?" 'Abd al-Rahman asked.

"When we returned from the monastery with Salma, we took her to a tent where she spent that night. The following morning, we took her to

Odo's reception quarters. I was one of the men standing guard by the door. At first, I peeked inside and saw a beautiful woman sitting next to him, and I later learned she was his daughter, Lumbaja, and that she had been living in the Arab camp before fleeing to her father that very night. When Salma entered, I was worried about her because of Odo's anger. But when I saw how gracious and respectful he was in greeting her, I was shocked. I heard her speak to him with daring and force, but he was patient with her, the way a lover is patient with his beloved. I heard him refer to her by a different name. Then he scolded her and ordered her to be returned to her tent. As she left the tent, she noticed me among the guards and gave me a secret signal to meet with her. I devised a scheme to get to her."

"'You're an Arab,' she said to me the second she saw me, 'so you must assist me in helping them. Go off to Duke Charles' camp and find out as much as you can, and then go to 'Abd al-Rahman with the information. Knowing the enemy's strengths will make things easier for them in battle.' She insisted that I go quickly, and so I did. I slept that night at Charles' camp. I spent yesterday and today snooping around, asking questions, and when night fell, I slipped away and came here to you, as you can see."

The two commanders marveled at Salma's astuteness, and they recalled her saying that she would be more helpful to them being in Odo's camp rather than remaining in the Arab camp.

"So what did you learn about their army?" 'Abd al-Rahman asked.

"That the commander of the army, my lord, is a fierce man named Charles, son of Pepin. He's the senior deputy to the King of Neustria, of the Merovingian dynasty. Given the weakness of this king, Charles seized power and gained control of the duchy of Austrasia beyond the Loire River. However, he wasn't satisfied with this duchy alone but also coveted the royal crown, and for this Odo became one of his major rivals. It was only in a moment of despair that Odo sought his help in resisting the Arabs. When he made the formal appeal, Charles mobilized an army from as many Frankish tribes as he could find, and amassed as many weapons he could lay his hands on."

"How big is their army?" the emir probed.

"I can't say for sure exactly how many there are, but I learned that it is most likely twice the size of your army. They comprise a number of tribes with different languages, customs, and values, even though they're all considered generally Frankish or European. However, more specifically, they include Austrasians, the original inhabitants of those parts, as well as Tuetons, Bructeri, Thuringians, Hessians, and others. Their coats of armor are made of skins, and their horses are girded in thick iron chest plates. Their weapons are long straight doubled-edged swords, sharp axes, arrows, and heavy spiked maces. They count among them foot soldiers and horsemen, although the former far outnumber the latter, who, by the way, are also the archers."

Roderic recounted all the information he was able to gather as 'Abd al-Rahman and Hani listened with rapt attention to every word he uttered. When he paused, Hani smiled and turned to 'Abd al-Rahman. "We're sure to be victorious since our cavalry is much larger. Although their bravery is well known and their skills with both bow and arrow and sword are indisputable, the Arab knight equals three of theirs. Besides, our infantry includes battalions of archers and lancers, and God grants victory to those whom He chooses."

'Abd al-Rahman turned to Roderic just as he was about to stand up. "Do you have any further information?"

"No, my lord. I'm going back to Odo's camp on Salma's instructions. Do you have a message for her?"

"Did she instruct you to return?"

"Yes, and she told me that if she learned something of vital importance to you, she would send me back to you."

"Please convey to her our greetings, and tell her that we will never forget this extraordinary service she has rendered to us," replied 'Abd al-Rahman.

Roderic stood up, asked permission to leave, and left the tent, with the translator following. 'Abd al-Rahman and Hani remained alone to discuss the battle plans. They agreed that a rapid offensive to preempt a Frankish attack was the best course of action.

The following morning at daybreak the bugle sounded and the Muslim battalions assembled in formation. 'Abd al-Rahman positioned the infantry at the center while the cavalry was to march on both sides. The commanders replaced turbans with helmets, girded themselves with swords, and mounted their horses forming lines according to tribal groups. 'Abd al-Rahman then addressed his officers.

"O commanders! We subdued all of Aquitaine, and victory was our ally. Now that the enemy has lost all hope of triumph, they seek the assistance of their bitter rival, the ruler of Austrasia. They bring to us their army, saving us the trouble of going to them. Over there, you see their camp with their forces assembled. What gave us victory over Aquitaine will give us victory once again. We have learned that they are weaker than we, in numbers and in weaponry. Victory depends upon steadfastness. Be patient and stand shoulder to shoulder, and God will make you triumphant. You will conquer many lands as long as the Muslims have an insatiable craving to conquer them, and you will achieve what God promised to his Prophet, that is, conquering the whole world. With that you will have glory that will live forever. You will achieve this *by the will of God. God is with those who are patient.*[13]"

✡ ✡ ✡

When 'Abd al-Rahman completed his brief speech to his corps of officers, Hani rode up to the front of the assembly, his face beaming with zealous enthusiasm. "Today is the day of our appointment with destiny, and we will prevail with patience and endurance. It behooves us to bear in mind that

---

13 This last sentence is a quote from Koran 2 ("al-Baqara," The Cow): 249: Many a time has a small band defeated a large horde by the will of God. God is with those who are patient. The same phrase also appears in Koran 8 ("al-Anfal," Spoils of War): 66. [Ahmed Ali]

we are embarking on something our predecessors failed to do, something for which our grandchildren will look upon with awe and envy, wishing they could have have been part of with body and soul. You will find me the weakest among you in resolve, the least among you in courage to sacrifice myself in the service of God—so powerful will you all be. If we triumph, then we will conquer a new world. If we are martyred, then we will be chosen in the eyes of God forever." He uttered these words, brimming with passion and fortified by the strength of conviction.

'Abd al-Rahman addressed the officers once again. "You must arouse your men and counsel them to be patient and steadfast. Speak to them of the honor and glory they will win from the tip of their swords. Remind them of the earthly rewards they will reap, far more than what they have already gained." Then he recited verses from the Koran to spark their zeal and courage. Enthused upon hearing mention of the spoils of war, the senior commander of the Berber tribes stepped forward. "Our lord, the Emir, is well aware that the Berbers are the most valiant of the Muslims and the fiercest on the battlefield. Since we are highly skilled marksmen, we request that you place us on the front lines!"

"We shall do precisely that," 'Abd al-Rahman responded in his desire to motivate them. He ordered that the Berbers march at the head of the procession, with bows in hand, and the Arab tribes follow with the cavalry marching by their sides.

Meanwhile, Charles was also preparing his troops to launch an attack against the Muslims. He and Odo debated over the best ways to utilize their armies. As soon as their scouts reported that the Muslims were in formation for battle, Charles organized his forces in row after row in the form of detachments, creating what looked like a thick human barricade. Many of these men were experienced soldiers, who had fought under the banner of Charles in several battles. They formed a line of defense, while the lancers were placed up front, in lines, one behind the other, to prevent the Arabs from penetrating that thick wall.

Chapter 16

War

Let us pause for a moment before the outbreak of war to review these two armies and how much they differ in race, language, and religion. Consider how they differ in the ways they eat, drink, and dress, and how far apart they are in values and conduct. One of these armies has brought together men from the far reaches of Asia and Africa, united only by the Islamic faith, and leads them into territories where they never before set foot and into cold and wet climates which they never experienced. They encounter in these lands men who don coats of armor and helmets made of animal skins, and who carry rectangular banners inscribed with Christian symbols. The other army hails from northern Europe and comprises various tribes, who for many years fought among themselves but have now united in common cause against a foreign enemy who has suddenly appeared at their doorstep with a new religion and an unfamiliar look. They are stunned by the strange sight of turbaned soldiers who form thickly compacted lines on the open field appearing like an ocean of crashing waves out of which jut banners with obscure writing they cannot read. If you could read the minds of these two armies, you would see them as hateful and violent. But both pray to God to grant them victory over the other. And if you consider the reasons that brought them to battle, you would see that it is none other than the irrational greed that differentiates man from animals. We know of no animal species that wages war against its own kind. Animals only attack one another over food, in order to save themselves from starvation, and for this they are justified. However, a man will kill his brother over something no more urgent than a whim, and he will kill for no other reason than self-satisfaction, for something we call power, fame, or glory, but certainly not to stave off hunger or to quench a thirst.

The sun rose that day and, according to estimates, it was Saturday in the month of October of the year 732 AD. The Arabs commenced their attack unleashing a hail of arrows upon the Franks. The Franks for their part didn't budge from their positions, facing the onslaught with steadfastness and resolve. The day passed and the two sides never joined in hand-to-hand combat except sporadically. They lined up on both sides, called out and shouted back and forth, but failed to understand each other as each side found the language of the other crude gibberish. One could say that the horses understood each other much better than the troops. They did succeed, however, in getting to know the enemy faces, but that did little to tamper their will for battle given the intensity of the enmity between them. At the end of the day, they withdrew only to continue their attacks the following morning.

Hani withdrew from the front lines dispirited, and he ordered the cavalry to return to their tents. He rode his stallion away from the battlefield and up a hill to survey the enemy. Suddenly he spotted a horseman, wrapped in an 'abaya racing toward him. Hani gripped the reins of his horse and examined the rider closely. He was astonished to see it was Maryam, and his heart beat ferociously.

"What brings you here, Maryam?" he shouted.

"I came to see my beloved Hani defeat the enemy and destroy their armies."

Hearing these words made him feel as though a spear had just been thrust into his chest, adding to the pain of guilt for having returned from the battlefield with nothing accomplished. Maryam was quick to sense this. "I saw you sprint into action like a lion on a hunt, but war has its ups and downs. I was expecting you to win today until you decided to put the Berber forces on the front lines. They'll never break through the Frankish lines. Only your cavalry will succeed at that. If you yourself lead them at the front lines, you'll decimate their defense, since their infantry is weak."

Hani saw the wisdom in Maryam's comment. In fact, he shared her view and was thinking of expressing it to 'Abd al-Rahman. He replied to her with a smile beaming with affection and admiration. "God bless the womb that bore you! I always saw in you the grace of women and the valor of men, but now I also see the acumen of a skilled leader. We will follow your suggestion tomorrow, God willing. We placed the Berbers on the front lines in order to flatter them, as you well understand our predicament with them. But tell me, why did you put yourself within striking range? While I was moving about in the thick of battle, I was imagining you back in the tent, waiting for me to return triumphant. But when we came back, as you see, I was disheartened. Had you been by my side, the outcome might have been different."

She took comfort in knowing that her presence near him gives him encouragement and strength.

"Tomorrow will be our day for victory," she replied.

"No," he protested. "Don't put yourself in danger. I can't bear the thought of you in the thick of battle, exposed to all the arrows flying in the air."

"And am I not to worry about you in the same way? How could I go on living if a catastrophe befell Hani? But let's leave that aside, tomorrow will be here soon enough." They continued to chat as they gradually made their way back to the camp. When they arrived, she bade him goodnight before going to her tent. He kept his gaze on her and her horse until they vanished from sight and into the darkness. He then proceeded to 'Abd al-Rahman's tent to discuss his and Maryam's opinion concerning the Berbers on the front lines. The emir summoned his other officers for consultations, and they all agreed with Hani's view.

✲ ✲ ✲

'Abd al-Rahman spent the night deep in thought, pondering all the possible outcomes and convincing himself that failure should be avoided at all costs. He was determined that if he saw his army falling behind, then he would challenge the commander of the Franks to a hand-to-hand duel. If he were to win, he thought, then the Arabs will be strengthened, and if he were to lose, then dying would be preferable to living. Hani, on the other hand, was more confident of victory, based on their information concerning the enemy's weaknesses. But hope springs eternal in the breast of youth more than in that of the aged.

When morning broke, the Muslim forces assembled for prayer and Koranic recitations. Then they organized the battalions. They placed the cavalry at the front lines and the infantry on both sides of them, the Berber forces forming the right flank and the Arabs the left. 'Abd al-Rahman, Hani, and the other members of the high command rode front and center. They advanced toward the Franks, who maintained the same formations as the previous day, with their cavalry forming both the right and left flanks. The Franks were the first to attack, pelting the Arabs with a swift and thick downpour of arrows that all but blocked out the rays of the sun. The Arabs continued their advance, braving the arrows until they reached the enemy front lines. Hani gave the signal to his horsemen, who gave free rein to their horses, spurring them into action while Hani took the lead, brandishing his sword atop his racing stallion. The Franks, unable to withstand this frontal attack, pulled back. As the two armies locked in battle it seemed as if the Arabs were gaining the upper hand. Hani's zeal and courage grew all the stronger, and seeing the enemy in this moment of weakness and retreat, he felt as though he was no more than herding sheep.

✡ ✡ ✡

At this very moment, Hani heard a voice that rattled him, a voice that shouted, "To God is victory, O Commander!" He turned in its direction and saw Maryam galloping on her horse, wrapped in an 'abaya, and wearing a turban over a headscarf. Only her eyes, forehead, nose and mouth could be seen, but there was no mistaking the flash of excitement beaming from her eyes. She withdrew her arm from beneath the 'abaya brandishing an unsheathed sword. In her other hand, she held a shield of thick, heavy leather. She plunged into battle as foot soldiers scrambled to clear her path as though she had descended from heaven. When Hani saw her in this way he was convinced she had become immeasurably stronger. But although feeling more confident as ever of victory, he was nonetheless fearful that she would be struck by an arrow. He continued to fight, prodding his men into action with assurances of victory. Even his stallion, sensing victory, was highly animated, neighing and panting as the sweat gushed from its neck and soaked its chest. The foam dripping from its mouth oozed down and mixed with the sweat on its girth, and Hani, aroused by the stallions' neighing, plunged deeper and deeper into the thick of battle. He thought that victory would be all the sweeter if he could take on Charles, hand to hand. He began to search for him, his eyes scanning the battlefield for his cloak, banner, and helmet with the large cross on top with which Charles stood out from all the other Franks. Hani caught sight of him from a distance, and it looked as though he was next to 'Abd al-Rahman. Hani was about to steer his horse in that direction when he heard Maryam scream. "Be careful, Commander. Look out, and turn around!"

He turned around quickly thinking she was warning him about a horseman trying to kill him from behind. But he only saw slaves and messengers scurrying about, those who crisscross the battlefield to pick up the arrows from the ground and bring them to the archers or to give assistance to a soldier who may have dropped his sword or bow—young men trained to maneuver between the horses hooves and dodge flying arrows. Hani turned around to find out why Maryam had called out to warn him. He saw her galloping on her horse as she chased one of these messengers who was running away with a dagger in hand all dripping with blood. When she caught up to him she severed his head with one blow of her sword. Hani was stunned as Maryam yelled out to him. "Get off your horse. It's been hit. Here, take mine." She then quickly dismounted.

Hani at first didn't understand what she was asking him to do, but when he turned to inspect his stallion he saw the blood gushing from its barrel the way water spouts from a water spring. His heart sank and he dismounted. One of his knights brought him another horse. He then told Maryam to get back on hers and she immediately obeyed. "May God punish that cross-eyed demon! At least we're now rid of him." Hani now understood that the cross-eyed servant disguised himself as a messenger and slew his horse. He leaned down to his stallion, al-Adham, and grieved bitterly its death, seeing it as the result of his hunger for victory at the expense of his horse. He jumped to his feet in his desire to keep his men from being discouraged.

Meanwhile, 'Abd al-Rahman was monitoring the forces from the center and was heartened to see his cavalry gaining the upper hand. He rode from one battalion to the other offering words of encouragement to his officers, cheering them and prodding them into action and raising their hopes with promises of glory. He paid special attention to the Berbers, given their ferocity and courage in battle, for nothing—neither a wall, a ditch, or a deluge—could stand in their way when they were on the attack.

✧ ✧ ✧

Charles by this time was thinking along the same lines as 'Abd al-Rahman. Seeing his troops growing weary in battle as the sun was beginning its late afternoon descent, he began to seek out the commander of the Arab forces for face-to-face combat. 'Abd al-Rahman caught sight of Charles. He recognized him by the banner that waved above his head. Charles, mounted on his horse as if it were a mountain, was armored in a coat of mail that looked like a heap of fish scales that wrapped around his chest, shoulders, and arms, covering his thighs and the front of his legs to his feet. A cross sat on the top of his helmet, and two metal chains that covered the sides of his face and the back of his head dangled from the sides. A sheet of iron that looked like a coat of mail hung from the front of the saddle, protecting his horse's chest. In his right hand, he raised an iron mace in the shape of a cross, and in his left, a banner with the insignia of the crucifix engraved on it. The pole of the banner rested on the left stirrup.

'Abd al-Rahman wore the Arab-style turban which, although soft and light, shielded him like a helmet. Wearing a chain of mail beneath his 'abaya and girded with sword and dagger, he was less encumbered and more nimble than Charles, and this appearance made him look just like any other soldier in the cavalry. His rival, on the other hand, stood out among his troops in his helmet, coat of mail, banner and horse. 'Abd al-Rahman recognized him immediately and called out to him with a shout that startled his horse. He began to charge with sword brandished in hand.

Charles fended off the blow with his mace and pulled back, but did not flee. 'Abd al-Rahman pursued him, wary that Charles's retreat could be a trap. He pulled back to prepare to strike him a decisive blow if he came back. Suddenly, an uproar erupted from the right flank of his army, where the Berber troops were fighting. The commotion grew to a frightening pitch, and he heard them shouting. "Our loot is gone! We're losing all our possessions." He turned around and saw them withdrawing from the battlefield, horsemen and foot soldiers alike. He raised his eyes to the heavens and shouted out to them to stay their ground, pleading with assurances that their possessions would be safe. But not a single one of them heeded his words, and the Arab ground forces, after their initial round of success, began to weaken. Witnessing such a sight, the Frankish forces counterattacked. Had it not been for Hani and his cavalry, the Arab army would have fallen completely apart.

As soon as he learnt why the Berbers had retreated, Hani made every effort to consolidate the infantry. Maryam, by his side, had by now removed her turban and head scarf and tossed aside her 'abaya, her female black robe in full view, and her hair cascading down her shoulders. She plunged into the middle of the battlefield brandishing her sword with her sleeves rolled up her forearms. "Shame on any Arab," she shouted, "who runs away like Berbers, who seek only the spoils of war. You're performing your duty of jihad whose booty is honor and victory, and you will reap both worldly and eternal rewards."

At first the troops thought she was a man, but as they beheld her beauty, grace, and courage, they envisioned her as an angel sent from heaven to assist them. They took heart and responded to her and Hani's appeals, resolving to remain steadfast in their fighting. Meanwhile, night was falling and the two armies were growing apart, as each side retreated to its camp.

☆ ☆ ☆

While the throngs of soldiers on both sides of the battlefield were returning to their tents, Hani went about searching for 'Abd al-Rahman. Not finding him, he asked about his whereabouts, but no one could give him an answer. He galloped on his horse looking for him in every direction, but not a trace of him was in sight. He returned and ordered his cavalry to go back to their stations, while he and Maryam dismounted. They set out on foot to search for him among the fallen soldiers on the battlefield, under the faint light of dusk. When the full moon rose, it beamed its light on the battleground, teeming with bodies, some dying, many dead. They walked among soldiers wounded or paralyzed, lying next to horses and mules killed in action. They searched everywhere but didn't find 'Abd al-Rahman. Then, all of a sudden, they heard the whinny of a horse that sounded just like his, coming from a distance. They were startled but hopeful, and looking in the direction from where it came, at the edge of the battlefield, they spotted a horse on its four legs, facing down toward the ground and neighing.

"That's the emir's horse," Hani shouted out. He ran toward it, with Maryam on his heels. When he reached it, it was standing over a shadowy figure he immediately recognized as 'Abd al-Rahman. He crouched down and took his hand and felt his pulse. His hand was rigid and cold. He was lying on his back with his arms stretched out. His eyes were glancing toward the east as if they were greeting the moonlight. When they saw an arrow lodged in his neck they knew how he was killed. Hani knelt beside his head.

"O, how I grieve for you, my commander, my father, my brother and comrade in arms, protector of the Muslims. You have earned a place in paradise as a martyr and holy warrior. May God will that I soon join you!"

✴ ✴ ✴

Maryam stood over the deceased commander lamenting his death while consoling herself with Hani's safety, pinning her hopes on his victory. If he triumphed in the battle, she thought, he would be the first commander of all the Arab army. And so she turned a deaf ear to Hani's prayer to join 'Abd al-Rahman in martyrdom.

"Let's put the mourning rituals aside since this is the business of women," she advised, "and return to the battlefield and re-energize the troops so that they do not fall. If we're blessed with victory tomorrow, God willing, then we will emerge triumphant, and devote ourselves to grieving for our losses." Hani knew she was right, but insisted that they bury 'Abd al-Rahman first. "When we get back to the camp," she replied, "we can send someone to bring back the body, then you can perform the prayers of the dead and bury him there."

She proceeded to leave the spot, with her arms exposed, oblivious to the chill of the autumn night. Hani followed as he dragged his sword behind him, his emotions in turmoil from the setback in the day's battle, and his grief and hopes all mixed with feelings of love and passion for Maryam, who walked by his side. She herself was experiencing similar sentiments while they made their way to the camp, with the battlefield to the right and Odo's camp far on the left. The battlefield had cleared of the soldiers, and the only sounds they heard were those of wailing and moaning. They saw a handful of slaves scavenging over the bodies, searching for weapons, a gold vessel, or a piece of jewelry. A corpse in a Frankish uniform caught Hani's attention when he nearly tripped over it. He wanted to be as far away as he could but suddenly noticed something familiar about its face. He examined it more closely and discovered it was the corpse of Roderic.

"Don't you recognize that face?" he cried out to Maryam in shock. he looked at it and replied that she did not.

"That's Roderic, Hassan's grandson, who brought us a message from your mother yesterday. She provided us with valuable information about the enemy forces, which helped us a great deal in battle today. She also sent word that she's now at Odo's headquarters, and that she's safe and being treated well. After he delivered the message, he rushed back to her, thinking she might need him for another urgent mission. But I wonder what brought him here today and how he was killed."

"I see something in his hand," Maryam shouted. "Maybe it's a letter he was carrying from my mother." She leaned down to grab the letter, but it seemed he was holding onto it with all his might and she couldn't extract it. She shuddered thinking that he still might be alive.

Hani stepped forward and released the letter from his grip. "He's been dead since morning," he said. He handed Maryam the letter, which was wrapped in leather casing.

"A letter," she cried out. "A letter from Mother. Let's read it." Hani stood beside her as she read it under the light of the moon.

To Commander 'Abd al-Rahman,

Greeting and Salutations:

> *I write to you in the wee hours of the morning, while everyone is still asleep. I spent all day yesterday gratified by what I witnessed of the Arabs' courage, and I am revived in my hopes for your victory. Then I came to learn what that so-called Maymuna conspired to do. Had she succeeded in her plot, the outcome would have been disastrous, God forbid! She arrived at her father's palace and informed him about the Berber half-heartedness toward Islam and their sole attachment to the booty. Then she advised him that if war broke out today and he detected any weakness on the part of his soldiers, he should dispatch a battalion to raid the tent where you store the booty, followed by a group of men masquerading as Arabs to yell out that the booty has been plundered. She also advised that Adlan the cross-eyed Berber take charge, since he knows very well how to disguise himself. He was the one, may God damn him, who was assigned to kill Hani's stallion as a way to demoralize and weaken the cavalry, the backbone of your army. The young Roderic informed me about this strategy of theirs, and so I'm sending him with this message. However, I fear that Adlan may strike him on the road just as he had struck his grandfather. I can't think of any way to avoid that. All I can do at this time is to inform you of what they're up to. If this message reaches you in time, you'll be able to foil their plot. I remain committed to your victory, God willing. If our efforts fail, God forbid, and if the Franks are given victory, then the Arabs will never again have a foothold in these lands. As for me, my mission in all of this will be finished, and I entrust Maryam to your care and protection. However, I wouldn't wish for her to live to endure an Arab defeat, nor would she wish that as well. If the Arabs fall and fail to cross the Loire River, then life will not be worth living. In the event that happens, do not come and look for me, because*

you will not find me. For those of us who are separated in this life will be united in the next.

Farewell!

☼ ☼ ☼

Maryam, stunned and trembling with fear after reading the letter, turned to Hani as the tears welled in her eyes. His head was bowed in pensive silence, and then he looked up at her. "Now we know why our army fell after we almost defeated the enemy."

"May God damn Lumbaja and her cross-eyed Adlan," she cried. "If it weren't for them, we would be in Charles's camp and crossing the Loire River by tomorrow."

"It's all our fault, Maryam, the fault of our army because they broke ranks in pursuing different goals, especially the Berbers. They only understand the pillage and looting in war. Were it not for 'Abd al-Rahman's intelligence, leadership, and patience, we would not have gotten this far. But our commander is dead, and I don't know what will become of us hereafter."

"It's true that his death is an enormous loss, but we shouldn't shun the task before us, and I will do everything I can to continue the battle."

"What we need from you is to rally the commanders to stand united and steadfast. I'm astonished to see the impact your words had on them in today's battle."

"I owe it all to you. If this army doesn't succeed, I won't be able to survive. This is what my mother warned in this letter."

"And me, can I survive by myself? But for now, I don't see any need for pessimism. Let's get back to the camp." They went back down the road, side by side, with Maryam's head still uncovered and her hair flowing down, not the least bit self-conscious.

As they approached the camp, neither the snorting of a camel nor a horse's whinny could be heard, nor did they see the light of a torch or any movement that would indicate the army's presence. But the tents were still pitched. They made their way into the commander's pavilion but found it silent and empty. They came out and inspected the areas immediately around it. Then they proceeded to Hani's tent, which was also deserted. In fact, the whole camp was a series of pitched tents in the middle of the desert without man or beast in sight. They continued to wander about, stunned and bewildered. After a while, Hani broke the silence.

"What's happening here? Where has the army gone, and all the servants? Do you think they went back to the tents along the Cher River to hunker down in a defensive position?"

"They may have done that. Shall we go there and see?" she replied.

In agreement, they walked through the tents, as if walking through the site of ancient ruins, and reached the banks of the Cher River, but once again not a soul was in sight.

"Even if we assume the Berbers fled in fear, where are the Arab troops? And where are all the women and children? How quickly they disappeared! Perhaps with 'Abd al-Rahman's death, they all retreated and lost the heart to fight on."

He put his head down, his heart heavy with despair, as he found himself at a loss for words. His heart was heavy with many matters far too numerous to count. Maryam continued in silence as she rode beside him, mulling over something she wanted to discuss with him. After some time riding through the tents, stomping on pieces of rope and tent pegs, both lost in their own thoughts, Hani spoke.

"We must bury our commander's corpse so that the vultures don't devour it, or that our enemy expose it to their advantage." He turned toward the battlefield, and they went directly to the place where the body lay. They worked together to lift it and bring it to a ditch in a separate area. They placed it into the hole and covered it with dirt, neither one of them uttering a word. There was such dignity and honor in the simplicity of this burial that their hearts, burning with the fires of sadness and despair, were nonetheless filled with love and affection."

✵ ✵ ✵

In total silence, they finished the burial as the moon shone in the middle of the night sky, its beams radiating like the light of day. "What do we do now, Hani?"

He sighed deeply. "If I had just fifty men, I would launch an attack on those two camps. I would attack all by myself even if it meant my demise. However I fear for Maryam that some harm might come to her if I were to be killed."

"Would Maryam survive after you were gone?" she asked. "That will not happen. But I read my mother's last words to me, and how lovingly she spoke of our being reunited in the hereafter. I have no doubt she is there at this very moment. And if you truly love Maryam and want to rest assured about her honor and well-being, then you will allow me to follow her if there is no chance for my survival. But Islam is in need of you, and all the faithful are in dire need of your sword and your strong arm."

His passion for her grew all the stronger as she uttered these words, and at that moment he nearly forgot everything else around him.

"The faithful are in need of the likes of you more than me. You're the daughter of a king and queen, and you've inherited their finest qualities. I swear, if only those cowards stood their ground and you were their guiding light shining through the dust clouds of battle, they would have achieved victory and crossed the Loire River. But we've been prevented from crossing it, and cut off from rejoining our forces. Will you do as I ask, Maryam?"

"I am at your service. I only refuse to live in this world if you depart it," she replied.

"Our army has fallen, and the survivors have fled, and in that escape, there is a survival which comforts only the coward's heart. Here we are joined together, and there is no one here to watch us. Both of us want to survive, but the only way for that is to escape. My soul rejects that. Our hearts dissolved longing for the day on which we would cross this river, because in crossing it we would stand united. So what's stopping us from reuniting in this river now?"

"Right in the middle," she cut in.

"Rather, in its abyss. As long as we're together, it doesn't matter to me where we are or how we are." As he said this he jumped up on 'Abd al-Rahman's horse and stretched out his hand for Maryam to jump up behind him. He spurred the horse as she held on to his 'abaya, and they made their way toward the Loire River on the outskirts of Tours. They arrived at a sandy bank where the soft waves of the river rippled gently ashore. The surface of the water glistened colorfully in the moonlight. They dismounted, and when Hani released the reins of the horse, it trotted back to the camp. They remained at that spot, isolated from the rest of the world. The wind was calm, and the only sound to be heard was the soft splashing of the waves against the bank. They removed their sandals and walked on the moist sand by the waters of the river. Hani took off his turban and 'abaya, now bareheaded and arms exposed just like Maryam. The hair on the back of his head was braided, which his turban had covered, and now it cascaded down his back just like hers. They walked along the sand until they reached the edge of the river, as the water splashed against their ankles. They stood there for a moment as Hani took Maryam's right hand, and feeling it cold and soft, he pressed both his hands on it. She shivered in excitement and fear. Her knees were knocking so much she could hardly stand. She leaned her head on Hani's shoulder, and his scent intoxicated her, just as the scent of her perfume intoxicated him. His face touched her hair, which tangled with the hair of his beard. He felt a shiver rush through his body like ants creeping through his flesh and bones. He feared that, overwhelmed by his emotions, his feet would betray him and he would fall. His left hand still clung to Maryam's right hand. He put his right hand on her shoulder, and they held each other up. While they remained silent, their love spoke. After a while, he lifted his head and looked into her eyes, which were languishing from emotion and welling in tears.

"Do you love me, Hani?" she asked in a soft voice.

With both hands, he held hers and pulled her closely to his chest. He was overcome with feelings and far removed from thoughts of war. "Yes, I truly love you."

"How wonderful and sweet love is."

"There is nothing sweeter than two hearts coming together. Are there in all of creation two people happier than we at this very moment? Come close to me, my beloved. Can you feel my heart beat the way I feel yours?" He spoke with one hand on her shoulder and the other holding her hand.

Maryam lifted her eyes toward the sky and saw the moon beaming brilliantly over the earth. She imagined on its face the picture of two lovers in embrace. "I see ourselves on the face of the moon. Look, Hani, can't you see two lovers just like us?"

"I don't see anything on earth that looks like us or feels the way we do."

"The way we feel is truly wondrous," she said, wiping the tears from her eyes. "We longed to be together and we strove to that end, but too much stood in our way. And now that we finally found each other, the fear of separation haunts us."

He looked her in the eye. "The only thing that will cure my aching heart after so much misery is that we unite in eternity never to part again. This can only happen if we succumb together. Will you join me in death, Maryam?"

Wrapped in embrace and staring into each other's eyes, she answered. "Death with you is life, my beloved. Ah, 'my beloved,' how often I took pleasure in repeating these two words in my solitude, and how much I ached to hear you utter them too."

"You speak the truth, for only two people truly in love know the real pleasure of these words. Our love for each other has allowed us to bask in the sweetness of these words, even though we're fettered by bonds that forbid us to reach what lies beyond. Had we been destined for victory and crossed this river, our union would have been longer and the realm of our pleasures wider. But we never felt any safety in separation, and we hardly lived to enjoy life's wonders. If we choose to die together embracing each other, then it will be like living in eternity, and separation will never ruin our lives."

"Then we must hurry and not prolong this waiting, lest something comes and stands in the way of our happiness." She reached into her pocket and took out the purse. She stared at it for several moments, then kissed it, pressed it to her bosom, and began to weep. "O mother, my mother, how I grieve for you, for the distress you endured in life, all the secrets, the pretending and vigilance. You departed a martyr to secrecy and love, keeping the promise of your beloved and honoring his will. Had I known all this before, I would have been shocked by your passion. But now that I've tasted the sweetness of love, I cannot blame you. Rather, I will do as you did, and I will carry out your will." She tucked the purse inside her robe. "This is your secret that will go with us to the ends of eternity."

Hani listened, watching her lips quiver and her eyes sparkle, sharing in all of her emotions. When she finished speaking, he passed his eyes over her nubile body. "Is it not wrong that this body be no more than food for the fish in the sea?"

"That would be preferable to having it fall prey to the beasts on land who call themselves human beings. Let's go quickly, Hani, lest our wish to live overtake us."

Hani and Maryam extended their arms and held each other around the waist as they walked, side by side, to the edge of the river. They walked into the water and felt its coldness and the slippery sand beneath their feet. As they waded into deep water, they held on more tightly and, clinging to each other, they became one body as they plunged into the depths as both reveled in repeating the name of their beloved. A minute later, the tips of their heads faded from the surface of the water as they sunk to the bottom of the river. From that moment on, only God knows what happened to them.

Meanwhile, the Frankish army, anticipating another attack by the Arabs on the following day, awoke to find only deserted fields and abandoned tents. They seized what remained of the spoils of war, and that was the last of their encounters with the Arabs in those parts.

The End

The Battle of Poitiers

Charles Martel and 'Abd al-Rahman

Study Guide

William Granara

1. Who was Jurji Zaidan?

Jurji Zaidan was born in Beirut, Lebanon in 1861 which, at that time, was part of a Syrian province in the Ottoman Empire. As a teenager he helped his father run a small restaurant. When he was nineteen years old, Zaidan enrolled in the medical school at what was then the Syrian Protestant College, now the American University in Beirut. However, after taking part in a student strike, he decided to leave the university. He soon left his native Lebanon and moved to Cairo. Like many Arab intellectuals of the time, Zaidan threw himself into the dynamic world of journalism, the most important cultural vehicle for the expression of nationalist aspirations throughout the urban centers of the Arab world. In 1892, he founded a cultural magazine, *al-Hilal* (The Crescent Moon) which continues to be published to this day.

Zaidan's professional life and career may be best understood through the nexus of politics and literature which became the hallmark of his legacy. In the political sphere, Zaidan is considered a pioneer in the Arab Nationalist movement (the *Nahda* or Arab Renaissance) whose aim was twofold to: (i) reclaim and articulate an identity among all Arab peoples who share a common language and history; and (ii) unite them politically and culturally against the old Ottoman order as well as against the rising tide of European political and cultural imperialism. On the literary scene, Zaidan is best remembered as the author of twenty two historical novels (including *The Battle of Poitiers*) set in the context of Arabo-Islamic historical events from pre-Islamic times to the nineteenth century. These novels, very popular to this day and regularly reprinted in the Arab world, were instrumental in fashioning an Arab consciousness in much of the Arab world. In addition to the novels, his prodigious output included scholarly books and articles in his magazine on a large number of topics: the history of Islamic civilization, and the history and development of languages, as well as on political, social, educational, and ethical issues. He thus played a very important role in making readers of Arabic more aware of the important events in their history and in developing a sense of national identity.

Jurji Zaidan died in Cairo, Egypt in 1914.

2. How may we understand 'Arab Nationalism' at the time of Jurji Zaidan?

Arab Nationalism, broadly defined, was a movement which began in the later years of the nineteenth century. The binding identity of Arab Nationalism is one of language: any person whose mother tongue is Arabic is an Arab, irrespective of race, religion, or ethnicity. While Jurji Zaidan was not a political activist, the brand of Arab Nationalism he promoted is often viewed as a reaction against pan-Ottomanism which commanded the allegiance of those still loyal to the idea of salvaging the Ottoman Empire, as well as to Turkish Nationalism, a movement that swept reformist-minded intellectuals in Istanbul since the 1870s, and which sought a political, cultural, and linguistic split between Turks, Arabs and other peoples of the Ottoman Empire. Arab Nationalism also sought to define itself as an alternative to pan-Islamism which espoused the belief that the Islamic faith was the dominant cultural and political force of the region that should form the basis of a modern nation. In this we see that many Arab Christian intellectuals, Jurji Zaidan among them, were strong proponents of this secular Arab nationalism. Finally, Arab nationalism aimed to curb movements toward regional nationalisms, especially in Egypt, Tunisia, Syria, and Iraq, that sought to promote local interests and thus diluted and even negated the move towards pan-Arab unity.

3. What is the *Nahda*?

The Arabic literary renaissance (*Nahda*) of the late nineteenth and early twentieth centuries was the secular literary and cultural offspring of the Islamic Reformist movements that aimed to reconcile traditional Arabo-Islamic beliefs and values with modern political, social and scientific ideas. The *Nahda*'s primary goal of creating an indigenous modern national literature was achieved through: (i) the reclamation, edition, and publication of the vast pre-modern Arab literary heritage (*al-turath*); and (ii) the translation, adaptation and indigenization of western modes of artistic and literary expression. The *Nahda* flourished in the major urban centers of Egypt, Syria, Iraq, and Tunisia where a growing urban, educated readership, inspired and stimulated by the proliferation of print media and the wide appeal of both the official and popular presses, developed a taste for new forms of creative writing.

The historical novel, a 'western import' for which Jurji Zaidan is best remembered and widely regarded as the Arab world's leading pioneer, perhaps serves as the finest illustration of the melding of indigenous Arabic culture with the imported western novel to fashion a modern Arab literature. Zaidan's intention in penning his historical novels, shared as well by other contemporaneous writers of modern Arab literature, was to educate his reader to the long and rich literature which Arabs produced throughout the centuries, and to instill a sense of pride in Arab history, culture, and identity.

4. Why is the Battle of Poitiers so important to both Muslims and Christians?

The Battle of Poitiers in 732 AD is often seen in the context of the epic struggles for world hegemony between Islam and Christendom. Less than a hundred years elapsed between the birth of Islam in 622 AD and the date of the Muslim invasion of Spain in 710 AD by which time the Islamic faith had spread rapidly to both east and west: Syria, Iraq and Egypt first, but then east towards India and west along the Northern shores of Africa. From then on, the Muslim caliphs were set on conquering the European continent *which was the only remaining part of the then known civilized world to which the Islamic faith had not spread.* They first tried to do so from the east with the siege of Constantinople in 717 AD in which the Muslim forces came close to success. With over twelve thousand land forces and eighteen hundred ships, Arabs, Persians and others managed to cross for the first time the Bosphorous, breaking the chains with which Byzantine emperors restricted access to the city and reaching the outskirts of Constantinople where they entrenched themselves for a long blockade. Muslim forces were defeated with a new instrument of war—torches of fire ("Greek fire") that were lobbed onto ships that effectively destroyed most of the Arab ships. And Artemius, the Byzantine emperor, foresaw the Arab blockade and had stocked sufficient wheat and grains to feed the city for three years, outlasting the Muslim forces' need for provisions.

Following that unsuccessful siege, the Umayyad Caliphate in Damascus resolved to reach Constantinople from the west by conquering a fragmented European continent that was backward and in disarray compared to the far stronger Byzantine Empire. Muslim forces in the Iberian Peninsula crossed the Pyrenees and conquered Bordeaux and other cities on their way to Tours near where the Battle of Poitiers was to take place.

In the above context, the Battle of Poitiers, or The Battle of the Martyrs' Path (*Ma'rakat Balad al-Shuhada'*) as it is called in Arabic, survives in modern memory as much through myth as through history. The earliest Latin chroniclers' view of divine intervention in this decisive Christian victory over the Muslim invasion has been eclipsed by a modern macro-historical narrative, most famously articulated by Edward Gibbon (*The History of the Rise and Fall of the Roman Empire*, 1781) that views the Battle of Poitiers as a victory of Christianity over Islam in Europe.

There were also other reasons that led the Arabs of Andalusia to cross the Pyrenees Mountains in France following their successful conquest of the Iberian peninsula which began in 711 AD. The newly settled Muslims of Andalusia wished to secure their northern borders against the potential of Christian counter-offensives. And the new Muslim conquerors wanted to replenish their coffers through the acquisition of the spoils of war that abounded in the churches and monasteries of Gaul.

The decisive Battle of Poitiers took place one day in late October 732 AD after seven days of skirmishes between the Arab and Frankish armies. The battle ended with a defeat for the Muslim army during which its commander, 'Abd al-Rahman al-Ghafiqi, was killed. Early the following morning, the Christian commander, Charles Martel, in his quest to complete his victory, lead his triumphant soldiers to the still erect tents of the Muslim camp, only to discover, with great disappointment, that the survivors had quietly fled in the dark of night.

Both the snippets of information culled from medieval sources and modern historical scholarship posit that the Arab cavalry, as skilled as it was, had grossly underestimated the vast, well-equipped, and battle-tested Frankish infantry. Arabic and Latin chroniclers also suggest that the Arab forces may have been unaccustomed to the hills and forests that dotted the local terrain, and ill prepared to function in the cold climate of north central France.

5. Who are the principle characters of *The Battle of Poitiers*?

(i) **'Abd al-Rahman al-Ghafiqi**: an Arab of Yemeni tribal origin, and senior military commander in the Umayyad army, assumes the position of governor-general of Andalusia in 726 AD. He is best remembered in both east and the west as the general who led the Muslims in the Battle of Poitiers in which he succumbed in 732 AD;

(ii) **Charles**: or Charles Martel, a.k.a. the Hammer (*Martellus*), as nicknamed by medieval Latin chroniclers, is the governor of the Frankish realm and commander of the Christian army fighting the Muslims at Poitiers;

(iii) **Hani**: a senior officer in the Muslim army, right hand to 'Abd al-Rahman, is the fictitious romantic hero of the novel;

(iv) **Odo**: (or Eudes the Great), Duke of Aquitaine, the French province located north of the Pyrenees, is former rival to Charles who seeks his alliance to repel the Muslim invasions;

(v) **Bustam**: commander of the Muslim Berber forces, and arch-rival to Hani, is the fictitious villain of the novel;

(vi) **Salma**: woman of mysterious identity, captured by the Muslims at the Battle of Bordeaux, and go-between the Christians and Muslims;

(vii) **Maryam**: daughter of Salma and is the fictitious romantic heroine of the novel;

(viii) **Lumbaja**: servant in the harem of 'Abd al-Rahman, is the (secret) daughter of Duke Odo, and villain of the novel.

6. What are the major themes of the novel?

Zaidan's *Battle of Poitiers,* as in all his historical novels, mixes actual historical events (the conquest of Bordeaux and the Battle of Poitiers), persons ('Abd al-Rahman, Charles, Odo and Lumbaja), and places (Bordeaux, Tours, etc.) with romantic modes of fiction (Hani and Maryam's love, Bustam's villainy). His use of the Arab conquest of Spain, with subtle references to the grand civilization of Andalusia the Arabs would eventually build in their eight centuries on European soil (711-1492 AD) is a fine example of how many contemporary Arab artists and intellectuals look back to their Andalusian past as a time of both extraordinary successes and failures and a model towards which Arab societies should strive.

Writing at a time of contentious debates among Arabs concerning their identity, the ways they wished to govern and be governed, their conflicting stances toward European colonialism and technological progress, and the direction of their future, Zaidan's novel addresses these issues by using the lessons of history to inculcate the values of unity, tolerance and justice:

- *Unity.* 'Abd al-Rahman and Hani's personal relationship transcends ancient Yemeni tribal factions, and their continuous attempts to appease the disaffected Berber contingents—albeit via a romanticized demonization of their role in the wars of conquest—nevertheless speak to a binary of division versus unity that marked Zaidan's own times.

- *Tolerance.* The constructions of the fictionalized Salma and Maryam give voice to the idea of tolerance and shared values between Muslims and Christians, as they do to an expansive definition of what it means to be *Arab* and *Muslim*; and

- *Justice.* 'Abd al-Rahman's character, from explicit military commander to implied ruler of the nation, embodies power and strength through compassion and justice.

Other questions to discuss concerning *The Battle of Poitiers*

1. Many readers of the novel would have known who won the Battle of Poitiers. But the novel still manages to create suspense. How?

2. Like the novels of Charles Dickens, *The Battle of Poitiers* originally appeared in separate episodes printed in a newspaper. How does Zaidan keep the action moving forward across episodes?

3. Zaidan's novels are based on the idea that a specific national group, the Arabs, have participated in something called Islamic civilization. Does this idea make sense? How does the novel support it? In what ways does it undermine it?

4. Like the press in many countries during Zaidan's time, the Arabic press helped readers create an image of themselves as citizens; as members of national, ethnic, or religious groups; and as men and women with specific gender roles. In what ways might *The Battle of Poitiers* have helped shape its readers?

Further Reading

Nicolle, David, *Poitiers AD 732: Charles Martel turns the Islamic Tide*, Oxford, UK: Osprey Publishing, 2008.

Watson, William E. *"The Battle of Tours Revisited"* Providence, *Studies in Western Civilization* v.2, n.1 (1993). (http://www.deremilitari.org/resources/articles/watson2.htm)

Thomas Philipp, *Jurji Zaidan's Secular Analysis of History and Language as Foundations of Arab Nationalism* (Forthcoming).